It was like being teleported back in time...

...back to a world of fairies, castles and dungeons, spells and sorcery. There was a sense of pure netherworld mysticism in the mansion, a hint of the dark ages when superstition had run rampant. Oddly enough Sara could have sworn that Warwick's hawklike eyes were actually watching her, following her every move.

Giving her head a determined shake, she walked on to the next poster. She got the same sense of being watched from the eyes of the evil Lord Dracos. And suddenly it occurred to her that the eerie sensation didn't stem from the posters at all. It felt real, as though there was someone else in the basement. Someone with human, malevolent eyes. Someone shooting daggers at her from a shadowy corner.

Then, through the dusky darkness of the timeworn halls, she heard it. A faint whisper that brushed across her soul like the touch of a ghostly hand.

"Forever shall Morganna sleep... For now and for all eternity... Forever shall the sorceress remain at rest... Forever..."

ABOUT THE AUTHOR

As far back as she can remember, Jenna Ryan has been dreaming up stories, everything from fairy tales to romantic mysteries. She's read Harlequin Intrigues since the line was introduced, and inspired by Anne Stuart's *Hand in Glove*, she set out to write one herself. A resident of Victoria, B.C., Jenna has worked as a model, an airline reservation agent, a tour escort and a lingerie salesperson.

Books by Jenna Ryan

HARLEQUIN INTRIGUE

88–CAST IN WAX

Suspended Animation

Jenna Ryan

Harlequin Books

TORONTO • NEW YORK • LONDON
AMSTERDAM • PARIS • SYDNEY • HAMBURG
STOCKHOLM • ATHENS • TOKYO • MILAN

To Kay and Bill, who have always believed

Harlequin Intrigue edition published October 1988

ISBN 0-373-22099-5

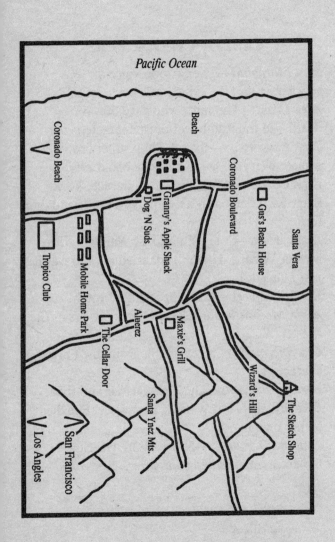

CAST OF CHARACTERS

Sara Moreland—The cartoon voice of Morganna and the evil curse's next victim.

Alex Cross—Animator who gave life—or death—to the Rainbow Forest characters.

Jack Kensington—Sketch Shop supervisor who wanted everything—anyway he could get it.

Noel Gordon—She filmed the characters and knew each one intimately, but was she friend or foe?

Dieter Haas—Sole animator of Warwick, the Master Wizard. His smile dazzled all, but was it just a facade?

Robin Danvers—A self-proclaimed witch.

Alvin Medwin—He believed in his powers as the Master Wizard.

Gus Sherman—Creator of the Rainbow Forest characters.

Forrest Clements—Gus's ex-partner and rival.

Elke Stevens—Morganna's first voice. She died by her own hand.

Jasmine O'Rourke—She was hired as Elke's replacement and died soon after....

Prologue

It was a cool rainy night on the California coast, the kind of night made for the cheery warmth of a crackling hearth. It was a night for curling up with a good book and a snifter of blackberry brandy. It was not a night to be standing alone in the rain outside a small-town train depot, praying the 11:15 would pull in early.

Shivering slightly, the woman on the platform angled the brim of her felt hat over her eyes and huddled deeper into her trench coat.

She should have said something, she realized that now. She should have made a general announcement to everyone at the Sketch Shop, told them she was quitting her job and ditching this town. Maybe then the nightmare would have ended. Maybe then she could have made a clean break, free at last from the gnawing tendrils of fear she could feel in her bones but not explain.

"God, help me," she murmured through taut colorless lips. "Let the train come early. Just this once, let it be ahead of schedule."

As if in answer to her plea, a shrill whistle sounded through the splashing rain. The woman stole a glance at her watch. 11:05. It was early by ten glorious minutes. Thank God and Amtrak. Her prayers had been answered.

Twining the fingers of one shaking hand around the strap of her leather handbag, she used the other to work the zipper open. She had her ticket and her wallet and all her credit cards with her. Everything that mattered was here. Tonight she would stay in Los Angeles. Tomorrow she would take a plane to Newark, and by evening she'd be safe at her mother's home in New Jersey. She could send for her belongings then—right after she called her boss and turned in her long-distance resignation. If she could dredge up the courage, she might even go so far as to tell old Gus—

The thought broke off abruptly as her searching fingers brushed against a folded sheet of paper stuck at an odd angle between the teeth of her comb. A choking lump of dread formed in her throat. In fearful slow motion, she peeled back the heavy corners.

It was Sketch Shop parchment, the kind used by the animators. Familiar paper with a recognizable figure on it: Morganna, the Medieval Sorceress, lying in a coffin, her fingers curled around the stem of a blood-red rose.

Oh Lord, this wasn't just some sick joke as she'd once thought. It was pure twisted evil. Cruelty in its basest form. Why hadn't she told someone? Why hadn't she said something?

The woman's entire body began to tremble. She wanted to scream, but she couldn't. She wanted to turn and run, but her feet were rooted to the platform. All she could do was stand and stare in desperate horror at the death mask before her. It was *her* death mask. A snapshot of *her* face, pasted atop a cartoon character's body.

Through the steady drizzle, the 11:15 approached, drawing ever closer to the quiet station. Suddenly she could run. She had to run. The evil was here. It was real, and it was after her!

Teetering on her leather soles, she let the paper drop, then made a frantic dash for the far end of the rain-slicked platform. She could see the glare of the train's lights through the mist, could hear the screech of brakes as the cars began grinding to a halt on the steel tracks. She made it to the platform's edge, just barely managing to stop herself from toppling over the side.

But then she sensed the menacing presence again, stronger and colder than ever before. It was behind her. She could feel it, lurking in the shadows of the redbrick depot. Lurking, waiting, watching like some cruel harbinger of death.

Drawing a deep terrified breath, she spun around. Her wide eyes scoured the darkness. There was no one by the depot. No one lurking in or out of the shadows. She was alone here. Alone and safe. Her imagination had been playing tricks on her after all.

With a heartfelt sigh of relief, she wrapped her arms around her quivering body and turned back to the tracks.

It was the last voluntary move she ever made.

Chapter One

Through the windshield of her borrowed MG, Sara Moreland caught her first glimpse of Gus Sherman's southern California animation studio. To the unprepared eye, it was an imposing sight. Housed in a huge old monolith and perched high atop a craggy bluff, affectionately dubbed Wizard's Hill by the residents of Santa Vera, the Sketch Shop stood out in stark, gray relief against the late-afternoon sky.

As she rounded the final bend in the steep, winding road leading to the aging mansion, she could see two massive turrets rising straight up from the jagged rocks on the cliff behind them. It was like straying into a scene from Gus's fabled Rainbow Forest, Sara reflected, brushing several strands of honey-blond hair from her cheeks. The shuttered windows seemed to gape down at her, almost menacing in their vacant surveillance of her approach. Slowly she let her gaze climb past stylish Tudor facings and gabled roofs to a number of high chimneys constructed entirely of worn brick.

The building, she knew, had to be more than a century old, and every one of those one-hundred-plus years appeared to have etched themselves into the rough stone foundations and the weathered lines of the outer walls. Even in the full light of day, it wouldn't have surprised her one bit to spot an enormous black thundercloud forming above the rooftop, with perhaps a few swooping bats thrown in for good measure. At the very least, she half expected to see Morganna, the Medieval Sorceress, emerging from the bordering woods. Morganna, clad in a long black cape, gliding soundlessly across the rocky ground, a large crow perched dutifully on one regal shoulder.

Giving her head a shake to dispel the fanciful images, Sara parked her car in the clearing that evidently served as the employees' parking lot. Yet in spite of herself, she couldn't quite shake the haunting sensation that gripped her.

Aside from a sporadic cluster of empty vehicles, there was no sign of life in the area. Even the sun shimmering off the leaves of the nearby trees couldn't diminish the eerie atmosphere that seemed to emanate from the very depths of the shadowy mansion.

Smiling to herself, she got out of her car, easing the damp cotton shirt from the center of her back. Gus couldn't have chosen a more appropriate setting for his studio if he'd tried, she thought, slamming the door closed with her free hand. Dead silence reigned on the bluff, a silence broken only by an occasional gust of wind sweeping from the canyon below and the inevitable drone of flies in the densely treed woods to her left. She wondered idly if the old cartoonist had come up with the Rainbow Forest's characters before or after he'd chosen the site for the Sketch Shop.

Probably before, she decided, recalling the colorful fairy tales he'd told her so often when she was a child. Tales of elves and fairies, wood nymphs and witches. Stories of magic and pixie dust almost as vivid as those he conjured up for his feature films.

The man was an absolute genius when it came to animation—which seemed fitting to Sara since he bore an amazing resemblance to Pinocchio's kindly creator, Gepetto, the wood-carver.

Sara had met Gus when she was eight. Yet as busy as he'd been back then working on a series of animated sequences for one of her father's unique ad campaigns, he'd always managed to find the time to fill her head with visions of the supernatural. Once, she remembered, still surveying the brooding mansion before her, he'd gotten truly inventive and had added a sorceress to the ranks of his usual woodland creatures. Not the infamous Morganna, but perhaps an early prototype he'd later expanded upon.

Morganna, the Medieval Sorceress.

Sara still couldn't believe she was actually going to be doing the character's coveted voice. To say the least, it would be a change from repertory theater. A change for her, and possibly a chance to help Gus out of his current financial problems. He wanted to save his beloved Sketch Shop, and she wanted to try her hand at something new. Maybe this would turn out well for both of them.

Drawing a deep breath, Sara took one last look at the sinister mansion in front of her. She had a feeling that working here was going to be a definite departure from the stage. She only hoped it would prove to be a pleasant one.

"THERE CAN BE NO ESCAPE for you this time, Morganna." From the center of a wide angled screen, the animated figure of Warwick, the Master Wizard, issued the dire warning to his black-cloaked apprentice, Morganna, the Medieval Sorceress. "As you can see," the cartoon character proclaimed imperiously, "I now possess the mighty Rainbow Scepter, against which even your great powers shall prove ineffective."

Amber eyes blazing, Morganna stood her ground. "Your magical tools don't frighten me, Warwick," she informed the aging wizard in a voice heavy with contempt. "Though you may possess the Rainbow Scepter, you do not have the strength necessary to destroy me. Croatia, who bears the knowledge of all the ages, could not do it when she guarded the Scepter, and neither, my former master, shall you." A crafty smile touched her scarlet lips. "That which you do, I shall swiftly undo," she promised in a silky whisper. "Heed my words well, Warwick. There is no diabolical conjuration in all this vast land formidable enough to hold me for more than a small stretch of time."

Beneath his tattered brown cape, Warwick's bony form straightened. Black eyes glittering, he raised the luminous Scepter. "Your self-confidence has made you strong, my young apprentice. But no more shall it serve you. This is your fate, Morganna, an end to your evil trickery: forever shall you remain in your castle chamber...forever trapped in the spell of the Moonstone Orb."

Having uttered that portentous statement, the ancient wizard aimed the Rainbow Scepter at an opaque crystal ball resting on a tall wooden pedestal before him. "Forever..." he incanted as the orb began to radiate a blood-red light. "A curse I place upon thee, Sorceress Morganna, for now and for all eternity. Never again shall you set foot in the Rainbow Forest. Dominion is mine alone. From this moment until the end of time..."

Warwick's crackling voice faded out, and slowly the vivid amber of Morganna's eyes gave way to the crimson shimmer of the Moonstone Orb.

As it did so, the lone person in the screening room hunched down into a thickly padded chair, gaze lowering to the crumpled sheet of parchment spread out so carefully across a neighboring seat. Smiling secretively, the shadowy figure reached out and traced a circle around the torn snapshot glued to Morganna's head.

"You learned the hard way, didn't you, Jasmine?" a whispered voice intoned mockingly, eyes locked on the woman's smiling face. "You thought you could come here and play Morganna. You thought I'd let you do that." A scowl replaced the smile on the speaker's face. "You did think that, didn't you? Didn't you, Jasmine O'Rourke?" Now the voice grew cold, almost accusing, the eyes bitterly hostile. But only for a moment. Only until the memory of Jasmine's death returned in a satisfying rush. Then the anger dissipated.

It was done. She was gone. She'd learned her lesson the hard way when she'd fallen in front of that train six weeks ago.

The hand hovering over the picture lifted slightly, blocking out the woman's porcelain-fine features, blocking out everything that no longer mattered. Blocking out everything except the lingering surge of evil.

The evil that was Morganna's curse.

Chapter Two

The meeting room on the fourth floor of the Sketch Shop was almost half-full when Alex Cross made his way there from the animation level late Wednesday afternoon. He was surprised that there were still so many people hanging around the studio. It was a hot day, most of the employees were avid sun worshippers, and Santa Vera had one of the nicest stretches of beach in southern California. So what were fifty of the workers doing here? For that matter, what was he doing here?

Behind him, Robin Danvers, one of the Shop's premier voices, tapped his back. "What's going on, Alex?" she demanded. Then she scowled. "Aw, don't tell me Jack is gonna give us another lecture. Blow your cigarette smoke all over him, will you? Maybe he'll cut his speech short." She gave her curly mane a disdainful toss. "Nepotism," she grunted in her usual stringent fashion. "Old Gus should have his aging head examined for making that little wart assistant production supervisor."

"You didn't have to come today, Robin," Alex said mildly, searching his pockets for the crumpled pack of Salems he knew was there.

"Sure I did. You never know. Maybe Jack's going to let me do Morganna's voice. God knows, I've waited long enough for the opportunity. Anyway, I figure no one else would touch it with a ten-foot pole, what with all the talk about Morganna's curse." Her dark eyes flashed. "It's my turn now," she announced, as if daring contradiction. "No curse in the world could ever touch me."

"Don't count on it, Robin." Dieter Haas brushed past her, a blue T-shirt slung over one bare, sun-bronzed shoulder. "What's up, Alex? Has old Gus finally decided to sell the Sketch Shop to the Cartoon Emporium?"

"Damned if I know." Alex finally located his cigarettes. "Probably not." He nodded in the direction of a young woman he'd never seen before. "Unless she's from the Emporium, I'd say Morganna's got herself a new voice."

"You think so?" Dieter's speculative gaze traveled down the length of the woman's body. "She looks pretty calm for someone who's stepping into a role that's supposed to have a curse attached to it."

"Morganna's curse?" Arching a wry brow, Alex regarded his longtime friend and coworker. "Come on, Dieter, you know that's nothing but a lot of bull. Some reporter at the *Gazette* just invented that story to sell more newspapers."

"Yeah, I know, but you can't really blame me. It's all I've been hearing about since Jasmine fell onto the railway tracks a few weeks ago."

Alex said nothing, just wandered over to one of the hardbacked chairs scattered about the room and straddled it. Like so many of the other people at the Shop, Dieter was starting to believe in Morganna's curse. Jasmine had been the second person to do the character's voice, and her death was a hot topic. But it was a tired subject as far as Alex was concerned. Jasmine O'Rourke had fallen in front of a train; it was as simple as that. Even if a small part of him wondered if her death had been accidental, that was still no reason to attribute it to anything as nebulous as a curse.

"My book, my book. Where did I put my notebook?" From the sofa beneath the bank of windows, Alvin Medwin began squirming around. He was an older man, seventy-five or more, and prone to memory lapses.

"Check your vest pocket," Alex suggested absently, his gaze focused on the fairy princess standing several feet in front of him.

She was a pretty woman. Tall and slender, blond and blue-eyed, but not quite the stereotypical California girl. He could still recognize a New Yorker. This woman was calm, cool and accustomed to being stared at.

"Ah, that's the ticket. Thank you, my boy, thank you. You were right, of course. It was in my vest pocket all along."

Alex shifted his gaze back to Alvin who was already busy flipping through the dog-eared pages of his ever present notebook. Throughout the twelve years Alex had known him, Alvin wrote down everything he heard and saw. He even made notes in the john, although what could possibly be of interest to him in the men's room was hard to imagine.

At the front of the meeting area, Jack Kensington cleared his throat, indicating that the fifty or so people present should quiet down. Naturally no one did. Voices continued to buzz from all corners.

"So, what's going on, Alex?" a female voice inquired. "Jack looks like he's about to announce he's running for office. Could it be we're finally gonna lose our resident swamp rat?"

Noel Gordon's sarcastic southern drawl accompanied a dangerous scritch of taut denim as she sank into a seat next to Alex's and dropped her canvas bag beside her. She had an ample figure and a tendency to wear clothes that were a size too small. A quirk born of vanity, it was easy enough to ignore in view of her refreshingly garrulous nature.

"Nope, we're gonna gain a new Morganna," Alex said, resting his arms on the back of his chair.

Noel's hazel eyes flicked to the newcomer. "I hope she's got more spunk than Jasmine," she stated flatly. "I suppose it would be asking too much for Morganna's curse to overshoot her and hit on Jack instead. Look at him, will ya? Drooling like a hound dog.''

"What's that, Noel? I didn't hear you. Drooling like a what?"

Alvin's pen was poised on an empty line in his notebook. Alex couldn't tell if he was writing down their conversation or merely intrigued by Noel's observation. Not that it really mattered. An absentminded eccentric, the man was harmless enough. He never made any of his notations public, just kept scribbling them down.

"Like a hound dog," Noel told him with a grin. "Hey, Dieter." Leaning over, she smacked the blond man's bare foot. "Give 'em a rebel yell or something, will ya? Jack's starting to bug me the way he's hopping around up there. Looks like an elf with an itch."

It was Alex's turn to grin. Before Dieter could draw a breath, Alex emitted an ear-splitting whistle, which effectively silenced the gathering.

Tugging at the vest of his fawn-colored suit, Jack cleared his throat again. "Thank you, Alex," he said in his smoothest politician voice. "Now if I can please have your attention, ladies and gentlemen, I have an announcement to make."

Alex watched Robin, who was lounging malevolently against the windowsill. Her glare was aimed directly at the new woman. She knew exactly what Jack's announcement was going to be, and she was obviously stewing about it already.

"First up," Jack began loudly, "I want you to know that Gus's bypass operation was a complete success. He'll be in the hospital for a while, but he plans to come back to Santa Vera as soon as the doctors will let him. Second, I would like you all to meet our newest staff member, Sara Moreland." He beamed at his audience, all dimples now that he was the center of attention. "Gus has hired her to do the voice of Morganna, the Medieval Sorceress. Sara's an—"

"Morganna, the Medieval Sorceress..." Alvin repeated, his pen flying across the lined paper. "Pardon me, miss." He made a motion with the tip of his pen to gain her attention. "How do you spell your name? With an 'h' or without?"

Although Jack's lips thinned at the interruption, the blonde didn't seem the least bit perturbed by it, Alex noted.

"Without," she said in a voice that resembled honeyed velvet.

"Without, Alvin," Noel relayed at a louder level. "You'll have to speak up, Sara," she called across the room. "Warwick here is running a little short on ear power." She sat back in her chair and waved an airy hand. "Carry on, Jack."

"Thank you," Jack said, the words coming out short and clipped. "Now where was I?"

"Sara's an..." Alex supplied, lighting his cigarette.

"Oh, yes, of course," Again he cleared his throat. "Sara is an actress from New York City."

"On or off Broadway?" Robin snarled from her seat by the window.

For the first time, Sara Moreland looked behind her. Alex gave her points for not flinching under the woman's glacial stare.

"Neither," she replied calmly. "I live in New York. I've been doing repertory theater in Maine for the past five years."

"Huh," Robin snorted. "You call that acting?"

Sara met her frosty eyes without falter. "I believe that's what it's called, yes. Why? Do you use a different word out here in California?"

"You want a different word?" Robin shot back. "I'll give you a few that'll turn—"

"Excuse me, ladies." Clearly annoyed now, Jack began drumming his fingers on the paneled wall. "Robin, as long as you're all stirred up, would you mind opening that window beside you? The movement might improve your temper while it cleans up the air in here." He glanced pointedly at Alex's glowing cigarette.

Unrepentant, Alex exhaled a lungful of smoke. His vices were nobody's business but his own, and being preached at wasn't something he accepted well. Besides, the air-conditioning system was sucking up the harmful residue quite nicely. Jack was just being a pain as usual.

Dieter tipped his chair back toward Alex and asked quietly, "Did Gus tell you anything about this?"

"No. Why?"

"Let's just say I don't trust Jack. He's been after Gus for the past year to sell the Sketch Shop to the Emporium down in L.A.. For someone who's not getting his way, he looks awfully smug."

"Smug nothing," Noel, overhearing the conversation, inserted. "He's just plain old smitten. Sara Moreland has class stamped all over that pretty face of hers. When Jack finally gets around to winning his daddy's support, won't she be a fine little lady to host his Washington parties?"

Alex couldn't see it, but he didn't bother to argue the point. Jack would never be elected to Congress, and even if by some fluke his old man did get him halfway there, Morganna's new "voice" appeared to have more sense than to climb on for the ride. Anyone who could parry Robin's barbs had to be fairly sharp.

"So what do you think, Alex?" Noel nudged his rib cage with her elbow. "Do you figure she'll make a good Morganna?"

He shrugged. "She has the right voice."

"Uh-huh." Dieter slanted him a cagey glance. "And she also has the right look."

Yes, she did, Alex acknowledged silently, careful to keep his expression neutral. Pretty as Sara Moreland was, he didn't intend to let his healthy male hormones take over. He'd done that once before in his life, and all it had gotten him was a lot of pain and bitterness he could well have done without.

Squelching the unpleasant memories of a time long past, he returned his contemplative gaze to Morganna's new "voice." And in spite of himself, he couldn't help wondering just how much old Gus had told her about the character's alleged curse.

MORGANNA'S CURSE . . .

Although she knew there could be no such thing, Sara couldn't help wondering how such a wild, superstitious rumor had ever managed to take root. True, the sorceress's original voice, Elke Stevens, had committed suicide three years before, after completing two of the films in Gus's planned Rainbow Forest trilogy. And it was also true that Jasmine O'Rourke had been hired to do Morganna's voice and had died in a fall from a train platform six weeks earlier. But for the life of her, Sara didn't see how those two things could possibly be ascribed to a curse.

She took a quick covert look at the people around her. According to Jack, about one third of the Sketch Shop's regular contingent was present at this Wednesday afternoon meeting. That meant there were probably close to one hundred and fifty workers on staff here. And from what little she'd been able to gather after talking with Gus and Jack, well over half of those workers believed there really was something to Morganna's curse.

But was there? she reflected doubtfully. Or had the gossip simply gotten out of hand in the wake of Jasmine O'Rourke's sudden death? The latter seemed likely to her. Particularly when she caught a sideways glimpse of the woman Jack had called Robin. Now, this person struck Sara as someone who believed in curses.

From her clingy tank top to her open-toed shoes, Robin was clad entirely in black. Bright red nail polish adorned her fingers and toes, and around her neck, attached to a silky black cord, hung what appeared to be a carved wolf's head. A riot of wild ebony curls surrounded her narrow face, and from her temples, two thick white wings swept upward, giving her the appearance of one of Count Dracula's infamous undead brides.

As Robin turned poisonous eyes in her direction, Sara forced herself to look away. She'd already had one heated confrontation with the woman today. This probably wasn't the best time for a second verbal clash. Absent or not, Gus had enough problems at the Shop without her adding to them.

She thought back briefly to her meeting with Gus in his Dallas hospital room four weeks earlier. Weakened by a chronic heart condition, he'd kept the conversation short and to the point. He needed someone to do Morganna, he'd told her, and he wanted her to take the part.

"I have to bring Morganna back to the Rainbow Forest," he'd said in his wonderfully gruff Texas drawl. "I just don't have any choice. The first two pictures in the trilogy were a resounding success, but without Morganna, the third one didn't work. Audiences didn't like it. Now I have to make a fourth film if I want to keep the Sketch Shop going."

Although Sara was hazy on the details, she knew that Gus had chosen to shelve the evil sorceress after Elke Stevens's suicide. He might never have revived the character had it not been for the failure of his last feature film. That in combination with the high cost of making animated motion pictures had pretty much forced his hand.

"Pardon me again, miss." From the sofa, the little man in the baggy, three-piece suit motioned to her once more, drawing her out of her reflective thoughts. "Did you say you were from New York or New Jersey?"

Twisting around in her seat, Sara smiled at him. With his fading English accent, receding cap of white hair, jowly cheeks and wire-rimmed glasses, he reminded her of an absentminded professor. "New York," she said, hoping she wouldn't have to shout to make herself heard above the rising chatter.

"Did you get that, Alvin?" The woman with the heavy southern accent came to perch herself on the arm of the sofa. "She's a New Yorker."

Alvin nodded. "Yes, yes, I have it. New York. There we are. It's all down in black and white now."

The woman grinned. "Just in case you forget where you come from," she said to Sara. Chuckling, she held out her hand. "By the way, I'm Noel Gordon. I work down in the camera department. And Alvin here—" she patted the man's plump shoulder "—does the voice of Morganna's nemesis, Warwick, the Master Wizard. For a while there, he thought he was going to have the spotlight all to himself again, just like he did in the third picture. Didn't you, Alvin?"

"Yes, well, no harm done," he said as he flipped the pages of his notebook. "Alex, my boy, are you still around?"

"Right here, Alvin," came the lazy reply, and Sara got her first good look at the man who'd nearly shattered her eardrums with his whistle moments before.

He was in his early thirties, she estimated, and probably well over six feet tall. His chestnut hair was long and layered and totally unkempt. Though his eyes were veiled by dark lashes, she could see they were an uncommon shade of hazy green. In faded denim jeans and a red cotton shirt, the tails of which were hanging over his waistband, he looked more like a vagabond than anything else. A messy, good-looking vagabond. She wondered vaguely what he did at the Sketch Shop.

"I've been meaning to speak to you about Warwick's nostrils," Alvin murmured, still flipping. "Now where did I . . . Ah, yes, here it is. 'Talk to Alex regarding Warwick's nostrils.' I wrote it down, you see. Right here, below the account of Jasmine's accident. My, what a long account that was."

Alex was an animator, Sara perceived. And Alvin was a ghoul. A lovable ghoul, but a ghoul nonetheless. He'd actually written about Jasmine's death. She had a feeling she'd better watch what she said around him.

"Warwick's nostrils, huh?" Alex reached forward and nudged the bare-chested blond Adonis in front of him. "Wake up, Dieter. This is your complaint, not mine."

"What?" Blinking, the blond man roused himself. "What complaint? Who's complaining?"

"Alvin. He says there's something wrong with Warwick."

"There is. Oh, yes, indeed, there is." Removing a heavy sheet of folded parchment from the pocket of his vest, Alvin thrust it at Sara. "You tell me what you think, miss. Tell me if you don't think Warwick could catch birds in nostrils like that."

Obligingly, Sara unfolded the paper. "I..." she began, then halted, impressed by the detailed artwork. "This is good. Who did this?"

"Alex, of course," Alvin told her with a definite nod. "Alex animates Warwick now. He's the best. But he does seem to be having a problem with nostrils these days, don't you, my boy?"

"Don't look at me, Alvin. I'm animating Morganna. Dieter's doing Warwick in this picture."

It was Alvin's turn to blink. "Preposterous!" he declared. "You've always done Warwick."

"No, not always," Alex reminded him patiently. "Only in the last film, and only because Morganna was temporarily shelved. Now that she's back, I'm doing her. Dieter's doing your character."

"No, no, no," Alvin objected. "That simply can't be. I don't have that written down anywhere. You must be mistaken. See here, my boy..."

"This is going to take forever, Sara," Noel drawled as Alvin continued to argue. "Since Jack appears to have lost control here, would you like me to show you around a bit?"

Sara took a look at the Shop's assistant production supervisor. Jack had lost it all right. He was currently embroiled in a heated discussion with the venomous-tongued woman who'd been sniping so bitterly from the sidelines. His absorption with her seemed to signal an end to this so-called meeting.

Nodding, Sara stood. "Sure," she said, glad she wouldn't have to suffer though the grand tour at Jack Kensington's hands. The man might be an administrative wizard, but his Dapper Dan mannerisms left a lot to be desired. With his perfectly groomed gold hair, rheumy blue eyes and fair skin, he looked like a sprite straight out of the Rainbow Forest. The fact that he was somehow related to Gus's wife undoubtedly accounted for his presence here at the studio. Under any other circumstances Sara couldn't see even the softhearted old Gus hiring him.

Noel led the way through the milling throng and out into the fourth-floor hallway. "This is the studio level," she disclosed over her shoulder. "The stages and sound booths are all up here." She indicated several glassed-in alcoves tucked behind a vast array of audio panels. "It's a little tricky getting your bearings at first, but you'll figure it out in time."

Would she? Sara wasn't so sure. "I have a lousy sense of direction," she said doubtfully. "How many corridors are there on this floor?"

Noel laughed. "Who knows? You see, this old mansion was built in 1855 by a miner who struck it rich up Sonora way. He designed himself a regular Gothic labyrinth to live in. When he died, the place was turned into a school for the performing arts. Unfortunately, in these parts, surfing and swimming are the major art forms. Old Gus took it over back in the seventies after he'd had his fill of Los Angeles. He's made a few modifications over the years, but basically, the layout's still intact. Down below's a little easier to navigate."

Sara peered through an arched doorway, which revealed a narrow staircase leading to the attic. "What's up there?" she questioned.

"The morgue."

"I beg your pardon?"

"Cartoon heaven," Noel clarified. "That's where we store the old drawings and tapes. If an animator's having problems, say, making one of the characters move, he or she can just move up here and take a look at how someone else did it."

"Sounds complicated."

"It can be, especially if you're new at it. Lucky for Gus, his staff's pretty loyal. There isn't much of a turnover at the Shop."

"Except for Morganna's voice," Sara noted dryly.

"That's right, honey," Noel concurred, clearly aware of the sorceress's purported curse. "Except for Morganna's voice."

With that weighty statement hanging in the air between them, the two women descended to the third floor.

Here, Sara spied one large central chamber with several smaller rooms shooting off from it. Unlike the soundstage area, this level had a completely human feeling to it. What she noticed most of all was the kaleidoscope of colors around her. Color and form splashed on a multitude of plastic sheets.

After explaining briefly how the various inks were applied to the drawings, Noel sent Sara a long, speculative look. "You can tell me to butt out if I'm being nosy," she said, "but just how is it you're here? Last any of us heard, Gus was vacillating between selling out to the Cartoon Emporium and coming up with a new sorceress to take Morganna's place."

Moving one shoulder, Sara replied, "I've known Gus for a long time, close to twenty years actually. My father has his own advertising agency in New York. An associate of his recommended that he talk to Gus about an animated ad he was trying to put together, so he packed my mother and me up and brought us out to the west coast with him for what he called an extended working vacation."

"Then I guess you know Gus pretty well, huh?"

"Well, yes and no," Sara admitted. "He used to come to New York sometimes after that, and whenever he did, I'd see him. But beyond that, I'm not terribly familiar with his work. At least, I wasn't," she amended, "until he called me from Dallas four weeks ago—right before he went into the hospital for bypass surgery."

"And that's when he asked you to do Morganna's voice?"

Sara nodded. "I guess he just wasn't ready to give up on that particular character yet."

"I guess not," Noel remarked, her eyes running with canny deliberation over Sara's jeans and white T-shirt. "You don't by any chance have a cape and red tights on under those clothes of yours, do you?"

Sara grinned. "You think I'll need them while I'm here?"

Shrugging, Noel fanned her face with a sheet of clear plastic. "You might," she allowed, her tone unreadable. "I suppose Gus told you all about Morganna's curse."

"He told me a little."

"Do you believe it's real?"

"The curse? No. Should I?"

"I guess that all depends. Some of us do. Some of us don't. And most of us are just glad we aren't doing her voice. Robin's about the only person I know who's chomping at the bit to play Morganna. Has been ever since Gus created the character eleven years ago."

"Robin," Sara repeated, frowning a little. "That's the woman who was talking to Jack when we left, isn't it? The one who does Princess Aurelia's voice?"

"Yep. Robin Danvers." Noel scanned the empty room, then to Sara's surprise began unfastening her jeans. "You see anyone of the male gender wandering around anywhere, you give me a good poke," she instructed, stripping down to a powder-blue, one-piece bathing suit. "Christie Brinkley hasn't got much to fear from me, but I'm too hot to worry about comparisons. Now, what else would you like to know?''

Sara perched herself on the corner of a cluttered desk, watching as Noel sucked in her stomach and tied the tails of her shirt around her waist. ''You were telling me about Robin Danvers.''

''No, I was finished with that subject, honey,'' Noel assured her. ''Besides, you can handle her. She'll give you a hard time at first, then she'll settle down to a steady stream of malevolent glares.''

''So I noticed,'' Sara murmured.

Noel chuckled. ''Don't worry, Sara. Mean looks aside, in a lot of ways, she's less creepy than Jack.''

Sara arched a disbelieving brow. ''You're sure about that, are you?''

''Uh-huh.'' Noel smiled. ''You see, Jack's a wheeler-dealer. He's been onto Gus to sell out to the Cartoon Emporium for the better part of a year now. He says a move like that would benefit all of us in the long run. I say it would benefit him most of all.'' She flung her jeans over her shoulder. ''What it boils down to is money and power. Jack likes 'em both. And honey,'' she added, arching a knowing brow, ''I'm very much afraid you're standing in his way right now. The last thing our conniving little mini-chief wants is a new Morganna messing up his plans.''

''His plans?'' Sara began, her curiosity aroused. However, she stopped speaking as Noel suddenly began peering around the huge room.

''My bag,'' she frowned, bending over the desk upon which Sara was still perched. ''Did I put it down when I took my jeans off? Or did I... Aw, damn, I did.'' She groaned. ''I left it upstairs.'' Emitting an aggrieved sigh, she began tugging on her pants. ''Wouldn't you know it? Just when I'm getting used to breathing again.''

Sara hid a smile. ''Do you want me to come with you?'' she asked, but Noel waved her off.

"No, it's okay. You wait here. Just don't stray too close to Robin's cat if you can help it."

Robin's cat? Sara followed the direction of Noel's departing nod, to a row of shelves laden with colorful pots of ink. There, in a typically feline crouch, sat a small Siamese cat, its blue eyes surveying every move she made.

It was a beautiful creature, sleek and perfectly marked. Had it not belonged to Robin Danvers, Sara would have ignored Noel's warning and tried to win its confidence. Somehow, though, she reflected wryly, she didn't think Robin would appreciate such a gesture.

Stretching her arms over her head, Sara slid from the desk and began poking through a pile of plastic sheets. She was lingering over a completed drawing of Morganna when she heard a woman talking on the far side of the stairwell door. Even allowing for her brief contact with Princess Aurelia's voice, she had no trouble recognizing the sarcastic lilt that belonged entirely to Robin Danvers.

She turned and saw Robin stepping across the threshold. "You might want to zip up your fly before you venture back into the meeting room," Robin trilled over her shoulder at the departing Noel. "Unless, of course, you're really looking for Alex rather than your purse."

Red lips drawn back into a taunting smile, she turned her gray eyes to Sara. There wasn't a trace of friendliness in her expression. Only a slight glimmer of surprise in the form of one elevated black brow.

"Well, what do you know?" she drawled, her tone resembling that of a serpent. "If it isn't our new Morganna. I see the curse hasn't wrought its deadly havoc on you yet."

Morganna's curse again. Well, why not? Sara thought. She'd expected this woman to believe in curses, hadn't she? Summoning up a smile, she met Robin's steely stare. "Sorry to disappoint you, but no, it hasn't gotten me."

Robin moved farther into the room, skirting Sara as a cat might skirt its quarry. "You can't escape its power, you know," she predicted, running the tips of her fingers lightly along a line of hanging plastic sheets. "Whatever you might or might not have heard about it, Morganna's curse is no rumor. It's real, lady, just as real as you and I."

"Is it?" Sara refused to be intimidated by this white-winged bride of Frankenstein. "Then if that's the case, why would you want to do the voice?" she countered coolly.

Robin regarded her through the fringe of her dark lashes. "Ah, yes, of course you'd know about that by this time, wouldn't you? Where Noel Gordon is concerned, there are no secrets." She moved one slender shoulder, covered now with a huge, drapy black jacket. "No matter. The point is, I can handle a curse."

"And you think I can't?" Sara retorted, keeping her tone even. There seemed little to be gained by letting the woman rile her.

Robin's laugh rang through the warm air. "Lady, I know you can't." She waved an airy hand. "Oh, maybe you'll hang on a bit longer than Jasmine, but beat a curse? Not a chance. You do know, don't you, that your most recent predecessor, Jasmine O'Rourke, was trying to leave town the night she accidentally died?"

Sara shrugged. "I heard she fell off a platform at the Santa Vera train depot, yes. But I don't see what that has to do with a curse."

"No?" Smiling, Robin strolled over to the shelf where her cat was still firmly ensconced. "Tell me then, Sara. What do you make of a woman who, for no discernable reason, would suddenly choose to pack up and leave town— Oh, pardon me," she interrupted herself with a low chuckle. "I say pack up and leave rather loosely, I'm afraid. You see, Jasmine didn't actually bother to pack. She just up and left. Poof!" Robin snapped her fingers. "Like a puff of smoke. No suitcases, not even an overnight bag. She simply—left. In the middle of the night. In the middle of the week. In the middle of taping a scene."

Sara had no idea what she was supposed to say to that. In truth, she really didn't know much about Jasmine

O'Rourke's death. Gus had very considerately left out the gory details when she'd spoken to him. Now, however, she wished he'd seen fit to give her just a few of the more pertinent facts.

"I still don't see what that has to do with me," Sara said at length, certain that Robin was attempting to unnerve her. "I hate to sound cold-blooded, but people die every day. And many of them in stranger ways than Jasmine O'Rourke."

"Yes, I daresay they do," Robin concurred, reaching up to lift her cat from the shelf. "But then again, none of those unfortunate people happened to be doing Morganna's voice when they died, did they? None of them," she added, "except for Jasmine O'Rourke. And three years before her, Elke Stevens. No," she said as she slowly turned back to Sara, "I'm afraid there's just no way around this. You do Morganna's voice; you bring Morganna's curse upon yourself. We know that, don't we, Pyewackett?" she crooned to the animal in her arms.

Sara hesitated. "Pyewackett?" she repeated dubiously. "That sounds like a name straight out of *Bell, Book and Candle*."

Robin's red lips curved into a wicked travesty of a smile. "It is," she replied, holding one hand up in front of her face and staring at Sara through the splay of her fingers. The smile took on definite overtones of malice as she arched her black brows. Then, at Sara's skeptical expression, she laughed once more. "You don't get it, do you? You haven't figured it out?"

Sara had a horrible sinking feeling that she had indeed figured it out. Nonetheless, she managed a composed, "Maybe it would be best if you just told me, Robin."

The woman tossed her ebony hair. "Oh, it's quite simple, really," she replied, her eyes steady on Sara's. She paused for effect, then announced in a low ominous tone, "I'm a witch."

Chapter Three

"You might have mentioned that Robin was a witch when I asked you about her," Sara muttered as she and Noel descended to the second-floor animation level.

Noel, who'd returned from upstairs mere seconds after Robin had made her sinister disclosure, gave the door in front of her a mighty shove. "If I had, would you have believed me?" she demanded, grinning broadly.

"I don't see why not." Sara sighed. "Tell me, are there any other denizens of darkness lurking around the Shop?"

"Nope, just Morganna's curse, and I gather you got quite an earful about that from Robin."

Sara couldn't resist a small smile. "I'm beginning to feel like an authority on the subject, and I haven't even started working yet."

"Well, it never hurts to know what you're getting into," Noel told her. "And speaking of getting into something: Welcome to Wonderland, Alice. This here's the Sketch Shop's answer to the Magic Kingdom. The animation level."

Slipping past Noel, Sara stepped through the door. As it had been on the floor above, the human feeling was very strong, except that here there was an added dose of magic and make-believe. Storyboards lined the paneled walls of the main room and every other partitioned-off room Sara could see. All the characters from the Rainbow Forest were present and accounted for: Croatia, Guardian of the Rainbow Scepter; Princess Aurelia; Dracos, Lord of the Purple Mist; Warwick, the Master Wizard; and of course, Morganna.

"Voices first, animation second," Noel informed her. "You do your job, then Alex takes over."

Sara spared the woman a brief, curious glance. "Alex, being Morganna's animator?"

"You got it, honey. You know, you're a very lucky lady in some ways. Alex Cross is the head of the animation department. He's also the best animator there is. Even Dieter's not as good—and he's good."

"Dieter who?"

"Dieter Haas, the healthy-looking blond guy who was taking a catnap during the meeting. He and Alex have worked together for years, both here and down at the Cartoon Emporium in Los Angeles."

Sara regarded the woman thoughtfully. "The Cartoon Emporium," she repeated. "Gus used to be partners with the man who owns it, didn't he?"

"Uh-huh. The man's name is Forrest Clements. And the industry buzz is that he's mighty keen to get his hands on the Sketch Shop. You see, when he and Gus split, Forrest lost a passel of popular characters. My feeling is he's just itching to get 'em back. I'm sure he sees dollar signs in Morganna's amber eyes. Unfortunately for him, Gus doesn't agree with his cheap animation tricks—which, I'm sure, is what led to their less-than-amicable split ten years ago."

For what it was worth, Sara digested that tidbit of information, along with all the other bits that had been imparted to her that afternoon. While Noel paused to examine some of the newer storyboard drawings, she wandered over to the wide window and gazed at the clearing below.

The view from the top of Wizard's Hill was incredible. The vibrant beach community of Santa Vera, stretched out like a shimmering jewel, was basking lazily in the late-afternoon sun. Set in a lush valley between the Pacific Ocean and the Santa Ynez Mountains, the atmosphere in the town smacked of the late fifties and early sixties, in direct contrast to the rather haunting atmosphere of the Sketch Shop. She'd passed food drive-ins on Coronado Boulevard where the car hops still wore roller skates, had seen surfboards crammed into the backseats of no less than five classic Chevy convertibles and heard Beach Boys' music blaring loudly at every turn. Although Los Angeles was just a stone's throw down the coast, there wasn't a trace of Hollywood glitter here. Only sun and sand and sea—and the aroma of Kingsford charcoal wafting from half the Mexican-tiled patios in the area.

Behind her, Sara heard the muted buzz of the telephone-intercom system, followed seconds later by a grunt of displeasure from Noel. "Arrogant little troll," she muttered, pulling on the jeans she'd recently removed for a second time. "Honey, I've gotta run downstairs and dig up a tape for Jack. Give me a couple minutes, and we'll finish our tour."

Sara nodded. "Is it all right if I wander around a bit on my own?"

"Uh-huh. Just try not to cross swords with Robin again, okay? I'm sure that underneath her nasty cracks she's really still smoking about Gus's decision to let you do Morganna's voice instead of her."

If there was one thing Sara didn't want to do just then, it was cross swords with Robin Danvers. She'd had more than enough of that particular woman for one day.

For ten minutes or so after Noel had left, Sara contented herself with exploring the animation area. Then she took a chance and went down the rear stairwell, past the main-floor reception area and into the basement. It probably wasn't a smart thing to do since there was very little light filtering in through the tiny windows, but as usual her curiosity got the better of her.

This was the camera department, she realized quickly, one of the more technologically advanced areas of the Shop. Like the fourth floor, the basement was a maze of winding halls and hidden chambers. There were several life-size posters of characters from the Rainbow Forest adorning the walls. Sara wandered from one to another, engrossed in the cartoon figures looming above her, completely caught up in the spell of Gus's medieval world.

It was like being teleported back centuries, back to a world of witches and fairies, castles and dungeons, spells and sorcery. Even the floors were constructed of old stones. There was a sense of netherworld mysticism here, a hint of the Dark Ages when superstition had run rampant. Oddly enough, Sara could have sworn that Warwick's hawklike eyes were actually watching her, following her every move. That was how strong the supernatural feeling was. How strong and how compelling.

Giving her head a determined shake, she left Warwick and walked on to the next poster. To her dismay, she got the same sense of being watched from the eyes of the evil Lord Dracos.

Inner gremlins, she told herself resolutely. That was all it was. She was letting all the talk about Morganna's curse rattle her. The eyes in the posters weren't real, and the curse was nothing more than a lot of superstitious nonsense.

Swallowing the lump of irrational apprehension that had risen in her throat, she tried to figure out exactly where she was. Somewhere in the center of the cellar, she presumed. But of course, she had absolutely no idea how she'd gotten there or which direction to take to get out. Squaring her shoulders, she endeavored to retrace her steps, all the while ignoring the ripples of unease skating up and down her spine.

This was absurd. The eerie sensations had to be all in her head. Her mistake lay in coming down here alone. The basement was a veritable dungeon, dark and damp and completely devoid of humanity. The only person she might reasonably expect to encounter in a place such as this was an ax-wielding henchman on the prowl for renegade prisoners.

Quickening her steps, she tried to use the posters as a guide. Warwick, Dracos, Morganna, Croatia... and then Dracos again. Damn, did every corridor in this place double back on itself?

She glanced warily at the malevolent Dracos behind her. His features were lean, almost to the point of being skeletal. Sharp black eyes glared down at her from beneath heavy brows. They were vicious eyes, brutal and cold.

Next to him, she spied a picture of Princess Aurelia. Perhaps her eyes didn't contain the same glint of malice as the evil Lord Dracos's did, but they reminded Sara all over again of Robin Danvers. And thinking about a witch was not particularly comforting in surroundings like these.

Controlling her nervousness with difficulty, she let her feet carry her along another cobbled passageway—a dark, haunting passageway that seemed to wind even deeper into the cellar.

Then suddenly, through the dusky darkness of the time-worn halls, she heard it. A faint whispered voice that brushed across her soul like the touch of a ghostly hand.

"Forever shall Morganna sleep... for now and for all eternity. Forever shall the sorceress remain at rest. Forever...."

AT LEAST AN HOUR ticked by before Alex contemplated leaving the Shop for the day. Stretching the cramped muscles in his neck and back, he roused himself from his drafting board, flipped his sketch pad closed and tried to focus on the Garfield wall clock one of the other animators had hung for a joke.

Six-ten. Yeah, it was time to leave all right. He still had to work on his Jeep tonight, and if he finished that little chore quickly enough, he wouldn't mind sitting in on a set or two over at the Cellar Door, Santa Vera's raunchiest underground nightclub. Dieter's combo might not be up to par with Bruce Springsteen's band, but banging away on the drums with them usually gave Alex a release, a chance to get away from the world of cartoon witches for a while.

Almost in tandem with that thought, Dieter grumbled his way down from the meeting room. "Nostrils," he was muttering crankily under his breath. "It'd serve the old goat right if I added a scene where Warwick's whole damned nose got bitten off by a buzzard."

Grinning, Alex tapped a cigarette out of his pocket, debated for a second, then shrugged and slid the filtered tip between his lips. What the hell. He couldn't live forever anyway. He might as well take what pleasure he could from his bad habits.

"Alvin's just being picky," he commented idly as Dieter tossed himself into a chair in the partitioned work area. "His feathers are ruffled because Warwick's not going to receive star billing in this picture."

"Tell me about it," Dieter sighed, chuckling as his customary good humor slowly reasserted itself. "I've just spent the better part of an hour listening to him howl about Warwick's downfall. It's his opinion that if Morganna has to overcome her one-film banishment from the Rainbow Forest, she should at least be subservient to the Master Wizard when she returns. I swear, Alex, I think the old man really believes he's Warwick."

"Forty years in the business can get to anyone," Alex replied, shrugging the observation off.

"Yeah, well he should've stuck to animating dancing cows at the Emporium. His crossover into the realm of voices is going to kill me. You wouldn't care to switch characters, would you?"

Alex leaned against the windowsill and eyed his friend sagely. "Would you?" he countered, and as expected, Dieter gave his head a faintly sad shake.

"No, I guess not." From his sprawled position he queried, "So what do you really think of Morganna's new voice? You figure she'll last longer than Jasmine?"

"She'd better," Alex said flatly, blowing out a stream of smoke. "We're so far behind schedule already that it's going to take a miracle to finish the film anywhere near the planned deadline."

Outside the partitioned walls, he heard the stairwell door clank open. A moment later, Noel stuck her head around one of the canvas screens. "Have either of you seen Sara?" she asked. "I told her she could poke around the place if she wanted to, but she seems to have vanished into thin air."

At their unrevealing shrugs, she came into the work area, plucked Alex's cigarette from his fingers and stuck it in her own mouth, drawing deeply on the menthol filter. "I wish you'd give these things up," she reproached him without rancor. "You're starting me down the road to temptation all over again."

Alex's answering grin held a trace of lazy amusement. "Just offering you an example to live down to, Noel," he drawled, giving his sore muscles one last stretch. "Something for your willpower to fight."

"Yeah, well speaking of willpower, how would you two sexy males like to help me find Morganna's mighty tempting missing voice. And don't give me that, 'Who, l'il ole me?' look, either of you. I saw you both gaping at her during the meeting. Assuming you're not quite dead, I'd hazard a guess that you noticed those big baby blues of hers. Now come on, let's find her so I can make sure she's got a roof over her head tonight. Her *own* roof," Noel added with a pointed look at Alex.

Although he suppressed a smile at her droll expression, Alex didn't miss the subtle hint of warning in Noel's voice. That she wanted something more from him than mere friendship was no secret, but then again, it wasn't a topic he particularly cared to delve into with her. As a rule, things were easy between them, and that was the way he intended to keep their relationship. Open and easy. He wasn't going to become involved with Noel or anyone else, not for a long, long time.

Once burned, he reflected wryly, crushing out his cigarette. He wasn't about to get singed by those same flames twice. He knew it and so did she. Fairy princess or not, a fleeting caution was doubtless as far as Noel would go in terms of one Sara Moreland.

Picking up his jacket, he followed his two coworkers to the central animation area.

"Your choice, Dieter," Noel was saying. "Do you wanna go up or down?"

"Up," Dieter stated. Then he glanced over his shoulder at Alex. "Last I saw of Alvin he was heading toward Jack's office on the main floor, still taking potshots at Warwick's nostrils. I think my ego's suffered enough of a bruising for one day. It's your turn to listen to him gripe."

"Fine." Noel made the decision. "Dieter, you check the morgue, I'll scout around the third floor and Alex can hunt through the basement."

The basement, huh? Well she might have made it that far, Alex allowed. If she had, though, it was doubtful she'd be able to find her way out in a big hurry. The place was a maze. A seasoned navigator would have a hard time untangling himself from the crisscross of converging passageways.

Tugging on his jacket, he started for the central stairwell, pausing briefly to grab a wedge of the chocolate layer cake Noel had brought in that morning. He made it as far as the muraled foyer on the ground floor before running into anyone. And even then, neither Alvin nor Robin, both of whom were en route to the front door, noticed him. As usual they were both immersed deeply in their own muttered thoughts.

"Fire and earth and wind and sea," Robin was chanting under her breath. "Force of nature—prophecy. Moon and tide at my decree. Force of life. So mote it be."

Alvin's quieter voice underscored Robin's rather eerie tones. "I, Warwick, Master of Wizards in the Rainbow Realm, do hereby banish thee, my treacherous apprentice, to the Mountain of Shadows. This is your fate, Morganna, an end to your evil trickery. Forever shall you remain in your castle chamber. Forever trapped in the spell of the Moonstone Orb...."

Reflectively Alex took another bite of cake. Most of Alvin's discourse had come straight from the final act of the second Rainbow Forest film. But who was really uttering those lines? he wondered. Alvin or Warwick? And more to the point, why were they being uttered at all?

Robin, Alex understood. She was always chanting about something particularly when she was upset. Alvin, however, was more difficult to read. He'd been complaining about Warwick's nostrils upstairs, and now he was apparently off on some other quirky tangent. The man was definitely not working on all cylinders.

"Alex, wait a minute. I want a word with you." Jack strutted out of his office like the pompous elf he was.

Not especially interested in anything the assistant production supervisor might have to say, Alex continued in his trek toward the basement. "I'm not here," he said around a mouthful of chocolate cake.

"What kind of answer is that?" Jack snapped. "Of course you're here, and I want to talk to you. It's about the latest offer from the Cartoon Emporium."

"Not my department, Jack," Alex tossed over his shoulder, pulling open the basement door. "If you want to talk sellout, phone Gus in Dallas. He owns this place, not me."

"Yeah, but he listens to you." Jack's Gucci loafers tapped double-time on the stone staircase. "You could make him understand the benefits of selling the Shop to Forrest Clements."

"Sorry, not interested."

Out of the corner of his eye, Alex saw Jack's pale hand snake out to make a grab for his arm. One warning glance had him snatching it back again. "Look, Alex," Jack began, clearing his throat. "I know we don't get along all that well, but think of old Gus for a minute. Think about Morganna's curse, for God's sake."

"There is no Morganna's curse."

"Oh? You're sure of that, are you?"

For the first time, Alex slowed his stride on the worn stairs. "What are you getting at?" he demanded, out of patience with Jack's dogged insistence that the curse was real. Jack's and everyone else's around this place.

"Just this," the shorter man said, his tone once more imperious. "It's my feeling that the whole Shop is under some ill-fated spell or other. Nothing supernatural, mind you, more like an over-extension of luck. Gus's standards are way too high. There's simply not enough money to maintain them. I think Jasmine's death was a sign of some sort, a signal to Gus to quit now, before he's forced to declare bankruptcy."

"Bull."

Jack's lips compressed to a thin line. "It's not bull, Alex. Okay, so maybe I'm being a little melodramatic, but you have to admit, Jasmine couldn't have picked a worse time to take a header in front of a train."

"Right. She should have waited until the picture was completed, *then* fallen off the depot platform."

"That's hardly what I meant," Jack grated, his cheeks mottling. "But while we're on the subject, what was she doing at the station in the first place? She should have been at her beach house studying her lines, or at the very least getting a good night's sleep. Alex, are you even listening to me?" he demanded testily.

"No." Taking another bite of cake, Alex peered into one of the dimly lit corridors that sprang off from the camera department. "Sara, are you down there?"

"Sara." Jack frowned. "What makes you think she's in the basement?"

Alex shrugged. "Same thing that makes you think the Shop's under some kind of an evil spell." He raised his voice. "Sara?"

"I give up," Jack muttered. "I'm going to go phone Gus."

"Do that," Alex suggested. "And while you're at it you might want to tell him all about your latest curse theory. Who knows, you may be working for the Cartoon Emporium sooner than you think. Of course, without Forrest Clements's payoff tucked in your pocket, you'll probably have to wait a while before you can launch any congressional campaigns, but at least you'll be moving up in the world."

The sarcasm in his tone wasn't lost on Jack. Without a word, he turned and tapped his way back up the stairs.

The ominous statements continued to haunt Alex long after the man had gone. An evil spell? Not a chance. But what about something else? It could just be that someone at the Shop was deliberately trying to sabotage the fourth film. There'd been enough minor accidents and spoiled tapes around here lately to support that theory. And then, there was the uncomfortable feeling he got in his gut whenever he recalled Jasmine O'Rourke's death....

Damn, but he wished he hadn't thought about that, Alex swore to himself. And how he hoped those little twinges of discomfort were unfounded.

Shoving the last bite of cake in his mouth, he moved deeper into the cellar maze.

FROM THE DEPTHS of a place that had to be a subbasement, Sara heard the distant sound of male voices. While she couldn't really pick out the details of the obviously heated discussion, at least she now had something she could latch on to. Hopefully a way out of this shadowy cavern.

One final shiver swept through her as she recalled the hideous whisper she'd heard earlier. The whisper that was still echoing eerily in her head. Who in God's name could possible have uttered those low raspy words? And why would anyone want to do it in the first place?

Allowing herself one final, fearful shudder, Sara honed in on the voices she could hear now. She was debating over which corridor to take to find the men behind them when, to her disconcertion, the conversation suddenly ceased.

With a muttered damn, she glanced sideways at Warwick's bearded visage. She'd passed the ancient wizard so many times in her circular travels down here that he was actually beginning to feel like an old friend—one whose hooded gaze had grown far less demonic once that creepy whisper had faded into the darkened reaches of the cellar. Now she was just plain lost. Lost and shaken and tired of searching for a way out.

"Sara?" A man's voice reached her from some indistinct passageway to her left. "Sara, it's Alex. Are you down here?"

Thank heaven. A human voice at last, speaking at a normal level. Breathing an enormous sigh of relief, she called back an echoing, "Over here."

"Keep talking to me, Morganna," he returned, a little closer now than before.

"What do you want me to talk about?"

"Doesn't matter. Tell me a dirty joke or something."

A dirty joke, huh? Well, why not? She'd heard hundreds of them from her fellow actors.

Leaning against the stone wall, she took a deep steadying breath. "Okay, here goes," she said. "There was this guy who decided to crash a party one night, but by the time he finally got there, he'd had so many martinis that he could hardly stand up, let alone remember what horrible things he might have done. The next morning he felt terrible. He had absolutely no idea whose party he'd crashed, only that whoever had thrown it owned an incredible gold toilet..." She paused, cutting herself off to enquire, "Are you anywhere near me yet, Alex?"

"Right here," he told her, pushing himself away from one of the pitted stone walls and out into the filtering light. "I wanted to hear the whole joke before I showed myself. What were you saying about a gold toilet?"

"Forget it," Sara murmured. "I made the whole thing up. I don't know any dirty jokes."

"Uh-huh." He grinned. "If that gold toilet is really a tuba in disguise, I'd say you know at least one."

She tried not to smile. "If you've already heard it, why were you hanging around waiting for the punch line?"

"I like the sound of your voice," he said, shrugging, and Sara believed him. Of course, she would have believed just about anything Alex Cross said to her at this moment. Although she couldn't be sure why, her instincts told her that his was not the voice that had issued the disquieting warning.

As Alex moved farther out of the shadows, she got a better look at him. He was wearing a black lightweight jacket over his red shirt now, but essentially he appeared as unkempt as before. As unkempt and every bit as good-looking. Now why, she wondered, puzzled, had she noticed that?

She had no time to ponder the question, for Alex was raising a mocking brow in her direction. "This is probably none of my business, Sara," he drawled, "but what exactly are you doing down here?"

"Waiting for Noel," she said automatically.

"Hell of a place to wait," he observed, his tone mildly skeptical. "Even Noel loses her bearings in this part of the basement."

Confused, Sara ventured a cautious, "I thought she worked down here."

"She does, but not this far down. In case you hadn't noticed, these halls slope into a subbasement, which is where we are right now."

Well, at least she'd been correct in her subbasement theory, Sara reflected. Too bad the slope wasn't just a bit more discernible. "How far down does it go?" she asked, casting dubious eyes deeper into the labyrinth.

"To the wine cellar. You're almost there. The builder, Ezra Soloman, had a fascination for mazes. He was also a fanatic when it came to hoarding his vintage grape." Alex propped one shoulder against the damp wall. "He figured that even if a thief could get to his coveted cellar, there'd be no way for him to get back out again."

"So why are there posters on the walls?"

"Because Alvin has a rotten sense of direction. He uses them to guide himself into the wine cellar."

Sara stared at him surprised. "You mean there's still wine there?"

Alex sent her a lazy grin. "Depends how often Alvin raids the place. When Gus is around, he keeps the shelves stocked. When he isn't, the supply tends to dwindle pretty fast."

"In other words, Warwick's voice is a lush," she interpreted bluntly. "Does Gus know about this?"

"Yes, Gus knows about this," Alex replied. "And no, he doesn't care. And offhand, I'd say Alvin's no more of a lush than anyone else at the Shop."

Which wasn't really saying much, Sara thought. Still, she let the matter slide. It was enough that the creepy feelings evoked by the invisible voice she'd heard had subsided. And Lord knew she was glad that Alex had taken the time to come looking for her.

"Maybe I'd better go find Noel," she murmured, conscious of his eyes sliding over her body, not quite sure how to read their expression.

Again that vaguely disconcerting grin curved his lips. "Might be a good idea," he said in an amused voice. "I assume you'll want to get yourself settled in sometime tonight." He straightened from the wall. "Gus did arrange accommodations for you, didn't he?"

Sara met his hazy green eyes. "Yes, he did. He told me there was an empty beach house I could use while I was here."

"One of the Apple Shack cabanas?"

"Yes, I think that's what he said."

"Did he also happen to mention that your predecessor, Jasmine O'Rourke, stayed there?"

No, he hadn't, but Sara wasn't prepared to let Alex or anyone else know that. She must be getting used to shocking news, she decided with an inward sigh. In any event she wasn't afraid of ghosts...or so she kept telling herself. "He might have," she allowed carefully. "I don't remember."

Alex regarded her through half-closed eyes. "I'll bet you don't," he murmured, then he shrugged. "Do you have a way to get there?"

She nodded. "I spent last night at a friend's place in San Francisco. Since she was going to be out of town for a while, she lent me her car."

"Do you want me to show you where you'll be living?"

Not really, she thought. Although she wasn't quite sure why, something about Alex Cross had the power to unnerve her. Something she didn't think she'd ever be able to explain, even to herself. The man was just a bit too sexy for her liking. Too sexy, too good-looking and much more distracting than any male had a right to be.

"Thanks, but I've put you to enough trouble already," she declined politely.

He moved one shoulder. "Suit yourself, but it's no trouble. I live on the beach—right next to where you'll be staying, in fact."

Sara grinned, not really certain why she wasn't surprised to find that out. "Better you than Robin," she replied brightly. "I'd much rather live next door to someone who animates witches than to someone who is one."

Alex's smile widened a bit at that, and Sara had to admit he had a beautiful smile. Not sun-god perfect like Dieter Haas's, but riveting just the same.

"I hate to be the bearer of bad news, Sara," he said, turning into a corridor she'd somehow missed before, "but Robin does live down near the beach. She rooms above the Apple Shack. When she's not working here, she moonlights up there as a fortune-teller. So if I were you," he added humorously, "I'd make a point of keeping my palms to myself and my tea leaves out of her sight."

"Thanks, I'll remember that," Sara replied. And with one final backward glance at the cracked stone walls of the cellar, she followed him up the sloped floor and out of the shadowy underground maze.

She didn't notice the slight movement that altered one of those darkened shadows, didn't see the fingers that curled themselves tightly around the corner of the passageway behind her. She didn't feel the hostile eyes that trailed her out of the murky subbasement. And she didn't hear the prescient whisper, uttered in a bitterly soft rasp.

"A curse I place on thee, Sara Moreland, for now and for all eternity. Dominion is mine alone. Mine...until the end of time...."

Chapter Four

"Okay, this is it." From the passenger seat of Sara's MG, Noel pointed to a cluster of white cabins situated on the upper fringe of a broad stretch of beach. "Just turn onto this little patch of gravel and park anywhere you can find a spot. Under the trees is good."

"Which cabin's mine?" Sara asked, easing the car to a halt beneath a thatch of swaying palms. For the time being, at least, her fears had been banished—aided, she knew, by Noel's upbeat presence. It was a state of mind she fully intended to maintain.

With her head, Noel indicated a small building ahead of them. "Yours is the one down front there, right next to Alex's." She gave her hand an aimless wave. "And that's Granny's Apple Shack up on Coronado Boulevard, beside the Dog'n Suds. 'Course dear old Granny's long since made the climb to the Pearly Gates, but the Shack's still going strong. It's run by a bone crusher from the city these days."

"A what?" Sara laughed.

"A wrestler. You know, like Hulk Hogan, only older and flabbier." Noel chuckled. "The Shack's a teahouse cum restaurant. If you're ever hungry for a good meal, that's the place to go."

Sara couldn't see ever being hungry enough to venture up to Granny's Apple Shack. Not when there was a self-proclaimed witch who told fortunes on the side likely waiting to dish out all sorts of dire prophecies. Suppressing a distasteful shudder, she turned to look at the other cabanas in the vicinity, listening as Noel cheerfully described their various occupants.

"This here is Santa Vera's answer to *Rear Window*, Sara," she said with a wide sweep of her arm. "You know, you're going to be living in the middle of quite a colorful collection of characters." She pointed to her right. "Over there in that little cabana, you've got yourself a skinny old man, who shuffles around the sand all day collecting empty beer bottles and seashells. And behind him, you've got an aging hippie who listens nonstop to scratchy Bob Dylan records and still believes she's at Woodstock."

"Wonderful." Sara grinned. "Now, let me make sure I've got this straight. I have a guy who draws sorceresses and wizards on one side of me, a wandering hermit on the other, a hippie behind him and a witch living over Granny's Apple Shack."

"Yep. You've also got a stand-up comedian behind the hippie, and next to him, a fading, silent-movie queen. Her place is the one with the rhinestone underwear flapping away on the clothesline. Oh, and then you've also got a starving artist a ways back from her. If you hear the lids on your garbage cans rattling in the dead of night, it'll probably just be Desmond scrounging for useful bits of trash."

"You seem awfully familiar with these people," Sara observed. "Do you live around here, too?"

"No, but let's just say I have a fondness for spending time with one of your closer neighbors." Noel raised a shrewd brow. "You getting my drift here, Sara?"

It would have been hard to miss. "Loud and clear," Sara confirmed, slamming the trunk and recalling Robin's snide comment beyond the stairwell door earlier. So Noel had a thing for Alex, did she? Interesting. And understandable. Alex Cross was a good-looking man.

Noel's round features relaxed into a pleasant smile. "I thought you might. Okay, now let's see about getting your things into your new cabana."

That, however, was easier said than done. One thing Sara had never been was a light packer. Her wardrobe accompanied her wherever she went. At the end of ten sweltering minutes, Noel rolled her eyes and tossed a final carryall onto the sofa in the spartanly furnished living room.

"You sure you and Jasmine weren't related?" she grumbled, albeit good-naturedly. "She was just like you. Used to carry around enough luggage to fill the cargo hold of a 747."

Sara shook her head, but her curiosity was piqued about her predecessor. "Tell me about Jasmine O'Rourke, Noel," she said, shoving the carryall aside so she could sit down. "Was she a good Morganna?"

"She was decent. Nowhere near as good as Elke."

"Did you like her?"

"Nope, couldn't stand the sight of her. Picture Rita Hayworth in her prime, and I'm sure you can guess a few of the reasons why. Don't get me wrong, though." Noel shrugged. "There were plenty of other things that bugged me about the woman."

"For example?"

"Her dippy giggle for one. You see, life was just one big hoot to dear Jasmine." Noel's smirk held a note of satisfaction. "I guess she must've known she was getting on people's nerves, though, 'cause about halfway through her two-week stay here, she kind of started quieting down. Hardly heard a titter that last week—thank God. Oh, and then there was the way she dressed—if you can call it dressing, that is. Miniskirts and low-cut halters were Jasmine's style. All in all, she pranced around in outfits that didn't rightly have enough material in them to be called a belt. And you gotta know she did a fair bit of prancing outside Alex's window."

Sara digested that information in silence, frowning slightly over something Robin had mentioned at the Shop. "Do you know what Jasmine was doing at the train station in the middle of the night?" she asked.

"Haven't got a clue," Noel said, drawing out each word she spoke in that heavy southern accent of hers. "Like I said, she clammed up real good that last week she was here. Kept looking at all of us like we were from outer space. Could be she just didn't feel comfortable around an animation studio. Or maybe some sleaze-ball Hollywood director offered her a role in an X-rated movie, and she decided to accept."

Possibly, but Sara had a feeling it hadn't been either of those things. Gus had spoken a little too highly of the woman for that to be the case. And if there was one thing she knew about Gus Sherman, it was that he was an impeccable judge of character. Besides, why would Jasmine have left town without any of her personal possessions? That was one of the things Sara simply couldn't understand, and the question lingered long after Noel had left, declining the offer of a lift home in favor of a little exercise.

An hour later, having more or less unpacked her clothes, and for the moment doused her curiosity, Sara took her first real look around her rented cabana.

For a beach shack, it was really quite nice. Open and airy, with windows everywhere. There were two in the bedroom, two in the kitchen, two enormous ones in the living room and even a small hexagonal one in the bathroom. The walls were painted a pale yellow and adorned with lithographs of Snow White and the Seven Dwarfs, Little Red Riding Hood and, on a more reminiscent note, Bobby Darin, decked out in a trench coat and a felt hat, with a shark fin rising in the darkened alley behind him. "Mack the Knife" and the Brothers Grimm, Sara reflected, amused. The landlord must be as much of a character as the rest of her neighbors.

After a quick trip to the Safeway on Coronado Boulevard, Sara settled herself in the breakfast nook and let her gaze roam over the pounding waves of the nearby Pacific Ocean. It was a pleasant sight, warm and summery, and Jan and Dean's "The Little Old Lady from Pasadena," wafting down from the Dog 'n Suds drive-in only made the southern California atmosphere that much stronger.

When she'd finished her meal and washed up the dishes, Sara wandered slowly toward her room, determined to finish hanging her clothes that night, equally determined not to dwell on Robin Danvers's morbid predictions about Morganna's curse, or the horrible whisper she'd heard down in the Sketch Shop's cellar.

As she entered the tiny chamber, Sara closed her eyes for a moment, savoring the fresh ocean breeze that washed across her face. The air here was subtly different than it was in Maine. Warmer and somehow not quite as salty.

Taking one final deep breath, she turned her attention to the scattering of open suitcases on the floor. She saw that one of the pale yellow curtains had billowed out and was flapping wildly across her overnight bag.

A little puzzled, Sara lifted her eyes to the window. Now, that was odd. She could have sworn she'd only opened that window halfway. Either her memory was failing, or the San Andreas fault worked its destructive magic in very strange and unusual ways along this stretch of the coast.

Reaching up, she dragged the sash back into place. Then she flipped the curtains aside and picked up her overnight case.

The only space in the room not laden with clothes was the vanity, and with a rueful smile at the explosion of colorful fabrics spilling out over the bed and nightstand, she dropped the soft-sided bag onto the empty wooden surface. One of these days, she'd have to learn how to pack—

The thought broke off sharply as Sara's eyes suddenly froze on the oval mirror before her. The curtains were still blowing softly in the evening breeze, blowing in vaporous golden tendrils across the mirror's frame. They fanned out slowly, veiling the silvery glass somewhat...but not quite enough to obliterate the jagged slashes of red scrawled upon it.

In numbed horror, Sara stared at the hideous scorings, her fingers digging convulsively into the leather strap of her overnight case, her breath seizing painfully in her throat.

"Oh, my God," she breathed, certain her heart was going to slam its way right out of her chest. "This can't be real!"

She remained there in front of the vanity, too stunned to move for several terrified seconds. Then adrenaline took over. Spinning around, she fled the room. Fled the cabana and ran across the sun-bleached veranda to the warm sand beyond.

A creeping darkness had invaded the California coast, but while there were lights shining in a dozen nearby windows, none of them looked overly welcoming to her—not after what Noel had told her about the people behind them.

Without pausing in her flight, she raced across the sand to Alex's front door, banging on it until her fists were raw and numb. "Alex!" She shouted his name above the opening strains of Perry Mason coming from inside. "Alex, answer the door!"

She was still banging on the rough wood when the bolt slid back. That the man who emerged was dripping wet and standing there clad only in a pair of hastily pulled-on jeans was a detail Sara scarcely noticed. Using both her hands, she grabbed his damp wrist and pulled. "Alex, you've got to come to my cabana with me. You've got to see what's in there."

A frown of confusion spread across his dark features. "What are you talking about?" he demanded, nevertheless taking a few forward steps.

Sara willed herself to calm down. Grinding her back teeth together, she managed a semi-rational, "Someone's been in my bedroom. There's a...a message...written on my mirror."

His lashes lowered, veiling the hazy green of his eyes. "What kind of message?"

"I...ah...two words." She swallowed the lump of panic in her throat. "It says: Morganna's curse. And it's written in red. You know, like blood."

"Jesus." The low oath burst from him like a gunshot blast. He drew her swiftly into his cabin. "All right," he said, reaching for his discarded red shirt. "You wait here. I'll go have a look."

He'd go have a look? No way. "I'm coming with you," Sara announced firmly. "I've been in enough murder-mystery plays to know exactly what happens to the person who stays behind and waits."

"Now why did I just know you were going to say that?" Alex murmured, taking her by the hand. "Okay, come on then. Let's go see if we can't figure out what's going on around here."

In bare feet, Alex moved soundlessly across the still-warm sand, and Sara stayed right on his heels all the way. Across the sand, along the open veranda and finally into her cabana.

There was only the glow of the lights of neighboring shacks to guide the way, and more than once Sara found herself bumping into unfamiliar tables and chairs. Alex, however, seemed to have no problem navigating the room. He headed unerringly toward the back of the cabin, paused for only a second to wait for her, then flipped on the overhead light.

It called for a tremendous effort on her part, but somehow Sara was able to summon up the nerve to peer over his broad shoulder. And what she saw—or rather, what she didn't see—made her eyes widen in utter disbelief.

"Oh no!" she moaned, only half-aware she'd spoken aloud. "It's just like the voice in the cellar." She continued to stare at the oval mirror, yet she knew all the staring in the world wouldn't change the truth. The window she'd half closed was open once more. The pale gold curtains were again blowing wildly in the warm breeze, plastering themselves across the vanity mirror.

But the glass was clean.

"I'M TELLING YOU, Alex, it was there, spelled out in jagged red letters: Morganna's curse. Those were the words I saw, and I'm not the type of person who imagines things like that." Sara couldn't sit still in Alex's cluttered cabana. Rising from the plump sofa with its collection of jeans and newspapers draped across the back, she stepped over a sleeping Alsatian to pace the carpet in front of the television.

Without lifting his head, Alex raised his eyes from the bottles he'd been sorting through on the kitchen counter. She was upset, no question. She'd also seen exactly what she said she did, of that he was certain. The mirror had been smudged in spots as if someone had just recently gone over it with a paper towel, and they'd both smelled the telltale traces of cleaner hanging in the air near the window. As well, he'd pointed out to her a couple of red smears on the outside pane. Whoever had been in there obviously hadn't had time to cover his or her tracks completely.

"Here, drink this," Alex said, coming out from behind the counter and handing Sara a glass. The subtle scent of roses and wildflowers he'd quickly come to associate with her hit him almost instantly, and he turned away to lounge against the wall on the far side of the narrow room. He liked the scent she wore. It reminded him of the tropics, and it belonged on a fairy princess. But now just wasn't a good time to be concentrating on Sara Moreland as a woman.

He kept his eyes on her while she absently took a sip of the drink he'd poured for her. He saw her pause and look into the glass. "What is this?" she asked, swirling the amber contents.

"I'm not sure," Alex conceded with a wry smile. "Some kid peeled all the labels off every bottle, jar and can in the place during a beach party here last week. I think it's Scotch and soda."

"I think it's Scotch and tonic, but it doesn't really matter." She took another sip before lifting her head and frowning at him. "Alex, what's going on? Why would someone want to do something like that?"

He shook his head and tasted his own drink. "I don't know why, Sara," he said slowly. "It could be someone's idea of a practical joke."

"It isn't very funny."

No, it wasn't. And neither was the whispered warning she'd heard in the cellar that afternoon. Alex decided to dig a bit deeper into that incident. She'd touched on it a few times while he'd been prowling around her bedroom. Now he wanted to hear the details.

"Tell me exactly what the voice in the cellar said to you," he prompted, leaving the wall and moving to straddle the arm of the sofa. "Something about sleeping forever?"

She sighed. "There were a lot of forevers thrown in there. Forever sleep, forever rest. For now and for all eternity.... Words like that. I kept hoping I'd imagined the whole thing, but I'm sure now I didn't."

"You're also sure it was a whispered voice you heard, and not Warwick's?"

"I honestly don't know." She gave her honey-blond hair a shake. "It was just a whispered warning. I couldn't recognize the voice behind it. It was like the message, though—there one moment, gone the next."

Alex let his thoughtful gaze travel to the TV where Perry Mason was cross-examining a prosecution witness. With his glass he motioned to the flickering screen. "It's the scrawny sea captain who did it," he said after swallowing a mouthful of his Scotch. A tentative smile curved Sara's lips, and Alex was obscurely pleased that she could follow his offbeat thought processes to a certain extent. Few other people could.

"He's just a wizened-up little old man, Alex. Is this your way of telling me that you think the bath-robed beachcomber Noel told me about earlier tonight is really a demon in disguise?"

"No, it's my way of telling you that any one of the innocent-looking people at the Sketch Shop might be your mirror-writing culprit. And God only knows how many other people in town might have let this curse story push them over the edge."

She lowered her lashes wearily. "Robin believes in Morganna's curse," she murmured at length. "At least she professes to believe in it. And she certainly could have sneaked into my cabana easily enough. After all, she does live around here."

"A lot of people that work at the Shop live around here, Sara," Alex told her, swallowing another mouthful of Scotch. "And Robin's not the only one who believes in Morganna's curse."

"A curse that leaves lipstick messages on mirrors and uses cleaner to wipe them off." Sara resumed her seat on the sofa. "It seems to me the supernatural would be a little neater than that. A little less obvious." She raised her eyes to his. "Someone's trying to scare me, Alex. It's the only answer. Someone wants me to leave town, and I haven't even started working yet."

Alex drained the contents of his glass then contemplated the black-and-white TV screen before him. "Someone's trying to scare you, and someone's messing around with the tapes at the Shop. Sounds more like sabotage than the supernatural to me."

"Tapes?" Sara's brow furrowed. "What tapes? What are you talking about?"

"I'm not sure. Maybe nothing." He regarded her through the veil of his lashes. Until now, he hadn't mentioned the damaged tapes to anyone. But then again, until now he'd had no reason to. The sound equipment at the Sketch Shop, though technologically current, wasn't infallible. And neither were the people who operated it. It was possible that the tapes he'd heard had been magnetized entirely by accident. But when he added to that a whispered warning and a disappearing lipstick message, the coincidence was just a little too glaring to be ignored.

"Alex, what did you mean when you said this sounded more like sabotage than the supernatural?" Sara persisted. "Do you honestly believe that someone could be trying to ruin Gus?"

"It's worth considering," Alex allowed, wishing he could rid himself of his gnawing suspicions. "I don't know how much Gus told you about the Shop, but ever since the failure of the third picture, he's been having trouble meeting the bills. Animated films cost a lot of money to produce, and Gus demands perfection in every aspect of the work we do."

"So where does the idea of sabotage come into this?"

Alex tried to sift through the jumble of theories in his head. He probably shouldn't have brought the subject up, he reflected dryly. He had little enough to go on. But, since he'd started this, the least he could do was try to explain the situation to Sara. She deserved that much after what she'd been through today.

"For the past several weeks, different things have been going wrong at the Shop," he began, rising from his perch and walking back into the kitchen. "Nothing major. Just a few panels short circuiting, fuses blowing, cameras breaking down and magnetic tapes distorting background sounds. It all started when work on the fourth Rainbow Forest picture got under way. Then," he noted, "two weeks into taping, Jasmine O'Rourke suddenly decided to leave town."

"And didn't make it," Sara added, fingers tightening around her glass. "Alex, is it . . . Do you think it's possible that someone might have pushed her from the train-depot platform?"

Dammit, he swore to himself, he didn't want to. . . But did he?

He poured a healthy measure of Scotch into his glass, lifted it and let the fiery liquid burn down his throat. "Murder, Sara?" he questioned, watching her closely, noting the rising apprehension in her eyes. Apprehension she was endeavoring to bank down. He came to stand in front of her, reaching out to touch her cheek with his thumb. "No, I don't," he half lied in an attempt to reassure her. "I think if there really is anything going on at the Shop, it has more to do with delay tactics than death." He dropped down beside her, resting his head against the sofa cushions. "Forrest Clements, Gus's ex-partner, wants to buy the studio, and Jack's been right there for the past year, trying to push a deal through."

"So you think maybe Jack is behind the technical breakdowns? Behind Morganna's curse?"

"Jack—or someone else," Alex conceded carefully. "A couple of the people at the Sketch Shop still work for Forrest on occasion."

Sara stared at him, puzzlement replacing the apprehension in her eyes. "What people?"

Alex shrugged. "Robin for one. And Dieter. Even Alvin used to go down to the Cartoon Emporium every once in a while to narrate Forrest's Saturday-morning spots, although he hasn't done that for a few years now."

"Still," Sara maintained, "any of them could be working for Forrest in ways other than the obvious, couldn't they?"

"Someone could be," Alex said gently. "There's no real proof that anyone's doing anything yet. The only thing that's certain is the voice you heard in the cellar and the message that was left on your mirror, both of which might have been someone's idea of a sick joke."

Sara wasn't convinced. "There's also Jasmine O'Rourke's sudden decision to leave town," she pointed out, and Alex knew instinctively where her mind was headed with that statement. Hers and his.

A renewed shaft of unease released itself from the pit of his stomach, but he kept his expression shielded as he sought out her eyes. "Don't dwell on it, Sara," he advised. "Jasmine was a flighty woman at best. Gus hired her because an old director friend of his thought her voice was a close match for Elke's. If he hadn't been so pressed for time, he probably would have taken a second look at her and realized that her devotion to her work wasn't half as strong as her devotion to herself. I know for a fact that she didn't appreciate the long hours she had to put in at the Shop. Chances are good she got tired of the extra overtime and decided to duck out. It's a good bet she really did slip and fall in front of that train."

To Alex's satisfaction, Sara appeared relieved to hear those things about Jasmine. After pouring her a more palatable drink, they finished watching Perry Mason, content for the moment to let the subject of sabotage slide.

It wasn't until he'd taken her back to her cabana, checked all the doors and windows twice and instructed her to yell at the top of her lungs if anything more happened that night, that he allowed his mind to acknowledge the questions still tumbling around in his mind.

Lighting a cigarette, only his fourth that day, he stretched out on his rumpled bed, rested his head on the hand of one bent arm and stared consideringly up at the swirling ceiling fan.

He tried to picture Jasmine somewhere other than outside his window, sashaying up to the pane in her string bikini. He tried to picture her lying face down on the railway tracks clad in a trench coat and a high-necked wool dress—a departure from her usual skimpy outfits. He tried, but he couldn't do it. He kept seeing Sara at his window in that black G-string. Sara, who for all her slender curves and fairy-princess freshness, struck him as infinitely more alluring than the coy and voluptuous Jasmine O'Rourke.

It could have been Sara lying on those tracks, he thought, controlling a shudder and angling a stream of smoke at the ceiling. Sara, instead of Jasmine, dead and buried now in the east.

"Jesus," he muttered, scrunching his eyes closed. Had the woman been murdered, or had she merely slipped and fallen in the rain? Was there really a crazed killer running around loose in Santa Vera, or was there a more calculating individual wandering around the town? Around the Sketch Shop? Someone, perhaps, with enough cold-blooded ambition to deem murder a mere means to an end? Someone like Jack Kensington, who was hot after old Gus to sell out to the Cartoon Emporium?

When he really thought about it, it really wouldn't be out of the question for Robin to be on Forrest Clements's payroll. Robin, or Dieter. Both of them still worked for the man on frequent occasions. Hell, they were on his payroll already, weren't they?

With a grunt, Alex levered himself up onto his elbows and stared into the black hole of his living room. He was jumping, he told himself angrily. Dieter was an old friend; they'd known each other since college. And Robin—well, for all her faults, she'd never struck him as anything more than a lot of smoke without much fire.

But what about Jack? he wondered, lying back down and drawing once more on his cigarette. What about Alvin, the most harmless-looking person in town? What about the old man's alter ego, Warwick?

And what about Noel? he tacked on darkly. If he was going to jump, he might as well jump all the way. Noel had hated Jasmine O'Rourke. It was possible, however unlikely, that she might have wanted the woman dead.

He closed his eyes against the pounding that had started in his temples. His thoughts had brought him full circle, back to Morganna's current voice. Back to Sara Moreland and the role she'd agreed to take on. Right back to superstitious talk of Morganna's curse. And no matter how hard he tried, he couldn't shake the uneasy notion that the talk had its roots in something far deeper than irrational fear.

ALL ALONG the southern California coast, foamy waves lapped the sandy shore. They were gentle waves tonight, soothing and warm. But with each one that washed up on the beach, there came an echoing of that now-familiar phrase.

Morganna's curse. Morganna's curse....

No, it wasn't a hoax or a superstitious tale or a mere hot-sheet headline. It was real, as real as old Gus's Sketch Shop. It was life and it was death. It was new, yet it was as old as time itself. It was whatever it had to be at any given moment.

From the dim reaches of the subconscious mind, the evil surged forth and stretched its sinuous tentacles. Its strength was astounding, its power fed by emotions too passionate to be fully comprehended. It knew what it had to do. There was no alternative to what must follow, nothing that could change the order of future events. The film must not be finished. Morganna must not return to the Rainbow Forest. Morganna's curse must wreak its deadly havoc yet again. That was how it would be.

Then, now and always....

Chapter Five

"That poor old coyote just can't win, can he? His rocket-powered roller skates sputtered out not six inches from the side of that cliff."

Plunking herself into a cross-legged position on Sara's living-room rug, Noel surveyed the early-morning antics of Wile E. Coyote, who was currently plunging off the side of a craggy mountain road under the scrutiny of the beeping Road Runner.

"I think that coyote would be better off mailing away for a carton of frozen entrées rather than any more Acme do-it-yourself kits," Sara observed, fighting a yawn and wishing she could feel half as wide awake as Noel looked.

Mornings were not her favorite time of day, especially not when she'd lain awake most of the previous night, listening to every wave that slapped the shoreline and every car and truck that rolled along Coronado Boulevard.

The only consolation to be had was that Alex lived so close by. It was doubtful that whoever had written the jagged message on her mirror could have broken in and caught her before her shouts for help reached his ears.

Through bleary eyes, she watched Noel peel back the plastic wrapper on a fresh Twinkie and take a big bite of the cream-filled cake. What little sleep Sara had managed to squeeze in the night before had been rudely interrupted by the woman's insistent pounding on her door fifteen min-

utes ago. It had taken that fifteen minutes for Sara to realize that the darkness of night had given way to hazy summer
sunlight.

"Will I have to get up at the crack of dawn every day?"
Sara asked, smiling a little as the cartoon coyote poured a
box of birdseed over a pile of ball bearings.

Noel regarded her in amusement. "If you call this the
crack of dawn, honey, then I'm afraid so," she drawled.
"Anything after nine o'clock's a late start at the Shop."

Sara struggled to focus on the sunflower wall clock beside her. Big hand on the two, small hand on the eight.
Okay, so it was past dawn. But as far as she was concerned,
this was still a ridiculous time to be getting up, even under
normal circumstances.

Squeezing her eyes closed, she blotted out the nightmare
images that had been dancing around in her hand for the
past several hours. Images of Morganna and slippery train-
depot platforms. Audio impressions of garbled tapes, visions of shorted-out panels and possible saboteurs lurking
in the dim reaches of the studio mansion.

Thankfully it wasn't as hard to do as she might have
expected. Noel was shoving a Twinkie at her, and already
she could hear the enthusiastic shouts of a dozen or more
early-morning surfers down on the beach. For now, she
vowed to keep an open mind about everything and everyone at the Sketch Shop. If any more odd things happened to
her, then and only then would she let her imagination go to
work.

"You get dressed, Sara," Noel ordered, switching the TV
channel to an old Jetsons cartoon. "Then you can give me
a lift to the Shop. My old clunker of a car hasn't worked
right since I accidentally pumped diesel fuel into it instead
of gas."

Swallowing a mouthful of cake, Sara glanced over at her.
"Where do you live, anyway, Noel?" she asked the woman
who was now absorbed in George Jetson's astral life.

"Over at the mobile-home park, about half a mile farther down the beach. You see, when old Gus first hired me seven years ago, I didn't know whether or not I was ready to put down roots here in California. I'd been teaching school in Yazoo city, Mississippi, till I met him. I knew it'd take a while to decide if I liked working at the Shop, and by the time I'd made the decision to stay, I couldn't see uprooting myself all over again. Besides, at the time, Alex was staying in the park, too."

"Why did he leave?"

"Bad memories, I suppose. A lot of us used to live there, Morganna's first voice included. Then, one night at a party, Elke took it into her head to slash her wrists. Just went out behind Alex's trailer, used a steak knife and cut herself open. A bunch of us found her there around 3 a.m. Alex waited till her body'd been taken away, then he packed up his duds and moved down here to the beach."

Who could blame him? Sara thought on a note of revulsion. She made a concerted effort to keep her next question casual. "Why did Elke Stevens kill herself, Noel? Does anyone know?"

"Not really. She'd been having throat problems. That might've had something to do with it. Seemed like she was always down at old Doc Wilshire's office for one thing or another. Still, it was the shock of the century to find her lying there in the dirt covered with blood."

Sara could believe that. Leaving Noel to George Jetson's latest adventure, she went into the bathroom for a much-needed wake-up shower. By quarter to nine she was back in the living room fastening the buttons on a red cotton jumpsuit.

"Good enough," Noel said in her customarily laconic fashion. "At least you're covered up. We should make it to the Shop just in time for you to suffer through Jack's pompous oratory. Survive that, and you're halfway home."

Sara almost wished she really were halfway home. But for Gus's sake, she resolved she would stick it out here in Santa

Vera. She loved the old man too much to turn tail and run like a frightened jackrabbit. This was one performance she was determined to see through to its conclusion. Besides, she reminded herself forcefully, nothing had really happened—yet. The smart thing to do right now was to keep an eye on everyone she possibly could at the Sketch Shop. With any luck at all, she'd be able to sail through this project without another hitch.

But as it turned out, she discovered there were hitches and there were *hitches*. The moment she and Noel arrived at the Shop, Jack Kensington made a big production of shepherding her into his main-floor office. It was a difficult scene for Sara to play first thing in the morning.

For the few seconds that he was standing near her, she couldn't resist looking down at him. He was quite short and probably not much older than Alex or Dieter. And with his bland, piquant features, he really did bear a striking resemblance to one of the sprites from Gus's fabled Rainbow Forest.

"Please, Sara." He smiled slickly, clearing his throat. "Have a seat."

"Without a word, Sara perched herself on the pub-style sofa. Jack wouldn't join her there—she knew that on an instinctive level—and silently she thanked Providence for the small favor. She didn't care for men like Jack. His pretentiousness was a bit overdone.

He went to sit on a huge swivel chair behind his desk. Whether he realized it or not, the enormity of the furnishings dwarfed him. "Now then," he began, steepling his fingers for effect, "let's you and I have a little chat, shall we? Did Gus explain to you what the part of Morganna would entail? Specifically, I mean."

Sara nodded. She wanted to keep this chat as brief as possible.

"And did he also tell you about the other women who've done the character's voice?"

"He told me they were both dead."

"Yes, of course, but did he happen to mention any of the details about Morganna's curse? I know we touched on the subject briefly when you arrived here yesterday, but I'm still not sure Gus made the situation clear to you."

"He mentioned a rumor," Sara murmured. "But I don't believe in curses, if that's what you're getting at." Behind her the door swung open, and her favorite person entered.

"You don't believe in curses, huh?" a woman's voice taunted with no lack of contempt. It was Robin, of course, dressed in shapeless black cotton, the two white wings standing out starkly in her ebony hair. "Give her the dirt, why don't you, Jack?" she continued mockingly. "All the gory little details Gus would never have spit out. Like how Elke carved her wrists up with a knife, and how dear Jasmine got her face smashed by that train."

Jack's elfin features reddened. "This is a private meeting, Robin," he snapped. "I don't appreciate your eavesdropping outside my office. What do you want, anyway?"

Robin assumed an air of mocking insouciance. "I came to tell sweet Sara here that she's wanted upstairs."

"Well, that's too bad—" Jack started, but was interrupted once again when Dieter Haas poked his head through the door.

"Is Alex in here?" he asked innocently enough, and Sara had to bite back a grin. Despite Robin's poisonous glower, the entire situation struck her as absurdly funny. Jack just didn't seem to be able to carry out his meetings as planned.

"No," Jack snarled in response to Dieter's query, "but I'm sure if we wait long enough he's bound to barge in." He tugged at his tie. "Now, if you and Robin don't mind, I'd like to speak to Sara. Alone."

"Fine with me," Robin sneered. "You might as well talk to her while you have the chance, Jack. Who knows when Morganna's curse will see fit to strike her down."

"Robin..." Jack warned, his face contorting with annoyance. "Will you please get out of here? You, too, Dieter," he barked.

Dieter grinned. "Hey, I only came looking for Alex."

"Well, he isn't here.... Oh hell!"

This, as Alvin, oblivious to the confusion, shambled in from the muraled foyer.

"Dudley Dooright," he was mumbling, his head bent over a sheet of parchment. "That's it. That's it exactly. That's what Warwick's nostrils look like." He peered near-sightedly into the office. "Alex, my boy, are you here?"

"No, he's not here," Jack all but spat. "He's—"

"—doing sketches of Goldilocks up on two," Robin interceded sardonically with a virulent glance in Sara's direction.

"Goldilocks?" Alvin blinked his myopic blue eyes. "No, no, my dear. I think you're mistaken. There's no Goldilocks in this picture. I would have written such an addition down."

As he began fumbling through his notebook, Sara rose to her feet. "Maybe we should talk later, Jack," she suggested.

Emitting a frustrated sigh, Jack gave his head a curt nod. "It would seem to be the only answer. Robin, take Sara up to the miming room. And Alvin, stop your damned babbling."

"Babbling? Babbling?" Alvin held aloft the sheet of parchment he was clutching. "I'll have you know, my boy, that Warwick is the star of this picture. I'll not allow his nostrils to be caricaturized. No indeed, I'll not allow that at all."

A smirking Robin preceded Sara out of the office. "Star of the picture," she muttered to Dieter in passing. "You'd better rip his head out of the sand, friend. When I take over the role of Morganna, I want him to know who the real star is."

Dieter merely shrugged and tapped Alvin's arm. Sara skirted them both and went out into the foyer.

Alvin thought Warwick was going to receive top billing in the feature; Robin was already planning to take the part of

Morganna; Robin and Dieter both had connections to the Cartoon Emporium, and Lord only knew what Jack might be planning. Something told Sara this was going to be one very long film.

Out in the wide entrance hall, Robin lounged in wait against the staircase railing, one arm folded loosely across her chest, the fingers of the other spread wide in front of her face. "I see a purple-gray cloud forming around you, Sara," she revealed, eyes narrowing to silvery slits. "The same purple-gray cloud that hangs over the Mountain of Shadows in the Rainbow Forest."

Sara glanced at the enormous mural that surrounded them. "You think I'm going to be swallowed up by Lord Dracos's Purple Mist, Robin?" she inquired, wondering a little about the woman's mental stability. "I thought you figured it would be Morganna's curse that would get to me."

"Oh, it will," Robin assured her, pushing herself from the railing. "But first the cloud must form." She lifted her face to the ceiling, holding her hands up in front of her, fingers curled like rigid talons. "Hail, hail, seeds of doubt. Purple shadows from without. Creeping roots inside of thee. As before. So shall it be."

For a startled moment, Sara wasn't sure whether to laugh or check over her head for any sign of a purple cloud. She wasn't even sure whether she dared move or not. Robin's odious chant hung heavily in the air for several long seconds after she'd finished speaking.

At last, she lowered her hands, and her eyes resumed their usual mocking gleam. "Come along, Sara," she said in Princess Aurelia's sugar-sweet voice. "Your new job awaits…and you wouldn't want to be late on your first day, now, would you?"

Laughing, she turned for the wide staircase. And after a quick precautionary look above her, Sara did the same.

"Eye of newt, tongue of bat, tooth of serpent, claw of rat. Magic potion, spirits past. Break the spell that Warwick cast. Far beyond this fated place. O'er haunted woods and inner space. Rise up my demon hordes. Make haste. The sands of time no more shall waste.''

For what seemed like the one hundredth time that day, Sara uttered the demonic incantation. With each word she spoke, she could feel Alex watching her, studying both her expressions and her movements as she acted out the film's opening scene in Morganna's eerily lit dungeon laboratory.

"Push the hood of your cape back a little, Sara," he instructed her from the front of the low stage where he'd been sketching her since early that morning. "I can't see your eyes."

Feeling more like a marionette than an actress, Sara rearranged her voluminous black cape and reached automatically for a vial on the rough wooden table in front of her. Although the mock-up of Morganna's dungeon was quite elaborate, she'd long ago lost interest in the dusky medieval decor. She was hot and irritable and growing tired of having every move she made scrutinized by a dozen pairs of critical eyes. After what seemed an eternity, the film's director dismissed his crew and called an end to the day's work.

"I think we've done plenty for now, you two," he said, gathering up his script and storyboard sketchbook. "We can work on the Forest scenes tomorrow."

Relieved, Sara began unsnapping her cape; however, before she could step out of it, Alex motioned to her from his stool. His sketch pad was still open, she noted wearily, and while everyone else was in the process of filing from the small room, he was showing no signs of following them.

"Just another half hour, Sara," he said, his charcoal pencil already beginning to outline Morganna's familiar form. "I still haven't quite figured out how to adjust the character's movements to fit your voice."

Sighing, Sara leaned her elbows on the table. "In that case, why don't I adjust my voice to fit the character's movements?"

Alex grinned. "That'd be a good trick. When you get it down pat, you might want to let Robin in on your secret. She'd sell her soul to master the art of tonal change."

At the mention of Robin, Sara grimaced. "At a guess, I'd say she's already sold her soul," she muttered, recalling the woman's baneful chant in the foyer that morning. "And as far as tonal change goes she might not have mastered that yet, but she seems to have casting spells down to a fine art."

Alex paused in his sketching and glanced up at her. "What was it she said to you, Sara? You never did tell me."

"I didn't have a chance." She pulled the black hood up over her head. "The director's been hovering around me all day. I feel like a claymation doll being shot frame by frame."

Chuckling, Alex hopped from his perch and crossed to the coffee machine to pour two cups of the strong black liquid. "You'll get used to it after a while," he assured her easily. "The first few days are always the toughest. It took Jasmine three just to get through the lab scene."

"That's probably because she kept expecting to find herself enveloped by a purple cloud," Sara stated flatly. She expelled a pent-up breath. "I'm not quite sure what Robin meant about purple shadows and creeping roots, but somehow I don't think she wants to see me succeed in my new role. You should have heard her, Alex. She sounded like the wicked queen in *Snow White and the Seven Dwarfs*."

"No, she didn't." Alex set his open sketch pad down on the table and handed her a cup of coffee. "If she'd sounded like that, Gus would've let her do Morganna when he first created the character. Robin's voice only works for certain roles. She's not particularly adept at subtleties or nuance."

A little puzzled, Sara pushed her hood back and stared at him. "I don't get it, Alex. Why does she want to do Morganna's voice so badly?"

He shrugged and blew on his coffee. "Because it's a good role, the kind that attracts attention to the person doing it. Elke had all sorts of outside offers when she was playing

Morganna. Voice-overs for TV, commercials, narratives for movies. Once she was even contacted about a part in a science-fiction film, dubbing the voice of the female android who was the main character. If she'd been an actress on top of that, she would have been all set."

Sara eyed him warily. "Is Robin by any chance an actress?"

"She used to be, twelve years ago. Gus found her when she was working on a soap opera in Los Angeles. The moment her character was killed off, he hired her to do the voice of Noni, the Wood Nymph, in one of his early features. He decided she'd make a perfect Princess Aurelia once he'd finished developing the Rainbow Forest characters."

"So she really could be trying to get rid of me, couldn't she?" Sara theorized, rubbing the side of her neck where the muscles had tensed up. "If I leave, Gus might be desperate enough to use her voice for Morganna. Then all the Hollywood doors would be open to her."

Alex gave his head a shake. To Sara's shock, he set his cup down and reached out to push her hand aside. His warm fingers replaced hers, moving firmly over her sore shoulder.

"It's possible," he said, standing just a little too close behind her for comfort. "Still, I've known Robin for a long time. She comes across like a wicked witch, but as far as I'm aware, her spells have never amounted to much. Besides, I find it hard to imagine her crawling through your bedroom window in order to write a message on your mirror. She'd be more apt to make a doll in your likeness and stick pins in its throat, hoping you'd lose your voice."

How wonderfully reassuring, Sara reflected, highly conscious of Alex's touch, equally conscious of the hazy green eyes staring down at her.

Wisely she lowered her gaze to the table, trying not to notice the way her skin tingled beneath his deft fingers. "I still think Robin wants to scare me," she maintained quietly. "You mentioned sabotage last night. Maybe what she wants is for Gus to sell the Shop to Forrest Clements. It could be that Forrest has promised to let her play Morganna if he can get his hands on Gus's characters."

"Maybe." Alex slid his hand to the nape of her neck and began working the stiff muscles there. "But that doesn't account for the damaged tapes I've heard. Robin's not a technician, Sara. Messing up tapes would be more Jack's style than hers. And he does need money to further his political dreams."

Jack needed money, and Robin wanted to be Morganna. Depending on how Sara looked at it, either of those two could be responsible for the recent problems at the studio and for the curse-related incidents she'd experienced. But then again, she amended, so could any number of the other people who worked here.

As the strain of the day began to ebb from Sara's body, she turned her attention to Alex's sketch pad. Still willing herself not to react to the pressure from his fingers, she flipped through the drawings he'd done, noting distantly the clean lines of Morganna's features and the remarkable detail etched into each one of them. The sorceress was perfect, from her almond-shaped eyes right down to the tips of her long oval fingernails. It was easy to see why Gus had wanted Alex to animate her. Very few people could have done justice to such a compelling character.

"Was it you who decided how Morganna should look?" Sara asked, risking a glance back at Alex's handsome face.

To her relief, he moved away from her a bit and picked up his coffee cup. "No, Gus did that," he said, leaning against the table. "His original drafts are in the red books up in the morgue, along with a bunch of sketches done by the other animators here. If you compared them with mine, you'd see the differences right away. No two people ever sketch the same way. That's why only one animator can draw any given character. And speaking of drawing—" he arched a wry brow in her direction "—do you think you can handle one more chant for me?"

If it would put some distance between them, Sara would have gladly uttered a whole book of chants for him.

"I guess so," she said, pulling the hood back into place.

The enigmatic smile that hovered for a moment on Alex's lips could have been the result of her reluctant agreement, but somehow Sara didn't think so. She would definitely have to watch herself around this man, she realized with a sigh. He was just a little too perceptive for her liking. And far too sexy for comfort.

"PURPLE SMOKE BY MY COMMAND. Curl and spread throughout the land. The Master Wizard's lair to seek. This curse remove. My vengeance wreak."

The incantation floated softly outward from the miming room, muffled only slightly as it passed through a closed door and reached the ears of the person standing just beyond it.

At the sound of the words, the evil railed, spurring the limbs of its carrier into action, embedding its vicious talons ever deeper into the mind of the human who coveted it.

This must be stopped, Morganna's curse decreed so stridently that the carrier felt certain the order would rattle the very foundations of the Sketch Shop. *We must make sure it stops. Go now,* it entreated harshly. *Do what must be done. Before Alex sees. Before he tries to interfere.*

Smiling cruelly, the human obeyed, turning from the door and climbing a narrow set of stairs to the attic morgue.

This was the evil's favorite place of all. It loved the feeling here, loved the dusty old-tome smell and floor-to-ceiling shelves of cartoon images. It was at home in this world. At home and happy.

But it had a purpose for being here today, it reminded both itself and the human sharply. There was a job to be done, a new phase of the curse to be implemented.

Death, the evil curse commanded, reveling in the sound of the deliciously malignant word. *The woman must die.* The arms and legs of its servant would see to that. *But first, there must be torment,* it cautioned, tempering its zeal a trifle. Torment and fear and uncertainty. Yes, indeed, that was how it must be, how Morganna's curse would make it be.

The smile on the carrier's face grew increasingly malevolent as a pair of hands reached high up into the dead shelves and withdrew a thick, leather-bound book of sketches....

Chapter Six

"Hey, Cabot. What have you been up to all day, huh?"

Alex strolled into his cabana, tossed his jacket on the sofa and fired a handful of Snausages at the expectant Alsation. Then, grinning, he continued on to the fridge and pulled out two cold beers. He threw one to Dieter who was just coming through the door. In return, Dieter handed over a thick wad of preliminary sketches.

"Warwick in all his glory," his friend announced with a grin. "Alvin's still not happy with the wizard's nostrils, but unless you want to take on another character, Alex, this is how the old guy's gonna look."

Sipping his beer, Alex studied the rough drafts. "The nostrils are fine, Dieter," he said finally, "but you're making his fingers look like claws again. Don't forget, these are supposed to be human characters."

Dieter glanced over his shoulder. "Oh, I don't know." He chuckled. "I think I like the claws better. Still, if you insist, I'll try for a more human effect. The last thing I need is for Alvin to get on my back about Warwick's hands." He guzzled his beer down, then lobbed the empty can into the kitchen sink. "So tell me, how'd it go with Sara today?" he queried humorously. "Noel says you two were holed up together in the miming room for most of it. According to her, you didn't spend half as much time on those same scenes with Jasmine."

"Noel said that, huh?" A wry smile curved Alex's lips. "What's she been doing? Standing outside the miming room with a stopwatch?"

Dieter raised a meaningful brow. "You know what she's doing, Alex," he said, reaching for his sketches. "And why. Unrequited love can make people do strange things. Noel just wants to find out whether or not she has a rival for your affections."

"My affections are none of Noel's business," Alex replied mildly, keeping his expression deliberately bland.

With a shrug, Dieter headed for the door. "Whatever. It's none of my business, either. I am supposed to tell you, however, that she's going to be at the luau tonight—just on the off-chance that your evening's not already booked up," he added teasingly before ducking out onto the porch.

Alex didn't bother responding to the parting shot. He simply watched Dieter as he bounded over to his old Chevy convertible and vaulted into the driver's seat.

Behind him, Cabot began to whine and paw at his leg. Absently Alex kicked the screen door open with his foot, finished off his beer and tugged the tails of his shirt from the waistband of his jeans. He would have turned for the bathroom had he not caught sight of Sara walking across the sand toward her cabana.

He surveyed her for a moment as she drew close. She was wearing a black, French-cut bathing suit that clung to her slender curves like a second skin, and her honey-blond hair was tumbling over her shoulders like a curtain of spun gold.

He paused there on the threshold, letting his eyes slide slowly down her legs. She had gorgeous legs—long, sleek and nicely tanned. More tanned than he might reasonably have expected.

Deep inside himself, Alex felt a sudden pang of something he hadn't experienced in years. It wasn't just lust this time, and he knew it. True, he'd have to have been dead for a year not to react to such an incredible body, but somehow he could sense the separation taking place between his hor-

mones and his emotions. Burned once or not, he was staring straight into the flames right now. Worse than that, he
was considering edging closer to them.

Reaching into his shirt pocket he withdrew a pack of Salems, flipped his beer can onto the counter to his right and
lit a cigarette. Through a blue-white veil of smoke he offered Sara a negligent smile.

"Water warm?" he inquired, wincing inwardly at the in-
ane question.

"Warmer than it is in the Atlantic," she replied with a
smile of her own, which drew him out onto the veranda. To
his disappointment, she slid her arms into the big blue shirt
she'd been carrying. "Your dog kept me company for a
while, but he took off like a shot when he saw your Jeep."

"He's a regular welcome wagon, all right," Alex agreed,
resting his hip against the rail. "Have you had any trouble
since you got home?"

She cast a quick, covert glance at her cabana. "Not so far,
but then I've only been here for half an hour." She bit her
lip. "I don't know why, Alex, but I have a horrible feeling
that whatever's going on isn't over yet."

No, it probably wasn't, Alex conceded inwardly. And that
might be dangerous, since neither of them could be sure yet
what "it" was.

"Tell you what, Sara," he proposed, a deceptively lazy
grin curving his lips. "Why don't you forget all about mirrors and voices for tonight, and come to the luau with me
for a couple of hours."

She raised her gaze to meet his. "Welcome to summer in
southern California, huh?"

He hid a wry smile behind his cigarette. "Yeah, well, this
is just the kickoff, but that's the general idea. By tomorrow
night, the party'll be getting a little raunchy, but the first
night's usually pretty tame."

She covered her disappointment well, yet Alex couldn't
help wondering if he might not be underestimating her a bit.
Just because she looked like a fairy princess didn't mean she

thought like one. Maybe tame wasn't her style... which could be either good or bad, he supposed, depending on how he chose to view her reaction. For the moment, however, he chose not to view it at all. He merely arched a dark brow in her direction, waiting to hear her decision.

She didn't take long to make one. "What time does this luau start?" she asked him, and he moved a shoulder offhandedly.

"It's already started. We can leave right now if you're ready."

She glanced at the cutoffs and sneakers in her hand and returned his shrug. "Then I guess we might as well get going," she said.

With a chuckle, Alex whistled for Cabot, shut the cabin door and went to join her on the sun-scorched sand.

DARKNESS HAD DESCENDED over the coast by the time they arrived at the luau. Some fifty feet below Coronado Boulevard, on the beach, Sara spied the orange glow of a huge crackling bonfire. The smell of burning wood and seaweed was strong in the night air. Out on the water, a group of surfers dipped and bobbed on the ocean waves, the torches they held shimmering like giant fireflies against the starlit sky.

Alex parked alongside a cherry-red Corvette, and hastily Sara slid from the seat out onto the cliff overlooking the sand.

It was a breathtaking view. Scantily clad bodies were everywhere, swimming, dancing, lounging on blankets. Near the water's edge a troupe of masked and caped fire jugglers did their best to keep flaming batons airborne, while at the base of the cliff a local band performed a rousing rendition of "The Lion Sleeps Tonight." She saw long tables groaning under the weight of ice- and beer-filled coolers, surfboards piled up near a rocky ledge and even a grass-skirted hula dancer shimmying to the beat of the drums.

"Aloha," Alex said, joining her on the edge of the cliff. He surveyed the crowd below. "Not much happening yet, but we could try a little night surfing if you're feeling adventuresome."

Sara stared at him. "You surf?"

He shrugged. "Everybody around here surfs."

"Even Jack?" Somehow she couldn't picture the spritely assistant production supervisor on a surfboard. She couldn't even picture him in a bathing suit—and didn't really want to, either.

"Jack bodysurfs out at Gus's beach house," Alex told her, trying not to smile. "There's a key to the place up at the Shop. Anyone who wants to can go out and spend time there. It's a big old house built high up on a palisade. When he's in town, Gus lives over on Hawthorne Road near the studio. He just holds on to the beach house so the people who work for him can enjoy it."

Sara descended the craggy cliffside steps ahead of him. "That sounds like Gus," she conceded, hopping onto the warm sand. "And that's what makes it so hard for me to believe anyone would want to ruin him. Do you really think that Jack might be doing something to the film's audio tapes?"

"I'm not positive, no. But he's the only one I can think of who'd sell his soul for money. And he is familiar with the Sketch Shop's sound equipment."

"That might account for the technical problems, Alex," Sara pointed out. "But what about Morganna's curse?"

"It's likely all part of the same thing," he said, dropping his arm over her shoulder. "Scare tactics and sabotage would work well together under the circumstances. Whatever the case, I heard some of those so-called bad tapes before they were ever handed over to Jack for final approval. If he's not doctoring them, I'd like to meet the magician who is."

Sara would rather meet the person who'd whispered the ominous warning to her in the cellar. Perhaps the same one

who'd left that red lipstick message on her mirror last night.
At the very least, she wanted to be certain that whoever was
behind those incidents had not been responsible for Jasmine O'Rourke's death.

She felt a tiny tremor slide down her spine. No matter how
many times she tried to dismiss the chilling notion that her
predecessor had not died accidentally, she couldn't quite do
it. The possibility of murder lingered despite her best efforts to push it away.

"Hey, Alex!" a drenched surfer called out from the water's edge. "The waves are great. You gonna come for a
ride?"

"Oh, yes, do go, Alex," a sardonic voice to Sara's left
purred. "I'll stay and keep Sara company." Robin, in an
open black caftan and a scarlet bikini, detached herself from
a circle of similarly clad people and sauntered over to them.
"It'll give us a chance to become better acquainted. I mean,
who knows how much time we'll have to do that given
Morganna's curse and all."

"Thanks for your concern, Robin," Sara replied, not
bothering to mask her sarcasm, "but I'm sure we'll have
plenty of time to get better acquainted."

"If not the inclination," Alex tacked on in a humorous
undertone that Robin couldn't possibly have heard. He
raised his voice. "You'll have to hold off for a while, Rob.
I promised Sara a surfing lesson tonight."

Robin's lips lifted into a bright red sneer. "A surfing sorceress? This I've gotta see."

So did Sara. "Alex, I don't think . . ." she began. Unfortunately the band started up again, drowning out her ob-
jection. Then Alex had her by the hand and was drawing her
down to the water.

"Come on, Sara," he drawled. "Lighten up and try it.
Who knows, you might like it. You can swim, can't you?"

"Well, yes, but . . ."

"Then there's no problem, right?"

Wrong. There was a big problem. She'd be stuck off-shore on a strip of waxed board with Alex sitting right behind her waiting for a wave to carry them back to the beach. In anyone else's company, that might have been an easy thing to do, but where Alex Cross was concerned, Sara's instincts warned her that there was no such thing as easy. This man was sensuality in motion. She could still feel his hands massaging the muscles in her shoulders and neck.

She watched as he pulled his navy shirt over his head rather than unbuttoning it, and found herself discarding her own clothes without half as much reluctance as she would have liked.

So he thought she should lighten up, huh? Okay, fine, she decided, grinning to herself. Surely whatever attraction she felt for him wasn't likely to get out of hand on a surfboard.

"Are you sure you're good enough to handle a novice?" she asked as he snagged a board from a passing cohort.

His beautiful green eyes swept over her. "No, but I think I can handle you. If you want a real lesson I'll get Dieter to take you out on the weekend."

"I take it he's good."

"The best," Alex confirmed. "He taught Elke how to surf and she was terrified of the water." With his head, he indicated a torch far out on the ocean. "That's him out there. When he catches a big one, he'll ride it right into shore."

"And what'll we be doing?"

"Wiping out, most likely."

Well, she'd asked, hadn't she? Leaving the general noise and confusion of the luau behind, Sara followed Alex's lead and plunged into the darkened water. She could feel several slippery tendrils of kelp brushing her legs as she waited for Alex to get himself positioned on the surfboard, could hear the lapping waves all around her mingling with the sounds of laughter and noise on the beach.

If there was anything at all to Morganna's curse, it wasn't making its presence felt tonight. This was a slice of pure summer magic. And Sara intended to savor every minute of it for as long as she possibly could. For as long as the curse's perpetrator would let her.

"THAT WAS GREAT, Alex." Sara laughed as she emerged from the buoyant salt water ten minutes later. "Short but great."

Alex tossed the surfboard onto the sand and dropped down beside it. "Five seconds worth of great," he replied. "If you had any conception of left and right, we might have stretched it to ten."

And if she hadn't been so aware of him on the board behind her, she might have been able to make the distinction between left and right. It was all relative, Sara decided, reaching for her shirt.

Noel Gordon detached herself from the throng by the fire and sauntered down to the water's edge. "Evening, you two," she greeted them, sinking to her knees next to Alex's shoulder. "I think the band could use a little help," she told him with a grimace for the tinny sound of an old Beach Boys classic being banged out near the cliff. "Do you feel like giving them a hand?"

"No." Alex lay back on the sand, one hand splayed across his chest. "But you can throw me a beer if you're heading in."

"You expect me to brave the mob for a can of beer?" Grinning, Noel winked at Sara. "Not a chance, honey. Not even for you." She glanced over at the leaping bonfire. "'Course we might be able to dance our way over to one of the coolers," she suggested hopefully.

At Alex's negative grunt, Sara regarded the swarming crowd some fifty feet away. "Dance, Noel?" she said doubtfully. "That looks more like a limbo contest than any dance I've ever seen."

"It is a limbo contest," Alex confirmed without moving. "The winner gets an all-expense-paid trip to Santa Vera's best chiropractor."

"Aw, you're just sore because this is one contest you can't win," Noel teased, giving his arm a playful slap.

"No, I'm sore because I just finished getting smacked by a surfboard," Alex shot back.

Noel's hazel eyes sparkled. "Thirty-three and over the hill already, huh? Getting smacked is a sure sign of age, Alex. Do you remember that night down at Ventura when you and Elke and Dieter and I crashed that beach party...?"

As Noel reminisced about an earlier time, Sara shifted her gaze to the limbo contest in progress by the snapping bonfire. The participants would have to be contortionists to bend back much further, she thought, tugging on her cutoffs. No wonder the conga line that was forming in front of the bandstand was growing longer by the minute. There weren't many people who could manage a two-foot clearance beneath the limbo pole.

Sara was lacing up her sneakers when Noel's low muffled curse caught her ear. She was glowering in the direction of the rocky embankment, staring at Jack Kensington in his dark blue Levis and a gray polo shirt. Jack in turn was sizing up a pretty young woman in a white knit bikini.

"Perverted little crayfish," Noel declared, turning her attention back to Alex.

Sara, however, continued to watch the man. Just when she suspected he was on the verge of zeroing in on the woman, Robin stomped across the sand and made a grab for his freckled arm. There was no question that whatever she was saying to him was being said in anger. Her mouth was a grim red slash; the fingers of one hand were curled into an angry fist at her side.

Now what could Robin possibly be so hot under the collar about? Sara wondered. Since there was only one way to find out, she scrambled to her feet and, without a word to either Alex or Noel, threaded her way through the throng, skirted the conga line and made her way to the bottom of the cliff.

". . . isn't the place for this, Robin," Jack was growling through clenched teeth.

"The hell it isn't," Robin spat, her witchy demeanor conspicuously absent. "Don't you treat me like some dim-witted flunky, you little wart. I played back the tape of Princess Aurelia's first scene this afternoon. Now you either listen to me, or I'll go find someone who will."

If Sara had expected a nasty retort from Jack, she was disappointed. He merely stiffened up and muttered a taut, "All right, fine. I'll listen. We'll talk. But not here."

No, talk here, Sara implored them silently. But her entreaty didn't work. She was forced to skulk along behind them at a discreet distance, across the sand and up the rough-hewn cliffside steps to Coronado Boulevard.

With a horde of people still pouring down to the beach, it was not an easy task. More than once she had to pause and move to the side so that a board-toting surfer could go past her. Unfortunately the delays were numerous and time-consuming. By the time she reached the top, Jack and Robin had disappeared from sight.

For a good fifteen minutes, Sara scoured the boulevard searching for any sign of the twosome, hoping to catch a glimpse of Robin's black caftan or Jack's blond hair. But her efforts were in vain. They'd simply vanished into the glittering lights of the neon-studded oceanside road.

In all likelihood, she reflected morosely, she'd just lost a golden opportunity to dig deeper into the confounding problems plaguing the Shop—and perhaps Morganna's curse, as well.

With a whispered, "Damn," she spun around and started back for the rocky steps. She'd almost reached them when she caught a glimpse of a dark shapeless figure standing about ten feet away from her on the edge of the sharp embankment.

Whoever it was, he or she was covered up completely in a long black robe and an enormous pagan mask. Three large, flaming torches were clutched in the figure's hand, but even they weren't moving.

Although Sara recognized the bamboo mask as belonging to the troupe of fire jugglers she'd seen earlier, this particular juggler showed no sign whatsoever of launching into a display of manual dexterity. The figure simply stood there on the side of the cliff, painted black eyes fastened on her face, following her as she moved closer to the steps.

Biting down hard on her lower lip, Sara fought the rising knot of fear in her stomach. There was nothing to be frightened of, she told herself fiercely. She was hardly alone up here. In any event, the juggler was probably just taking a break.

She stole a surreptitious look over her shoulder. It startled her a little to realize that there wasn't a soul in the area. Even the traffic on the boulevard had subsided.

She risked a glance at the cliff steps beside her, and as she did, the figure moved for the first time. She saw it raise all three torches and point them directly at her face.

"There can be no escape," a voice rasped from beneath the bamboo mask. "Death. Destruction. Despair. The end of life as we know it. Unceasing doom."

Oh God, please, Sara prayed, groping for the metal railing that ran along the rim of the cliff. *Please don't let this person be anything more than a crackpot.* Even the worst prophecy of doom would be preferable to another run-in with Morganna's curse.

"There can be no escape," the raspy voice repeated. "No escape from death..."

As the figure took a menacing step toward her, Sara's fingers at last made contact with the solid railing. Without a backward glance, she plunged down the rocky steps and into the safety of the passing conga line.

Lowering the torches, the caped figure watched her go, painted eyes trailing her across the sand. Then, from beneath the bamboo mask, a raw burst of laughter crackled through the warm evening air.

"Run Sara Moreland," a voice enjoined her, its muted mirth spilling forth into the darkness. "Run, while you still can. It won't be long now before you never run again...."

IT WASN'T UNTIL a full hour later, after she'd made it safely back to the beach and been accidentally swept into the conga line that Sara finally managed to locate Alex. Noel, she noted instantly, had disappeared. Alex and Dieter were chatting now, talking shop over by one of the groaning tables.

"Had enough, Sara?" Alex asked her, his navy shirt back in place over his tanned chest.

She nodded, still a little uncertain about her *Twilight Zone* encounter on the cliff. "I think so," she said.

"Okay then, we might as well take off." He arched a questioning brow in Dieter's direction. "You need a lift?"

"Yeah, I guess." Dieter shrugged. "There's not much happening tonight."

Oh yes, there was, Sara thought unhappily. Maybe a lot more than anyone knew. It just wasn't happening down here. She cast one last look up at the cliff. The masked figure had long since vanished, as had Robin and Jack. But Sara's trepidation remained. Dammit, what was going on here anyway?

She didn't say much as Alex drove back to the Apple Shack cabanas, didn't even cringe when they were very nearly sideswiped by a group of teens in a white T-bird.

Most of the cabins were lit when Alex swung the Jeep in behind a leaning palm. After bidding the two men a goodnight, Sara trudged up onto her porch. She flicked on the lights and tried not to care that the Jeep was pulling out again, heading farther up the coast road to the beach house where Dieter evidently lived.

Immersed in a flood of questions she couldn't hope to answer, she pulled a sheet of paper from the mail slot, strolled into the kitchen, poured herself a glass of wine and tore open a bag of pretzels.

This was all so confusing. Sara knew someone at the Shop had to be up to something. But was it Jack? And if it was, where did Robin fit into the picture? It sounded as though Ms. Danvers, too, suspected that the audio tapes had been tampered with, but did that necessarily mean she was innocent of any wrongdoing?

Sara thought for a moment about the murder-mystery plays she'd done on stage. It was always some little clue, or a bunch of little clues, that ultimately gave the killer away. Of course, in this case, she hoped and prayed that there wasn't any killer, but the basic premise was the same. She had to make a point of reading people better, of looking beyond the surface and trying to discover what evil might be lurking there. It could be Jack who was behind everything that had happened, and then again, it might not be him at all.

In her mind, she saw again the cloaked figure on the cliff and heard its rasping prophecies. She recalled, too, the ominous whispered warning she'd received yesterday in the cellar and the scrawled lipstick message on her mirror last night. And she remembered Robin's eerie chant that morning. The chant of a vindictive witch—from a woman who claimed to believe in the power of Morganna's curse.

A sliver of unease prickled up Sara's back, and she turned away from the ocean view, her eyes lighting for a second on the phone stand beside her, on the sheet of paper she'd just pulled from the mail slot.

Something about that paper suddenly seemed strikingly familiar. It was an ivory color, she realized, not white. More like parchment than a throwaway leaflet. And it had partially unfolded itself in the few seconds it had been sitting there. She could see now the bold black lines of the drawing it contained.

Haltingly she reached for it, forcing her fingers to smooth out the creases, forcing her eyes to regard those long black lines. Breath held, she moved closer and absorbed the sight of the entire sketch.

It took her less than a second to identify it, much longer than that to understand what the drawing portended.

The rough sketch before her was of Morganna. Morganna, the Medieval Sorceress, clad in her usual long black robe. A featureless Morganna whose slender fingers were twined around the stem of a beautiful red rose. And next to the evil sorceress sat a dark wooden box.

No, not a box Sara's shocked brain informed her. A casket! This faceless Morganna was standing beside a closed wooden casket.

Chapter Seven

"And they say Santa's elves work their little butts off making kiddies happy." Noel offered the droll remark as she and Sara were leaving the fourth-floor lunchroom early Saturday afternoon. "What're you in for today, anyway?"

"More taping with Alvin and Robin. Alvin keeps trying to ad-lib Warwick's lines." Sara grinned. "The script supervisor's having fits."

"Well, at least that makes things interesting. I'm stuck down in the basement listening to my counterpart's updated version of *The Perils of Pauline*. I tell ya, honey, life just ain't a bed of roses for some people."

No, it wasn't, Sara acknowledged wordlessly. She should know. She'd spent most of yesterday and this morning jumping at shadows. Not that anything terrible had happened to her since she'd discovered the charcoal drawing Thursday night, but she couldn't seem to shake the gnawing fear that something might any time now.

Whoever was tormenting her obviously had a reason. More than likely this was all part of some elaborate, twisted plot to get her out of town, she reflected bitterly as she and Noel parted company in the deserted hallway.

There was only a skeleton staff working at the Shop on Saturday, probably no more than thirty people in the entire building. Her confidence bolstered by the brilliant rays of sunlight streaming through the windows, Sara made a detour between the soundstages to the stairwell leading to the attic morgue.

She'd put this off long enough. She had half an hour before she was due back in the booth. Now would be as good a time as any to search for a few answers.

As she mounted the narrow stairs, she wondered if she ought not to have confided in Alex about this latest bizarre episode in Morganna's curse. Then she felt the folded sketch in her pocket and knew she didn't dare.

While she found it virtually impossible to believe, it was within the realm of possibility that Alex Cross could somehow be mixed up in this nastiness. She'd seen enough of his sketches on Thursday to feel certain that the one left in her mail slot had been drawn by his hand. Of course, he'd have to be awfully stupid to have slipped her a sketch that he'd done, but then whoever said twisted minds couldn't suffer from bouts of stupidity?

And the person behind Morganna's curse was definitely twisted, she judged grimly. No one except a depraved individual would ever resort to such cruel tactics in order to achieve their goals.

Upon reaching the stuffy morgue, Sara began wandering through the towering rows of floor-to-ceiling shelves in search of the red books that Alex had mentioned on Thursday. All the drawings of Morganna done by the various animators at the Sketch Shop were contained in those books, he'd told her. He'd also said that if she compared his work to anyone else's, she'd see the differences immediately. She only hoped that those differences were more subtle than he'd led her to believe, that in someone else's work she would find a close match for the sketch she had in her possession.

Determinedly she prowled the dusty attic. It didn't take much time for her to locate the high shelves where the red books were stored. They stood out in bold contrast to the brown and black leather-bound tomes around them.

In a corner of the room next to a collection of metal film canisters, she located a wobbly old ladder. After dragging it across the floor, she scrambled up several rungs. By clinging to the rough wooden shelves, she was able to keep her balance, while at the same time prising one of the thicker tomes free. The parchment sheets were all laminated to help preserve them, but at least Sara knew she was on the right track. The sketches were certainly basic enough. Too bad they were drawings of Warwick rather than Morganna.

She moved cautiously along the high shelf. At the end of a stuffy, dusty fifteen minutes, she'd unearthed all sorts of Morgannas, none of which resembled her copy of the sorceress and none of which had been drawn by Alex.

Dieter's versions had claws for fingers. Hers didn't. Gus's were exceptionally well endowed. Hers wasn't. Some of the Morgannas had shoulder-length hair. Others had hair that flowed past their waists. She even stumbled across a shaky drawing of the sorceress done by Alvin Medwin ten years ago. His Morganna looked a bit like a skeleton, she thought. But again, Sara's didn't. So where did that leave her? she wondered, inching the ladder over a bit more. And did it really prove anything one way or another? Her instincts told her no. Still, she kept moving down the row.

Using both hands, she wedged out another thick, leather-bound tome. Oddly enough, this one didn't seem as dusty as its predecessors. Moreover, the pictures it contained seemed frighteningly familiar, even though they hadn't been in any of the Rainbow Forest films.

She laid the book down on the top of the ladder, planted herself semi-securely on a rickety rung and flipped through the plastic-coated pages. Inside the cover, she saw Warwick waving the Rainbow Scepter at Morganna, who appeared horrified by the sight of it. Both characters were down in the sorceress's cobwebbed dungeon laboratory, and near one of the walls stood something that strongly resembled a casket.

Sara turned the page. Morganna was standing directly in front of the casket now, her own glowing wand in her hands. In the second picture, she'd raised the wand.

She turned to the next page. There, Warwick was aiming the all-powerful Rainbow Scepter at Morganna. And suddenly the sorceress's smaller wand was transformed into a rose—a black-and-white rose, but a rose, nonetheless.

Unfolding her picture once more, Sara laid it out flat and compared the sketches. Although she was no expert, she couldn't see much difference between her drawing and the one in this book. In fact, she reflected grimly, she couldn't see any difference at all.

Her eyes lowered reluctantly to the bottom right corner of the page, and she squeezed them shut when she saw the initials written there.

A. C.—Alex Cross. The featureless drawing of Morganna that she'd received had indeed been done by Alex.

"Damn," she swore in a frustrated rush of breath. Why did it have to be his? Why not someone else's? Anyone else's.

Disturbed, Sara refolded the parchment and stuck it back into the pocket of her cream denim pants. Then she slapped the thick red book closed, glaring at the leather cover, wishing she could reduce the thing to a pile of ashes.

Squaring her shoulders, she picked up the book, steadying herself to slide it back into place on the shelf. Then a sharp jolt below her had her losing her grip on the binding and clawing at the wooden ledge for support. Startled, she looked down, certain that the floor must be caving in.

But it wasn't the floor—and it wasn't the wobbly ladder. One of the heavy leather books had been jammed against the ladder's unsteady left leg. She watched in horrified fascination as the book slid soundlessly back into the shelf, then felt her muscles constrict when it suddenly flew back out again.

The violent contact broke her momentary paralysis. Frantically she endeavored to scramble from her perch, a strangled gasp breaking from her throat as the book once again slammed against the ladder's leg.

Beneath her, she could feel the ladder teetering precariously. Teetering and swaying, cracking loudly under her weight. With one final, mighty blow from the apparently self-propelled book, the aging wood split, sending her tumbling, plummeting to the dusty floor below.

The last thing she recalled before a curtain of darkness closed around her was a low, ominous whisper: "Beware Morganna's curse...."

"BEWARE MORGANNA'S CURSE, Sara Moreland..."

The words came again, but this time less ominously, this time not in a whisper. It was of no consequence, because Sara was unconscious. She could see nothing, hear nothing. And perhaps this was how it should end for her. A prophetic death up in the Sketch Shop morgue.

Do it now, the evil commanded regally. *Let us be rid of her once and for all. Let it be over.*

Slowly the curse's human carrier bent over Sara's inert form. A hand slid around her throat, feeling for a pulse, finding it. Strong and steady, in no danger of faltering.

Do it, the evil prodded. *No one will ever know. It will be just as it was with Jasmine O'Rourke, only faster, sooner.*

"And out of order," the carrier pointed out, fingers tightening obediently around Sara's throat. "Are you sure you want it done here? Now? The suffering has scarcely even begun."

It doesn't matter, the evil retorted, rather stridently. *Think of Alex. He isn't blind. He'll figure it out. It isn't the same as it was before. Alex likes this woman. We must do it. We must kill her while we have the chance.*

Even as the order was issued, Sara moaned slightly and stirred. Automatically the fingers on her throat clamped down a little harder.

"You're sure?" the carrier queried around a smile of anticipation. "You won't be angry if I finish it here?"

The answer never had a chance to form. From the attic stairwell, there came the sound of a door opening. And the decision was made academic.

Resentment spewed forth as the carrier's fingers released their grip and reached for the book Sara had been searching through. A pair of glazed eyes sought out the window and the fire escape beyond.

Within seconds, Sara Moreland was alone in the morgue. Alone and alive.

For now.

"SARA. COME ON, HONEY, wake up."

The words seemed to be coming from a million miles away. Groaning, Sara's muscles gave a reflexive jerk, away from the hands that were lifting her. But even in a semi-conscious state, she could tell that these were not cruel hands. Not the hands of a murderer. They weren't closing about her throat.

Closing about her throat!

Alertness returned with a jolt, and she struggled to sit up on the floor. Had she imagined someone's hands around her neck?

"Take it easy, Sara." Alex's calm voice was a soothing balm to her screaming nerves. At least it was until she remembered the sketches she'd found. "Just sit still for a minute," he instructed her when she tried to pull away. "And don't move." With gentle fingers he probed the bruise high on her forehead, beneath her hair. "Do you feel dizzy?"

She gave her head a tentative shake, tempted to bolt for the door. Somehow she forced herself to remain calm. Regardless of the sketches she'd found, she didn't think Alex wanted to kill her. "No, I'm fine," she replied, her voice subdued.

"You don't look fine."

"Well, I am. Really. I'm all right, Alex. How—ouch—how did you know I was up here?" she demanded accusingly.

His hazy eyes were unreadable in the dusky light. Unreadable but not malicious. After helping her to an upright position, he sat back on his haunches and regarded her with a slight frown. "One of the techs said he'd seen you heading this way about twenty minutes ago." A frown invaded his dark features. "What are you doing in the morgue, anyway?" he asked, his gaze not leaving her face.

"I was—" she winced "—looking for a picture."

Contemplatively he ran the side of his hand across his lower lip. "What picture?"

Sara hesitated. Should she show it to him or not? She swallowed, then made her decision. "This one." Her vision clearer now, she extracted the folded sheet of parchment from her pocket and handed it to him. "Someone left it in my mail slot Thursday night. I wanted to compare it to some of the other drawings in here."

Alex spared the sketch only the briefest of glances before raising his eyes to her face once again. His expression gave nothing away, and Sara couldn't begin to imagine what he was thinking.

"You didn't just fall off the ladder, did you, Sara?" he prompted softly, his eyes taking in the open window ahead of him.

She lowered her lashes. "I don't think so."

"That's what I figured." Placing his hands around her waist, Alex lifted her to her feet. Then, keeping an arm firmly about her waist, he propelled her away from the shelves. "Come on, we're getting out of here."

"No, wait," Sara protested, twisting herself around. "The book. Bring the book."

"What book?"

"The one..." Her voice trailed off as she scoured the empty floor. "Where is it? I was looking at it right before I fell. I saw the picture in it."

Alex gave her a long, discerning stare before following her eyes to the red, leather bound books above them. "The dead shelves," he murmured just loud enough for her to hear. "Which book was it?"

Sara rubbed her temple. "The one where Morganna's in her dungeon laboratory. The one where her wand's turned into a rose. The one with the casket in it." She stared at him, trying not to look like a judge about to pronounce a guilty verdict. "You did those pictures, didn't you, Alex?"

He offered no denial, but she had a feeling he knew what she was thinking. "Uh-huh," he murmured, tightening his grip on her waist.

She shivered, praying her instincts about him were right. "Oh, Lord, this is creepy," she said. "Let's get out of here."

He said nothing, just helped her down the stairs and into the empty lunchroom. She was seated at one of the Formica-topped tables before it occurred to her that she was supposed to be taping this afternoon.

"Don't worry about it," Alex drawled from the cupboard where he was digging out a first-aid kit. "I'll tell the director you have a headache. He can go with Robin and Alvin for now."

If it wasn't for her friendship with Gus, the director could go with Robin and Alvin for good, as far as Sara was concerned. She wasn't accustomed to being shaken off ladders and knocked out. Not to mention taunted with faceless sketches, whispered voices and lipstick messages.

First-aid kit in hand, Alex moved to stand in front of her, tipping her head back slightly and brushing the hair away from her forehead. He radiated a smoldering kind of sensuality that made breathing next to impossible and accusation out of the question. Sara had to force her eyes up and away from the taut denim stretched across his sleekly muscled thighs, which wasn't easy considering how close he was to her.

She focused instead on the rumpled flannel of his red-and-black plaid shirt. It wasn't any better for her pulse rate, but at least it was an innocent enough place to be staring.

As he swabbed her scrapes with peroxide, she ventured a thin, "Alex, how could someone draw an exact copy of a sketch you'd done?"

"Hold still," he told her. Then he lifted a shoulder. "There are any number of ways, none of which would require a scrap of artistic talent. Most likely the drawing you have is a photocopy."

Her head shot up, sending a shaft of pain right down to her shoulders. She ignored it and demanded, "You mean someone inserted a sheet of parchment into the photocopier and copied the original onto it?"

"Sure, why not?"

"But mine's a charcoal sketch."

Alex finished applying the peroxide, gave her bruise one last inspection, then pulled up a chair next to her. From his shirt pocket, he produced a charcoal pencil with an eraser on the end. He bent over her sketch. "There you go, honey," he remarked at length. "It's just a copy that's been gone over in charcoal."

Sara surveyed the erasure mark, which revealed a permanent copy line beneath it. "The face has been blotted out," she noted slowly. "Do you have any answers for that one?"

Alex tapped his pencil on the table. "For which one? The fact that it's been blotted out, or how it was done?"

A faint grin touched her lips. "No, I think I can figure out how to cover up a set of features. What I want to know is why anyone would do it. And why color in the rose?"

Alex placed the parchment on end and studied it through half-closed eyes. "The rose—I don't know. But the features I can take a guess at."

Sara shifted uncomfortably in her seat. "Do I want to hear this?"

"Probably not, but you'd better." He ran a finger around the sorceress's blank face. "I don't think this is supposed to be Morganna standing by that coffin."

Sara gritted her teeth. "I had a feeling you were going to say that. It's me, isn't it? Morganna's voice, not Morganna herself."

Alex nodded. "You—or Jasmine," he added, looking sideways at her. "I hate to say this, but you could be right about her death. She changed the second week she was here. It could be she was scared. What's happening to you might very well have been happening to her."

He returned his gaze to the sketch. "I think it's time we said something to the police."

"No," Sara protested immediately. "Alex, we can't call the police."

He glared at her. "Why the hell not?"

"Because we don't have proof of anything. You said yourself, this could be the work of some sick practical joker."

"And you still believe that?"

"Well, no, not really," she admitted, touching the bruise on her temple. "But I still don't think it would help to get the police involved. If they start poking around the Shop asking questions, production will be slowed down even more. It might actually have to be stopped. And if you're right about this being the work of a saboteur, that would probably be exactly what he wants."

Alex looked as though he wanted to dispute her argument, but Alvin's sudden appearance in the lunchroom doorway prevented any further conversation between them. The old man was clutching his pen, and both his glasses and tie were askew.

"Ah, there it is, there it is!" he exclaimed, rushing over to the counter by the fridge where his notebook sat. "I thought I'd lost it." He scooped the book up and brought it with him to the table. "I'm glad I've found you, Sara," he announced loudly. "I've been wanting to talk to you."

"Not now, Alvin," Alex said, his tone remarkably patient. "Sara's got a headache. I was just about to take her home." Without Alvin noticing, he refolded the copied sketch and slid it into the back pocket of his faded jeans. "Talk to her Monday, okay?"

"Monday? Well, yes, of course, if you're not feeling well, my girl." Alvin gave his glasses an absent poke and began scribbling in his notebook. "Speak to Sara Monday regarding Morganna's disrespectful attitude toward..." he paused. "How do you spell disrespectful, Alex? My memory seems to be failing me these days."

"D-i-s..." Alex frowned. "What do you mean, Morganna's attitude?" he demanded. "What did Sara say that makes you think she's being disrespectful?"

Alvin blinked his eyes like an owl. "Oh, my word, Sara hasn't been disrespectful in the least," he declared. "No indeed, not in the least. It's that impudent apprentice of mine who's been acting up. From the moment she escaped the spell of the Moonstone Orb, she's been causing nothing but trouble. She must be put in her place, Alex. Yes, indeed, she must."

Sara fingered the bruise above her temple. "Put in her place how?" she asked warily. "Do you want her out of the Rainbow Forest, Alvin?"

"Yes, well, that's always a possibility. But, of course, it isn't altogether necessary. No, indeed. Warwick would be quite satisfied if Morganna were simply to give him the respect that's his due. The pupil must never outshine the teacher, you see." He peered nearsightedly at Sara. "You do see that, don't you, my girl? Heavens, yes, you must. You're much more polite than your predecessor. She didn't understand, but I feel certain you do. Respect, that's the ticket. Respect and obedience."

Sara regarded the man suspiciously. Alvin had an almost fanatical gleam in his bright blue eyes, and his heavy jowls were quivering with the force of his emotions.

But he was nothing more than a harmless little old man, she reminded herself. An eccentric. On top of which, he'd never given any indication that he believed in Morganna's curse. There was no reason for her to think he might be trying to get rid of her in order to land Warwick a bigger part in the movie.

No, Jack was the best bet for saboteur. Jack and his political aspirations, his quest for money and power, his overblown ego and pompous speech. Alex was already convinced that Jack was messing up the audio tapes. Might he not also be attempting to pad that destruction by trying to frighten her into leaving town? That would be one sure way of putting a fatal crimp in the picture's progress, of crippling it and forcing the sellout that everyone around here seemed to think he wanted.

The answer to that was a resounding yes. However, Sara couldn't quash the eerie notion that there was more to Morganna's curse than met the eye, more to it than the surface motivations of money and power and deceitful manipulation. It was a terrifying thought, and mentally she slapped herself for even entertaining it.

With a modicum of urging from Alex, Alvin ambled off, back in the direction of the recording booths, mumbling under his breath all the way.

"Respect," he repeated, shaking his white head. "Respect and obedience. That's the ticket. Yes, indeed, people must be taught to respect their elders."

When Alvin was gone, Alex closed the first-aid kit with a metallic click, which echoed in the pervading silence of the empty room. "No police, huh?" he said, sending her a wry, knowing look. "All right, Sara. For what it's worth, I see your point. But I think it's time we both got out of here."

Mutely Sara nodded. She couldn't have agreed more.

THROUGH ONE of the less conspicuous windows of the Sketch Shop, Morganna's curse watched the woman leave. The curse and its carrier. The evil and its human corollary.

We weren't quick enough, the evil scorned, straining to get a better view from the human's eyes. *Look at that. Alex is with her. See him with her? See what your slow mortal reflexes have allowed? She could have been dead. We could have ended it. But, no, you had to question my orders, didn't you? And what did it get us? Nothing. Nothing but—*

"Stop!" the carrier commanded coldly. "We will end it. And I wasn't all that slow. You're the one who enjoys suffering. It was because of you that I didn't kill her."

The evil fell silent, content to let its human appendage brood. *Perhaps the mortal carrier was right, after all. Jasmine's death had brought with it no satisfying bit of misery. This one, on the other hand, just might. Yes, indeed. This one just might.*

The evil knew. It saw. It understood. And soon the human would understand, too. Soon there would be no more questioning of orders. Soon, this malleable creature would submit completely. Soon enough, Morganna's curse would hold sway. Forever.

Chapter Eight

The air in the small room was sweltering. Hot and close and filled with the smell of crushed leaves.

High on a shelf, three thick white candles, melted down to mere stubs, radiated a weird incandescent glow, outlining a round blackened pot and the misshapen root being dangled above it.

In the obscurity of the shrouded chamber, a voice rose up in chant while the grotesque root spiraled closer to the smoking brew below it. In slow motion, the hand holding it dipped and rose and dipped again. Three times up and three times down. Until finally the root was swallowed up by the steaming bubbles.

Until the potion was complete.

"OKAY, TRY IT NOW, Sara," Alex called to her from beneath the upraised hood of his jeep.

Absorbed in the fantasy world of his sketchbook, Sara twisted the key in the ignition. There was no response, just a repeated click that interrupted Smoky Robinson on the Jeep's radio.

"Were you always good at cartooning, Alex?" she asked him as he readjusted the wires of the defective starter.

"I always liked it." She heard the lazy thread of amusement in his voice. "Our barn walls had George of the Jungle crayoned all over them when I was a kid."

Scooping the hair off her neck, Sara flipped through the sketch pad, fascinated by the sight of Morganna who seemed to be moving right before her eyes. "I take it you grew up on a farm," she surmised, propping one bare foot up against the dashboard.

"Just outside Farmington, Iowa." Alex came out from under the hood, wiping his hands on a grimy, oil-smeared rag. "My folks sold out when I was eighteen and moved to town. Otherwise, I'd probably still be plowing fields, planting corn and sweating out the droughts." He rested his elbows on the lowered window, touching her temple gently with his forefinger. "How's your head?"

Sara smiled, forcing her eyes away from the broad expanse of his bare chest. "Better. In fact..." She peered past his shoulder and up to the Apple Shack. "I was thinking of going to see Robin. I've never had my fortune told before."

"Yeah?" Again the lazy amusement was evident in Alex's voice. "Now why would you want to let her do the honors when there are three other less venomous fortune-tellers working there?"

"I want to find out what she and Jack were talking about the night of the luau," Sara replied promptly. "I told you, Alex. Robin said something about listening to one of the tapes of Princess Aurelia's first scene. I'm curious to know what exactly it was that upset her when she heard it."

"And you figure she'll tell you, huh?"

Sara refused to be deterred. "She might. Particularly if I agree to let her give me her nastiest palm reading in return."

"Uh-huh." Alex tossed the rag he'd been holding aside and trapped her chin between his knuckle and thumb, turning her head slightly, impaling her with his hazy green eyes. "I think you're playing with purple fire where Robin is concerned," he commented wryly. "For all you know, it could have been her who knocked you off that ladder yesterday."

"In which case, I'd like to make sure she doesn't try the same thing again."

Alex grinned, releasing her. "I suppose that's fair enough," he conceded. He returned to the front of the Jeep and slammed the hood closed, allowing Sara a clear view of his tanned back and shoulders.

Why was it, she wondered with a small sigh, that dirt and sweat and scruffiness in general was suddenly beginning to have such a profound effect on her? Yes, the man had an incredible body, all sinew and bone and smooth, lean muscle. And yes, he moved with all the ease and grace of a mountain lion in its prime. But his hair was too long, his eyes were too knowing and his touch was too distracting...

Giving her head a shake, Sara pushed the door open, climbed out of the Jeep and bent down to retrieve her sneakers. She focused her gaze on the distant Apple Shack, then glanced over at Alex who was pulling on a khaki shirt—and watching her through those beautiful, unrevealing eyes of his.

"I'm going," she said, straightening and dusting off her palms. "Do you want to come with me?"

"To face the witch?" He took a considering look at the building up on the boulevard, then held out his hand to her. "Honey, I wouldn't miss this for the world."

GRANNY'S APPLE SHACK was a large rambling building, a combination teahouse, restaurant and herbal-potion dispensary, with a fortune-telling sideshow thrown in for good measure.

The tearoom to the right of the entryway was dark and devoid of customers by five o'clock on a Sunday afternoon. The restaurant to the left, though, was brimming with activity. Wicker light fixtures suspended from the ceiling cast a warm orange glow over the rattan chairs and tables below. The smell of herbs and spices was strong, as was the aroma of carrot soup and freshly baked rolls for which the Shack was famous.

From across the narrow cash counter in the foyer, Sara studied intently the labels on a vast array of tiny bottles. "What is all this stuff, Alex?" she asked him.

He let his gaze travel into the restaurant. He'd seen a black Caddy outside that had an awfully familiar look about it. "Herbal teas and earth remedies mostly. Maybe a love potion or two." He stopped speaking, his eyes zeroing in on a large man seated at one of the window tables. Bingo. The Cartoon Emporium's owner here in the Apple Shack.

A glance over his shoulder revealed that Sara was still perusing the bottles. With an absent, "Wait here, honey, I'll be right back," he went down the two carpeted steps into the dining area.

The large man caught sight of him almost immediately and lifted his beer glass in a welcoming salute. "Well, how're ya doing there, boy?" he exclaimed in a booming west-Texas bass. "Wonderful to see you again. Sit yerself on down, and let me buy you a cold one."

Alex pulled out one of the rattan chairs. "I'll have a Coors, Forrest," he said with no particular inflection, adding a blunt, "What're you doing in Santa Vera?"

Forrest Clements leaned back in his seat, unbuttoned his vest and gave his beer belly a satisfied pat. "Came up to enjoy some of Granny's delicious cooking, what else?"

"I can think of a few other reasons."

The man threw back his bushy gray head and roared. The laughter was a smoke screen, and Alex wasn't buying. "You got a right suspicious mind there, Alex," Forrest declared just a little too boisterously to be real. "I thought you mid-west-farmer types were supposed to be more trusting than that."

"I buried my trust in a cornfield a long time ago, Forrest," Alex replied easily. "Why are you here?"

"Well now, I just told you, boy. The Shack serves up the meanest hunter's stew this side of Amarillo."

Alex kept his grin amicable. "Bull."

"Well it might be that," Forrest chortled, "but I like it just the same." As if to justify his statement, he broke open a warm roll and dipped it into the bowl of stew before him. "I hear tell old Gus ain't been feeling so hot lately," he said as he chewed. "Robin tells me he's in Dallas recovering from heart surgery, while you folks here try and piece together a fourth feature."

Alex swallowed a mouthful of the beer he'd just been served. "We're doing better than that, Forrest," he drawled. "Taping's already started."

"Thanks to a little actress from the east." Bushy brows lifted above slate-gray eyes. "You figure this new Morganna of yours can help save the Shop, do you? You'll pardon me, boy, if that don't wash the way it should. Robin says you got yourself a devil of a curse hanging over you these days."

"Robin seems to have an awful lot to say," Alex noted, his tone dry. Forrest merely slapped his meaty thigh and laughed.

"Well, hell, boy, she's not alone there. Dieter says the same thing."

Alex shrugged. "I don't care what Robin and Dieter have said, Forrest. I want to know what you're doing in Santa Vera." He regarded the man through half-closed eyes. "You might as well tell me. You know, one way or another, I'm gonna find out."

"Ya, I'll just bet you will, too." Forrest hitched his thumbs in the pockets of his vest and tilted his chair back on two legs. It groaned threateningly beneath his two hundred and fifty bulky pounds. "All righty, I'll spit it out then. I came for the Heart Association fund-raiser your mayor is throwing at the Tropico Club tomorrow night...and I came to see how the film's doing. Ain't no deep dark secret that I'd like to buy me the Sketch Shop." His hooded eyes gleamed. "And it ain't no crime, either, Alex," he added with a trace of a cagey smile. "I'm just looking for a good investment, is all. If he were in my shoes, Gus'd do the same thing.''

"Like hell he would," Alex said softly, draining his glass.

He glanced at the entrance to the restaurant. Sara had vanished from sight. He wondered if she'd gone looking for Robin. It seemed likely.

Forcing his attention back to Forrest, he said, "There's someone at the Shop who's been messing around with the tapes. I know it, and so do you."

"That's a might libelous-sounding statement there, son," Forrest declared. "You got yourself any proof of that?"

Alex didn't answer. He merely offered a bland smile and lit a cigarette. The man was sweating; Alex could see the telltale beads of moisture on Forrest's upper lip and forehead. Great. Now, all he had to do was find an indisputable way to connect the Cartoon Emporium's owner with the saboteur at the Sketch Shop...and figure out how to tie both people to what was happening to Sara. Nothing to it, right?

Keeping his smile in place, and his eyes on the foyer, he ordered another beer.

FROM THE ENTRANCEWAY, Sara could see Alex drinking beer with an enormous sixtyish man wearing a brown, three-piece suit and a pair of expensive, leather cowboy boots. It looked to her like they were having an intense discussion about something, but even though her curiosity was killing her, she managed to refrain from interrupting them. Instead she slipped through a beaded atrium and into a wide corridor that led back from the tearoom. Robin, she felt sure, had to be here somewhere.

Since the Apple Shack was a public place and there was no one around to stop her, she didn't suppose this could be considered trespassing. Nonetheless she made a point of treading carefully on the tiled floor.

She might have made it all the way down the hall to the staircase at the end without being detected if Robin's

Siamese cat hadn't suddenly pounced at her from one of the Japanese-style rooms to her right.

Pyewackett's blue eyes gleamed in the crystalline lights from above, and Sara suspected that the whiny meow that emanated from the animal's throat would have been loud enough to reach the upper levels of the building. Certainly it was more than enough to alert Robin Danvers. The woman appeared from the shadowy chamber seconds after the cat, her eyes every bit as glittery and cold as those of her feline familiar.

"What do you want?" Robin demanded harshly. "I'm busy."

Sara didn't doubt that for a second. Not after she got a good look at Robin's face.

The blush on the woman's cheeks resembled two wide slashes of scarlet paint. Her eyes were dramatically outlined in pure black kohl, with two of the lines curving upward to touch her brows. On one high cheekbone she'd drawn a golden quarter moon, and her body was completely enfolded by a sweeping black cape.

The only thing missing was a broomstick, and Sara fully expected to see that come flying into the hallway at any second.

"I want to talk to you," Sara said in a calm tone of voice that amazed even her.

"I told you, I'm busy," Robin repeated coldly.

Busy whipping up some vile witch's brew, no doubt, Sara reflected, taking note of the sickly sweet odor spilling outward from the darkened chamber.

"I heard you and Jack talking at the luau," Sara persisted, in the hope of piquing Robin's curiosity. "You told him you'd heard one of the tapes of Princess Aurelia's first scene."

Robin's expression revealed nothing, but at least she was listening. "So?" she grated, raising one black brow.

"So, I think you know something."

"I know many things." At last, Robin's voice assumed its customary mystical tinge. "Things you couldn't begin to understand. I know about the forces that exist in nature and about those that exist within each of us. Forces of life and death. Forces of good. And—" her voice level dropped to a menacing whisper "—most of all, the forces of evil."

Sara resolved not to back away from the cloaked woman. She'd be damned if she'd let a witch force her into retreating—even if the idea was a tempting one.

"What about the forces of willful destruction, Robin?" she shot back more fearlessly than she felt. "What do you know about distorted audio tapes?"

Robin's gray eyes shimmered. "Not half as much as I know about Morganna's curse," she promised. One red-tipped finger drew a slow, deliberate circle in the air around Sara's face. "You've got the look, Sara Moreland. The look of a troubled soul. Just like Jasmine." Her lips parted into a humorless smile. "Yes, just like Jasmine. As I told you before, you do Morganna's voice; you bring upon yourself Morganna's curse." Her features grew sinister, almost grotesque. "Just like Jasmine did."

Swallowing hard, Sara ventured a cautious, "What about the first Morganna, Robin? Was Elke Stevens also a victim of Morganna's so-called curse?"

"So-called?" With her long nails, Robin scraped a design on the papered wall beside her. "You still don't believe, do you? What a fool you are, Sara. Elke's dead, isn't she? And Jasmine's dead, too. And both deaths occurred when Gus tried to bring Morganna back to the Rainbow Forest. Are you really so blind to reality? The sorceress was banished. She's under an evil spell—a curse. It's spilling over into life. Into your life this time."

Sara's temper snapped. "Oh, come on, Robin," she retorted, exasperated. "You sound like someone from the Dark Ages. Cartoon characters can't possibly be cursed, and neither can people. It was a reporter who coined the phrase

'Morganna's curse.' You can't expect me to believe in a newspaper headline.''

Robin lowered her mascara-coated lashes. "Believe what you want to, Sara. Ignore what you want to. Excuse what you want to. But remember this: two women are dead. Two of Morganna's voices. And now you're doing that voice. In my book, that makes you a target. And unless you know how to deflect them, as I do, curses like this one can kill. They will kill. Morganna's curse already has. Twice.

EVEN A FRANTIC ATTEMPT at logic couldn't keep Robin's sinister portents from flying around in Sara's head. After extolling the evil power of Morganna's curse, the woman closed the door behind her, and with a leveling glare in Sara's direction, snapped a large padlock into place.

"Mirror mirror on the wall, who's the meanest witch of all?" Noel's teasing voice floated along the corridor. "What's the matter, Robin? Did your caldron boil over or something?"

Robin whirled on her, but her expression showed nothing more than mild disdain. "Stick to your own concerns, Noel," she advised coolly. "I'm sure you have plenty of them to keep your mind fully occupied." She waved her hand. "Now, why don't you just run along and buy yourself a love potion—for all the good it'll do you," she tacked on in a silky undertone.

Noel's lips thinned, but of course Robin didn't wait around for a response to her gibe. With a lilting laugh, she gave her cape a billowing sweep, picked up her cat and sailed off around a bend in the wide hallway.

Sucking in her cheeks, Noel sauntered through the beaded atrium. "You must've riled her some, Sara. That look I saw in her eyes when I came in could've melted lead."

Despite her trepidation, Sara couldn't help grinning. "Lead maybe, Noel, but not Morganna's curse. She's convinced it's out there waiting to pounce on me."

"Waiting and hoping," Noel predicted, drawing close. "So what're you and Alex doing up here anyway?" she asked. "When Dieter and I finished slaving our weekend away at the Shop, we figured we'd stop by the beach and see if you two might like to head on out to Gus's beach house for a barbecue. I gotta tell you, it surprised me when Flora, the flower child, said she'd seen you both moseying up to the Apple Shack. Now, tell me, honey, that you didn't decide to confront Robin just because she's been needling you a little at work."

"It crossed my mind," Sara lied. She glanced in the direction of the restaurant. "Is Alex still in there with that man?"

"He and Dieter are both in there," Noel disclosed. "And that man they're with is none other than Forrest Clements, Gus's fast-talking ex-partner and the owner of the Cartoon Emporium."

Forrest Clements? In Santa Vera? That was nervy of him. "The guy must be a vulture," Sara noted in disgust. "The Shop's not even up for sale."

"Well, not yet anyway," Noel agreed. "Old Forrest's probably just sizing up a floundering carcass, hoping to speed the death roll up a bit by hanging around, making people nervous. Trouble with that is, all he's gonna wind up doing is bugging everyone in sight. If he's not mighty careful, even Dieter and Robin'll desert him."

Unless one or the other of them happens to be on the payroll, above and beyond the making of cartoons at the Emporium, Sara thought darkly. Just because Dieter was Alex's friend didn't necessarily mean he couldn't be bought. And Robin might very well be after something more important to her than money. She wanted to do Morganna's voice. Perhaps that was her incentive, her kickback for helping to sabotage the film. A curse, phony or not, could be an expedient means to an end, more effective in many ways than damaging audio tapes, as Jack was perhaps doing.

She preceded Noel back to the cash desk, noting with satisfaction that the cowboy-booted Forrest Clements, grunting gutturally, was on his way out the door under a heavy cloud of Brüt. Whatever Alex had said to him obviously hadn't sat well with the man. Seconds later, he'd squeezed himself behind the wheel of a shiny black Cadillac and was roaring off down Coronado Boulevard.

"The original Texas longhorn," Dieter was saying to Alex as Sara and Noel approached their table. He chuckled. "A little of his cock-and-bull story goes a long way."

"From Santa Vera to Los Angeles and right across to Amarillo," Alex agreed, pulling out chairs for Sara and Noel. "Did you talk to Robin?" he inquired of Sara when she'd settled in beside him.

"I guess you could call it that."

Dieter picked up his California cooler. "Why would you want to talk to Robin?" he asked, clearly perplexed.

Sara wasn't quite ready to confide in anyone who had ties to the Cartoon Emporium. She couldn't really see Dieter being involved in a plot to ruin Gus, but she wasn't prepared to take any chances just yet. She settled for a vague, "We had a disagreement about one of the early scenes in the script on Saturday. I thought we should get it straightened out before tomorrow."

"Diplomacy in action," Alex murmured, and the double meaning wasn't lost on Sara. With a sardonic smile intended solely for her eyes, he leaned over her shoulder and surveyed the tabletop menu. "Maybe we should trash the barbecue idea and eat here instead. You hungry, honey?"

Was she hungry? Well, yes, she was. But she was also incredibly conscious of Alex sitting so disturbingly close beside her. She could smell the clean scent of soap on his skin, could feel the warmth of his breath on her cheek and the ends of his long hair where it brushed her skin. And she couldn't resist stealing a glance at him in profile.

No, she thought, he definitely didn't possess any of Dieter's beachboy qualities. This man had grown up under a completely different kind of sun. Sara could see him working the land with his hands—the same hands that could create a world of magic and mystery on paper. Hands she suddenly longed to press herself against, to have tangled in her hair, holding her, caressing her....

A jumble of vaguely erotic thoughts whirled through her mind. Intimate and sensual thoughts over which she had not a speck of control. Try as she might, she couldn't put them down to mere physical attraction. Not with Alex. Not anymore. His scruffy, vagabond appeal went far beyond the surface, and she knew it.

She sighed to herself. Why did life always have to be so complicated?

FROM THE ENTRANCE to the restaurant, Robin Danvers stood and watched the foursome. Eyes hooded, features pulled into an enigmatic mask, she stared at Morganna's current voice. Stared at the woman who'd won the part. She could feel the tempest of emotions clawing at her insides. The struggle, the simmering anger, the wanting...the knowing. Oh yes, the knowing.

One hand moved to the pocket of her cape, to the worn leather pouch tucked inside. She fingered it lovingly. And slowly, inexorably, a trace of a bittersweet smile touched the corners of her red-painted mouth.

Chapter Nine

Wake up! The evil strode right into the center of its carrier's dreams, shattering them into a thousand colorful pieces.

Beneath a rumpled cotton sheet, the carrier shifted position, eyes closed, listening to the strident summons that cut through the filmy haze of a restless night. It was 5 a.m. and still dark, but the promise of dawn hung warmly in the sultry summer air.

Are you awake? The evil voice questioned, and the human nodded. *All right, then, get up.* Morganna's curse gave the mind it controlled a vigorous shake. *You have work to do—and we both know how slow your motor functions can be,* it tacked on with no lack of jeering acrimony.

It forced the human out of bed and over to the closet where a huge poster of the amber-eyed Morganna hung on the inside of the door.

See me at my best, the evil enticed pleasurably. *See the power Alex has given me. The strength. No more the mere cartoon character, I am a force unto myself. Unto you. Together we will destroy those who would threaten us. Now go and get dressed. The day unfolds, and we must be ready to greet it.*

Limbs twitching with anticipation, the carrier left the closet. By 7 a.m. the first task of the morning had been taken care of. Now the human had only to watch and wait. Morganna's curse would take care of the rest.

"HEY THERE, BOY!" Forest Clements's loud bass heralded his arrival on the Sketch Shop's animation level at eight o'clock Monday morning. "You the only early bird around this old mausoleum?"

Alex finished off the slice of cold pizza that was his breakfast and dropped onto the stool behind his sketch board. "I don't recall your people starting much before ten down at the Emporium, Forrest," he noted dryly. "I also don't recall much overtime being recorded."

"Don't need overtime with a full staff of workers, son. Seems to me old Gus falls a mite shy in that respect."

"Yeah?" Alex took a sip of his steaming coffee and held the man's gaze. "I suppose someone here keeps you fairly well informed on our numbers, huh?"

The big Texan walked over to the window. "There you go again, Alex, flinging those nasty innuendos. If you weren't such a talented sprout, I might just be of a mind not to make you such a lucrative offer."

"I'm not interested in any of your offers," Alex said, flipping open his sketch pad.

"Double your salary, boy," Forrest coaxed. "Hell, you could buy yerself a spread up north, do a little farming in your off time, raise chickens—all those things you land scratchers from Iowa like to do."

"You're barking up the wrong tree, Forrest," Dieter said, strolling into the partitioned office and over to the sink to wash his hands. "Not everyone's into money."

Forrest's expression grew ugly. "You quieten down there, Dieter," he ordered. "You ain't suffering any at my expense. If I were to double the salary I pay you, you'd drop this here place like a hot potato."

Dieter chuckled, arching a shrewd brow at Alex. "Touchy, isn't he? Tell me, Forrest, what is it you really want? Gus's people or his characters?"

The older man's laugh was strained. "Well, now, I'd say it's about six of one, half dozen of the other. Can't have Warwick without either you or Alex—or Dracos or Aurelia, either, for that matter. And there's only one person I know can do justice to the beautiful Morganna." He looked straight at Alex. "Think about it, son. You could be cruising down easy street in a gold-plated Mercedes, and all you have to do to get there is have a nice, friendly chat with old Gus."

Alex didn't say anything to that, just sent the man a cold stare, which had him expelling a resigned breath and leaving the room.

When Forrest was gone, Dieter picked up a clean towel and began drying his hands. "He must really want this place. I didn't think he'd do that. Has he ever tried that double-your-salary bit before?"

"Back during the split. Not since then."

"You know he wants you to do Morganna for him, don't you?"

Alex slid from his stool and headed out to the central area for a coffee refill. "He'd settle for you, if you'd be willing to do her."

"Well then he's gonna have a long wait," Dieter stated flatly. "I'm not interested in animating any cursed characters. Besides, we both know what happened the last time I drew Morganna."

Alex glanced over his shoulder at Dieter's hardened features. His friend had sketched Morganna for one week at the beginning of the third feature. One week's worth preliminaries—right before Elke Stevens killed herself. He'd never drawn the character again.

"It's just a story, Dieter," Alex said. "You were doing Morganna when Elke died, but I was the one drawing her when Jasmine died. You can't seriously believe Elke's death had anything to do with the fact that you were animating the sorceress at the time."

Dieter's eyes widened, sparkling as a trace of amusement danced through them. "Hell, who said I was worried about that? You can call me superstitious if you want to, Alex, but I just don't want to mess around with any weird hexes. I'm having enough trouble with Warwick's nostrils." He paused and lounged against the doorjamb. "Forrest seemed awfully sure of himself," he said. "Do you think he's talked Gus into changing his mind?"

Alex hunted through a three-day-old plate of doughnuts next to the coffee machine. "Not a chance," he said, popping a dried piece of cupcake in his mouth. "Gus'll never sell out. The only way Forrest will get his hands on this place is if old Gus is forced to declare bankruptcy."

Dieter picked up a fudge brownie. "Yeah, I suppose that's true." He took a bite of the chocolate square, then grinned. "Are you going to the Heart Association fund-raiser tonight?"

"I imagine so."

"You gonna take Sara?"

Alex lifted one shoulder. "If she wants to go."

Dieter eyed him cannily. "Noel won't like that very much, you know."

"Noel's a big girl, Dieter. She knows how I feel."

"Does she?" Dieter murmured. "I wonder."

"I PLEAD WITH THEE, Morganna. Do not summon the clouds of the Purple Mist. Has your banishment taught you nothing? You oppose the Master Wizard, but can you not see that it is his evil deeds you carry out? It is Warwick who shall benefit most from your cruelty. Please, Morganna. Hear me and..." Robin paused to scowl at her script. "What the hell?" she demanded. "Hear me, and...get thee to a nunnery?"

"Stop tape. Cut." The director sounded exasperated. "Five minutes, everyone. Robin, one more mess of Princess Aurelia's lines, and I'm getting Jack up here."

Robin flashed an obscene gesture behind the man's back. "Jerk!" she shouted, waving her script at the smoked-glass window. "You didn't even ask me what was wrong."

Sara stretched her arms out in front of her. "What's wrong, Robin?" she obliged, almost glad to hear the woman in a cranky mood. Anything was better than listening to her doomsday prophecies about Morganna's curse.

Robin threw her script over. "Read that," she snarled. "You tell me what it says."

"Please, Morganna. Hear me and—" Sara turned the page "—get thee to a nunnery." She frowned. "Who typed that in?"

"Well, it sure wasn't me. I'd have told you to get thee to a nest of cobras or a patch of quicksand, but never to a nunnery." Snatching her script back, Robin jumped down from her perch. "Someone had better have a good answer for this. These scripts were in Jack's office safe all weekend. Where is that man anyway? I'll skewer his pointed ears if he knows anything about this."

Sara heard her stomp out, but she'd already turned her attention back to her own script. "Spare me your insufferable pleas, Princess," she murmured as Morganna. "What I do is done for Warwick least of all. He shall feel the full weight of my wrath soon enough. And all the better—" she flipped the page "—to eat you with, my child—"

She stared at the last line. It came from "Little Red Riding Hood." Certainly it had no place in this story. What was going on? Slapping the script closed, she exited the booth and made the descent to the animation level.

Not unexpectedly, Alex was at his drafting board, drinking coffee, eating Glossettes and half watching the first installment of the Rainbow Forest trilogy on video. Even so, his pencil was flying across the parchment sheet in front of him.

As Sara entered the partitioned work area, he looked up from his sketch pad.

"Someone's been tampering with the scripts," she said, handing him her copy of the morning's scenes.

"More of Morganna's curse?" he questioned, a frown invading his features.

Sara gnawed her lip consideringly. "I'm not sure. Robin's lines were messed up, too."

"Flash, Alex." Dieter stuck his head around the canvas screen. "One of the panels has shorted on four. The place is going nuts."

Short circuits? Altered scripts? Something told Sara that this was going to be a hectic day.

The telephone intercom buzzed, and Alex put it on the speaker. Noel's voice issued forth in a blast of southern fury. "Alex, is that little warthog of a production supervisor back from Oxnard yet? We've got a camera down here that sounds like it's gasping its last breath."

"Terrific," Alex muttered. He raised his voice, "Get one of the techs down to look at it, Noel." He stopped and scowled at the speaker. "What do you mean, is Jack back from Oxnard yet? When did he go there?"

"Who knows," Noel grumbled. "Friday afternoon sometime. And come to think of it, I don't care if he's back or not. I just want this camera fixed."

Alvin appeared around the canvas screen. "Alex, my boy," he announced. "I have to speak to you."

"Not now, Alvin," Alex returned impatiently.

The old man looked offended. "Now, see here, my boy. This is extremely serious."

Alex motioned with his head, and Sara drew Alvin away from the partition with a gentle, "Why don't you tell me what you were going to tell me on Saturday? Something about Morganna's disrespectful attitude, wasn't it?"

"She probably made a crack about Warwick's nostrils." Dieter grinned, ducking behind Sara and into Alex's office.

"Nostrils?" Alvin picked up on the word instantly, laid his book on an empty drafting board and began thumbing through it. "Has Morganna been commenting on War-wick's nostrils behind my back?"

Sara shook her head. "I don't think so, Alvin. She's been too busy trying to steal the Rainbow Scepter to worry about Warwick's nostrils. Now, what is it you wanted to say about her attitude?"

"Morganna's attitude." The old man echoed, still hunting through his book. "Morganna's— Ah, yes, here it is, here it is. 'Speak to Sara—' Oh my! Oh my heavens," he interrupted himself to exclaim. "I must be off. Yes, indeed, I must." He patted Sara's arm absently. "Carry on, my young apprentice. Mind your master. We shall talk later." With that, he scuttled off toward the rear stairwell in his ill-fitting, three-piece suit.

Sara stared after him in disbelief. He reminded her of the White Rabbit scurrying away for a late date. She'd never seen the man move so fast. His mind might be going, but his motor functions were still intact.

Her eyes returned to the empty drafting board and came to rest on Alvin's notebook. "Alvin, wait," she began, then stopped. He was long gone. In any event, without his trusty book, he'd be lost. He'd be back inside of two minutes searching frantically for it.

Then again, she amended, maybe he wouldn't.

Alvin's heavy handwriting was perfectly legible. Sara had no difficulty reading the last entry he'd made and no qualms about doing so when she saw what he'd written: ('Meet Forrest Clements at 10:30.') Then a couple of words she couldn't discern, followed by: ('Be sure to bring a bottle of California Cabarnet.')

California Cabarnet?

The wine cellar! Alvin was going to get a bottle of wine to take to a meeting with Forrest Clements. For all Sara knew, they might even be meeting down there.

Meeting for what reason, though? she wondered. Was it possible that Alvin was responsible for the delays on the film? For the odd string of occurrences being directed at her under the guise of Morganna's curse?

He was rather eccentric, she reminded herself flatly. And he did resent Morganna's return to the Rainbow Forest. It was conceivable that he might be acting on Forrest Clements's behalf as part of a deal to procure the Sketch Shop, while at the same time guaranteeing Warwick star billing in an upcoming feature.

God, it was even within the realm of possibility that the old man was acting on his own initiative here. As far as Sara could determine, Morganna's curse seemed strangely disconnected from whatever else was going on at the Shop. The delay tactics were affecting everyone; Morganna's curse appeared to be aimed solely at her. Even if Alvin wasn't behind the technical breakdowns, he could still be behind the curse.

Well, she decided, casting a quick look beyond the canvas screen to Alex's now-empty office area, there was only one way to find out what, if anything, Alvin was up to. She'd have to go down to the wine cellar and see if she could pick up his trail there.

She passed a stormy-faced Robin on the stairs. "Extended coffee break," the woman grunted. "A panel's shorted on four."

"So I heard. Did you find Jack?"

"In his office, all flushed and indignant. Alex tossed me out."

Sara was genuinely surprised. Robin wasn't known for backing down easily. She would have expected the wicked witch of the west coast to have her fangs buried deep in Jack's pale neck at this moment, Alex notwithstanding.

Hunching her black-clad shoulders, Robin continued up the stairs while Sara continued down. The basement, when she reached it, was cool and dark, a sharp contrast to the blue sky and sunshine outside. Glad of the denim jacket she wouldn't have worn had it not been for the rather frigid climes of the fourth-floor recording booths, Sara threaded her way through the camera department, barely avoiding a head-on collision with Noel.

"Listen to that thing, will ya?" Noel declared. "Thousands of dollars worth of camera equipment, and it sounds like Artoo Detoo with hiccups."

Sara didn't have time to stop and listen to the wheezing machine. Or to Noel, for that matter. Alvin already had a good head start on her, and from what Alex had told her, there were at least seven corridors leading in and out of the subbasement labyrinth. If she didn't find him quickly, he might slip past her. She slowed just enough to ask Noel if she'd seen Warwick's aging voice.

"Sorry, no, I haven't seen Alvin, Sara. Hey, someone shut that thing off before it pops a blood vessel." Noel hastened over to the shuddering camera, and drawing a deep breath, Sara made her apprehensive foray into the stone passageways.

Down, she told herself repeatedly. Remember you're going down. Down to get in; up to get out. Too bad she hadn't thought to swipe a couple of dried-up doughnuts from the animation area. She could have tried Hansel and Gretel's trick and left a trail of crumbs behind her to guide herself back if she got herself twisted around in the shadowy passages.

As she ventured farther into the subbasement, the noises from the camera department gradually faded out until the only thing she could hear was the sound of her sneakers on the cracked cement floor. Keeping an eye on the Rainbow Forest posters, she descended deeper and deeper into the murky cellar.

She knew it had to be her imagination, but she could have sworn that the corridors were becoming narrower. Narrower, quieter—and more menacing. Like the gnarled tree limbs in the animated Rainbow Forest, the walls seemed almost alive, as if they harbored a thousand invisible eyes, which were all covertly watching her. She was tempted to shout one of Morganna's baleful incantations at the stones to keep them from closing in around her.

She didn't. Instead she continued to walk, certain that Alvin had to be poking through Gus's wine reserves in search of a bottle of California Cabernet. In her mind, she struggled to summon up images of white orchids and summer meadows. She tried to think about the Rainbow Forest's winged pixies with their smiling faces and melodious voices.

She tried—and failed. The orchids kept turning black; the Forest meadows became barren English moors, and the pixies' faces became ravaged caricatures of Lord Dracos and the shriveled-up Croatia.

Suddenly, from the dim reaches of a distant chamber, she heard a creak, the sound of a heavy wooden door swinging open or closed on its rusty hinges. Alvin? Maybe. Perhaps she was coming up on the wine cellar at last.

Still, her jumpy mind informed her in a spurt of fearful uncertainty, she probably shouldn't let relief take over too quickly. The old man might not be half as daft as she suspected. What if Alvin really was the essence of Morganna's curse? What if he'd purposely left his notebook on that drafting board, knowing she would read it and attempt to follow him down here? What if there really was no relation between the happenings at the Shop and Morganna's curse?

Her nerve ends began to tingle; her senses grew more alert. The rubber soles of her sneakers made squelching sounds on the concrete floor, and even telling herself that she was acting like a child didn't help. This place gave her the creeps. Any minute now, she fully expected the walls to develop limbs, sinuous arms and skeletal, claw-tipped fingers that would snake out and grab her... As they'd grabbed Jasmine? As they'd pushed her from the depot platform?

Nothing was worth this, Sara decided abruptly, slowing her footsteps in the narrow passageway. Of course, she was being ridiculous, but who wouldn't be in surroundings like these? It was dark and cold and eerily silent in the cellar.

And while the walls weren't likely to attack, there was a good chance that whoever had shaken her off the ladder in the morgue might.

She stopped walking, resting her hand on a worn cornerstone. But then the creaking door hinges caught her attention once more, and she found herself being drawn forward. Drawn toward a chamber at the end of the dingy corridor. A chamber with a door that was slightly ajar.

Sara crept along the passageway, her eyes never leaving the door. When she finally reached it, she squeezed through the opening without making a sound.

Enormous wooden wine casks rose up in front and to the left of her. Fifteen, maybe twenty of them in all. A single forty-watt bulb suspended on a frayed and twisted cord illuminated the room just enough for her to spot the rough-hewn shelves beyond the kegs. And from those shelves came the unmistakable sound of clinking glass.

She was forming Alvin's name on her lips when the old man suddenly materialized around the side of the racks, a bottle of Cabarnet in one hand and a bottle of Chablis in the other.

"My book," he said, blinking at her in confusion. "Where is my book?"

A shaky sigh of relief escaped Sara's throat. So much for living walls and visions of Alvin on a demonic rampage. He looked more like a disoriented Daffy Duck than a walking curse. Of course, she reminded herself, Daffy was an awfully greedy little duck. Very self-serving, intent on having his own way....

"It's upstairs, Alvin," she said, keeping her eyes on him. "In the animation area."

"Ah, yes, of course. Upstairs." He stared at the bottles in his hands. "Where am I going?"

"To meet Forrest Clements?" Sara suggested.

"To meet...? Oh, my word! I'm late. Yes, I am. Late, late, late." He made a beeline for the door, where he paused to look back at her. For a second, his eyes gleamed. "Remember, my dear. Respect and obedience. That's the ticket. We shall talk later. Yes, yes, later.''

Sara heard him mumbling to himself as he went out into the corridor. Something about Warwick and wine and being late and needing his book for reference.

Shaking off the feeling of trepidation that assailed her, she reached up to pull the chain on the light bulb. She would have preferred to leave it on; however, with all the electrical shorts taking place in the Shop, she didn't want to risk having a fire start down here.

Once the chamber had been plunged into darkness, she gave her eyes precisely three seconds to adjust, then, shivering slightly, shoved her hands in the pockets of her denim jacket and started for the door, intending to trail Alvin at a discreet distance.

She'd taken perhaps two steps when her fingers felt a folded piece of paper in the left-hand pocket. Heavy paper. Thick—like parchment.

Spinning around, she made a grab for the chain, at the same time yanking the paper out of her pocket and shaking it open. Even in forty watts of light, she had no trouble identifying the sketch. It was Morganna...again. Faceless...again.

And this time the casket next to her was wide open.

Chapter Ten

Sara felt her cheeks pale and wondered idly if she were to prick herself what color her blood would be. Ghostly white, no doubt. She could well imagine her own features stamped on Morganna's blank face. Features as lifeless as the wilted red rose the sorceress was clutching.

Heart pounding in her chest like an erratic bass drum, she crumpled the sketch. She didn't know how it had gotten into her jacket pocket, or who had put it there, or when. She only knew that she had to get out of the cellar. Now. Before whoever or whatever was the controlling force behind this madness could—

The thought skidded abruptly to a halt as a dreadful rumble ahead of her shattered the stillness of the dank chamber. The wine kegs, stacked and roped together moments before, were beginning to tremble. One after the other, they quivered and shifted. And then they began to roll. Thousands of pounds of aged wood, rolling toward the wine shelves. Toward her!

"What the...?" she began, but didn't finish. Stepping back, she came flat up against the edge of one of the shelves, and it was either make a dash for the rear of the room or be crushed by the huge, lumbering casks.

Desperation sent Sara scrambling for a dusty, cob-webbed corner, for the only escape route she could see. There was another door behind the racks, a slatted door with a huge, brass handle that made a grainy, rasping noise as she worked at turning it.

"Open," she begged the door out loud, as one of the kegs demolished a loaded shelf in its path. "Damn you, open!"

It did. And not a moment too soon. With a final creaking groan, the bolt slid back, and Sara dashed inside, followed by a spray of purplish red wine and a shower of shattered glass. She wedged the door closed mere seconds before something—a cask or one of the battered racks—slammed into it.

There wasn't a particle of light in the room. Nothing but black, musty air that had Sara conjuring up visions of castle dungeons and graveyard ghouls. Cautiously she inched her way along the uneven stone wall, away from the door. The casks were still butting against it, but despite the pounding the bolt held. And after the longest few minutes of her life, the crashes finally ceased.

In her hand, Sara felt the crumpled parchment. A sick prank? she wondered shakily, not believing that for a second. A warning? A threat? What? What did the thing mean? Who was doing this to her? And why?

For five fearful minutes, she stood motionless in the chamber, pressed against the cold wall, waiting for—something. She didn't know what, but she couldn't force her muscles to move. Those casks couldn't possibly have untied themselves. Someone had to have done it. And that someone might be waiting on the other side of the door.

So she stood there, and listened, and waited, until a certain measure of calm restored mobility to her limbs. Then, slowly, silently, she crept over to the door.

There was no sound from the wine cellar, no crunching of glass or sloshing of feet across a wine-soaked floor. Holding her breath, Sara twisted the brass handle and pulled.

One of the heavy, wooden casks rolled in a little as its brace gave, startling her, but beyond that nothing moved. By picking her way carefully over the toppled shelves, broken bottles and splintered barrels, she was able to crawl across the room. More than once, her knee or foot dislodged a teetering bottle, breaking it and splattering her with California grape, but thankfully, the door to the cellar was still open, and the light was still burning at the end of its crimped cord. If there was someone waiting to spring out at her, at least she'd have sufficient forewarning to do something about it. Belatedly she wound her fingers around the neck of a bottle of dessert wine and clutched it like a weapon.

She heard it then—just beyond the demolished cellar. Leather brogans creeping along the corridor. The muffled sounds of approach, followed by a grotesque shadow that rose like an awakening demon on the walls above the fallen wine reserves.

Sara's fingers tightened convulsively around the bottle's neck. The shadow moved, coming closer and closer, filling the entryway. And then, he was standing on the threshold, looking dismayed and confused, perhaps a trifle embarrassed.

Alvin's bright blue eyes stared at Sara from behind the lenses of his glasses. "I took the wrong wine," he said.

"DIRTY OLD MAN!" Noel banged her way into the rest room off the camera department, rubbing her ample backside angrily. "He pinched me! Do you believe that? The old coot pinched me!" She halted and frowned at Sara who was brushing splinters of green glass from her hair. "What happened to you?" Noel demanded. "You look like you got caught in a cloudburst of purple rain."

Sara spared her stained jeans, shirt and jacket a cursory glance, then lifted her eyes back to the mirror. She could tell Noel the truth, but she knew she wasn't going to do that. Right now, she didn't trust a single person in this house of horrors. "I tripped and bumped into a rack of wine in the cellar," she lied. "A couple of the bottles fell and broke."

"Hmph," Noel snorted, patting her butt. "Well at least the bottles didn't reach out and pinch you. Dirty old man!

Can't turn your back on him for a second. Slap and tickle my foot. I shoulda kicked him where it counts is what I shoulda done. Old coot! I hope he chokes on a crab leg at the fund-raiser tonight."

Sara plucked a shard of glass from her hair. "I assume you're talking about Forrest Clements."

"You got it, honey," Noel declared, still rubbing. "If I'd known he was coming downstairs, I'd have holed up in the control room for another hour. Being alone in a closet's gotta be better than having Forrest's pincers snapping on you."

That depended on what type of closet you were alone in, Sara thought with no lack of acrimony. If she'd ever really been alone, that was. In all fairness, she supposed Alvin's timely appearance at the wine-cellar door could have been a coincidence. Certainly he hadn't seemed the least bit fazed by the mess he'd encountered upon stepping across the threshold. And, after a few bad turns, he *had* led her out of the hellhole. Still, that didn't mean he hadn't started the avalanche of kegs in the first place. Nor did it mean he hadn't been the one to slip the sketch into her pocket.

"Have you seen Alex anywhere?" Sara asked on a spurt of renewed indignation and fear. Noel merely scowled at her own reflection and shook her head.

"Haven't seen anyone except that old Emporium bear claw since the techs hauled our belching camera away to the repair room. I'm telling you, Sara, if I get a bruise, I'm gonna blacken both of Forrest Clements's eyes. He'll be a hobbling panda bear by the time I'm finished with him."

Grunting, Noel stomped into one of the cubicles, and Sara, with a resolute sweep of her hair, exited the washroom. She didn't want to stay down here a second longer than she had to.

She found Robin and a couple of other people pacing the floor in the muraled foyer outside Jack's office. Evidently they were all waiting to see him.

Robin's lips immediately pulled back into an ethereal smile. "Shades of the Purple Mist," she murmured, buffing her nails against the sleeve of her black blouse. "Looks like I've still got my touch, doesn't it?"

Sara was in no mood for a mystical confrontation. "Back off, Robin," she warned. "Is Alex in there?"

"No, he's up on four, ripping apart a panel," one of the other pacers supplied, while Robin just stood with her hands on her hips and gloated.

Ignoring the smugly satisfied look, Sara marched over to the central staircase and started up. She was sick and tired of being jerked around by whatever lunatic was behind these so-called accidents. She'd be damned if she was going to be scared out of town by anyone. And definitely not by someone who relied on a curse to cover up for his or her malicious deeds.

ALEX SHOVED HIMSELF out from under the sound panel, a piece of scorched wire in his mouth and a pair of wire clippers in his hand. Through a swarm of engineers and production workers, he saw Sara coming around the side of one of the glass booths, and he frowned at her.

"What happened to you? You look like a victim of the Purple—"

"Please, don't say it, Alex," she interrupted. "I've heard more than enough purple cracks for one day."

He tossed the wire onto the panel. "Finish up here, huh?" he said to one of the older men. Then to Sara, he murmured, "Come on, honey. I want to hear this story."

She looked up at him as they walked back toward the stairwell. "Can we go someplace else? Someplace other than here, I mean?"

Alex didn't like the tone of her voice. It was too tense, too tight, and her expression was too controlled. She'd been through something in the past hour and obviously whatever it was hadn't been pleasant. Damn, he should have kept a closer eye on her. She hadn't just fallen from that ladder in the morgue; he hated to think what might have happened now.

"I'll get my keys," he told her, taking her by the hand. "I might even be able to dig up something you can change into."

She managed a small grin, which he was more than a little relieved to see. "Thanks. I have a feeling purple tie-dyeing is out of style this year."

Alex said nothing, just took her to his office and found a clean white shirt in the cabinet beneath his sink. He even quelled the urge to sneak a look at her while she stripped off her denim jacket and blouse. Sometimes, he reflected wryly, he amazed himself.

Moments later, they were driving down Wizard's Hill, and Alex was still waiting for Sara to speak. She didn't. Instead, she pulled a crumpled piece of parchment from the pocket of her jeans, smoothed it out and held it up in front of the dashboard.

"Beware Morganna's curse," she said simply.

"Damn," he swore through clenched teeth.

"THERE ARE A LOT OF PEOPLE who could have slipped the sketch into my pocket, Alex," Sara remarked from a booth in Maxie's Grill. It was a popular eatery in the center of town, crowded, but not with surfers or sun worshippers. This was where the grizzled locals congregated to talk over old times and enjoy Maxie's hash browns and meatball stew. Most of the talk, however, took place at the counter. The rear booths were private, and the low wail of jukebox tunes covered a quiet conversation nicely.

Alex toyed with a saltshaker in front of him, his eyes straying to the aproned chef who was flipping sizzling hash browns on an open griddle. Sara looked adorable in his shirt. If he focused on her, he wouldn't be able to think straight. And that was a luxury he couldn't afford right now. "Did you run into Forrest Clements at all today?" he asked her absently.

She shook her head. "No. But Noel told me he was down in the camera department. He could have made it to the wine cellar, I suppose, untied the casks and left without anyone seeing him."

"It's possible," Alex allowed, his response doubtful. "I don't buy it, though. Forrest isn't the type to do his own dirty work. Besides—" he picked up the crumpled sketch "—this is another of my preliminary sketches. Another photocopy drawn over in charcoal. Forrest wouldn't have had access to it."

"You mean because it came from the book that's missing from the morgue? The one that was taken on Saturday?"

Alex's nod was grim. "He wasn't even in town when you were knocked off that ladder."

"Are you sure he wasn't?"

Well, now that was a thought, Alex conceded. Just because he hadn't seen the man until Sunday didn't mean he hadn't arrived before that. Still . . . "He wouldn't risk it, Sara. I've known the guy for years. He doesn't operate that way. People with money usually don't take chances on getting caught. If Forrest's up to anything at all, it's a good bet he's hired someone to take the chances for him."

"Well, that tells us a lot, doesn't it?" Forlornly, Sara propped her elbows up on the table. "All we really know is that Forrest Clements might be paying someone at the Shop to ruin the film, in the hope of forcing Gus into bankruptcy. That's not very much to go on, Alex."

No, it wasn't, Alex concurred silently. He took a long reflective drink of his coffee, acknowledging the gnawing in his stomach for the first time that day.

Although he tried, he couldn't quite convince himself that the wine-cellar incident was related to the breakdowns that had occurred that morning. It was an unsettling feeling, and unsubstantiated, because he had absolutely no proof of anything. Regardless, he couldn't dispel it.

Swearing to himself, he finished his coffee and took a look at Sara across from him in the booth. A whispered warning, a mirror message, two sketches, two "accidents" and a host of setbacks on the film. Maybe connected. Maybe not. Whatever the case, there was definitely something going down at Gus's Sketch Shop. Something dangerous, possibly deadly. Something that had to be stopped.

Keeping his expression shielded, he arched a dark brow at Sara. "How would you feel about going to a fund-raiser tonight?"

She met his eyes. "To catch a crook, Alex?"

"Maybe. It's a place to start anyway. Forrest's going to be there. And so are a lot of other people from the Shop."

She lowered her lashes, staring into her coffee cup. "You don't really think that the sketches have anything to do with the other incidents at the studio, do you?"

Reaching over, he tipped her head back with his forefinger and thumb, looking straight into her blue eyes. "I don't know, Sara," he said. "But I guarantee you, we're going to find out."

DOWN IN THE WINE CELLAR, the evil surveyed the destruction it had wreaked. It had mixed emotions about the results.

Sara was still alive, and that was bad. But she must be at her wit's end by now, and that was lovely.

Ah, to have seen, at close range, the moment she'd discovered the second sketch. Morganna's curse squirmed inwardly at the colorful picture it conjured. How truly stimulating it would have been to watch. How revitalizing. Sadly though, a clear view of her reaction had not been possible. Not if the carrier's identity was to remain a secret.

After staring at the devastated cellar through the human's eyes for another few seconds, the evil put a clamp on its fanciful musings.

All right, that's enough, it stated rather haughtily. *There's nothing to be gained from either imagination or hindsight.*

Obviously she isn't dead. We must accept that and move forward from here.

"Yes, we have to move forward." The carrier agreed, and despite its disappointment, the evil couldn't resist smiling a little.

What a perfect refuge it had found in this muddled mind. How easily such a mind could be manipulated. Perhaps, the evil reflected slyly, it would consider staying here permanently.

It said nothing of its plans to its carrier, however, just prodded the human's limbs with a single determined thought. A thought that consisted of four meaningful words.

Sara Moreland must die!

A SWIM AND A COOL SHOWER had the last vestiges of tension ebbing from Sara's body. By quarter to eight, she had her hair blown into loose, shiny waves, her makeup on and her cocktail-length dress laid out on the bed, just waiting to be stepped into.

It was a beautiful dress, simple, yet elegant enough to give her the boost she would need to make it through the evening. After slipping into it, she eyed her reflection critically in the long closet mirror.

As she clasped a braided, white-gold chain around her neck, she smiled to herself. Her dress was strapless and snug. A smoky blue velvet, it was a color that was a near match for her eyes. A slit in the back gave her the freedom to walk—and to dance, she hoped. But only with a select few men, she resolved. Preferably with Alex for most of the evening.

She wondered vaguely if she'd be able to swing that, then decided she might be wiser not to dwell on what might or might not happen at the Tropico Club. She was thinking about Alex Cross too much as it was and in ways that had nothing to do with the problems she'd been encountering in her role as Morganna. If she wasn't careful, those thoughts would cross the line into impossible fantasy, and then she'd really be in deep water.

A glance through her bedroom window revealed that Alex's cabin was lit up like a Christmas tree. Rather than stand around dwelling on things she had no control over, Sara slipped into her silver-blue high-heeled sandals, picked up her evening bag and matching velvet wrap and began making her way across the hard sand path.

There was an orange-red glow over the ocean, the air was wonderfully warm, and someone close by was barbecuing ribs over an open grill. From Coronado Boulevard, she heard a Phil Spector classic blasting on a car stereo, and she couldn't help feeling like she'd been dropped into the middle of an old beach movie. Didn't anyone in this town ever listen to contemporary music?

Sara saw Alex through his open screen door long before he caught sight of her. He was wearing jeans and no shirt. His feet were bare; his long, layered hair was damp and appealingly rumpled. He was smoking a cigarette and spooning out food for his expectant dog.

Maybe it was some obscure quality he possessed that heightened her awareness of him, she reflected. Maybe it was the easy, graceful way he moved, or those lazy smiles of his or his beautiful, sexy green eyes. Whatever it was, Sara didn't know how much longer she'd be able to keep her tangled emotions at bay. And in many respects, that thought was as unsettling as the ones connected to Morganna's curse.

Alex rose from his crouch, and his hazy green eyes turned in the direction of the screen door. For a moment, he just stared at Sara while Cabot gobbled his dinner. Then a slow smile touched his lips, and he murmured an appreciative, "Blue velvet. You look gorgeous, Sara."

Blushing slightly at the compliment, she glanced at his jeans. "Aren't we supposed to be leaving about now?" she asked, congratulating herself on her composure. Alex's eyes were still grazing her body, bringing an uncustomary warmth to her skin, to her throat, to her cheeks.

He lifted his enigmatic gaze to her face. "Uh-huh. I'm just running late. I was held up at the Shop." He crushed out his cigarette and motioned toward a tape deck on the coffee table. "I got hold of one of the audio tapes in Jack's office. Go ahead and listen to it while I get dressed. And help yourself to a glass of wine. There's a bottle in the fridge."

After the incident in the cellar, the last thing Sara wanted to do was look at a bottle of wine. She sat down on the sofa instead and turned the tape machine on.

She could feel Alex behind her, pausing near the kitchen counter. He didn't say a word, just let her listen to the subtly slurred sounds issuing forth from the speakers.

The scene didn't involve any of the principal voices. It was Rainbow Forest chatter: talking trees conversing with wood nymphs, elves and a host of furry, four-legged creatures. Yet, even to Sara's inexperienced ear, the voices seemed wrong. They faded perceptibly in some places and blasted loudly in others. It was like listening to a warped record album, and there was little doubt in Sara's mind that this was not a tape suitable for use in the film.

Five minutes later Alex came back into the room in his tuxedo, and it was Sara's turn to stare. He looked incredible. Even Cabot raised his head and blinked at his owner.

Alex grinned at their disbelieving expressions. "Come on, you two," he drawled. "Give me a break. I wasn't born in jeans, you know."

Nudging herself mentally, Sara smiled. "You have to give us a moment to adjust, Alex. I never expected to see a tux on the beach."

"And I never expected to see blue velvet," he countered humorously, picking up his keys. "Life's full of surprises, Sara. Let's just hope this is the last of them for tonight."

Belatedly Sara reached down and shut off the tape recorder. Silently she echoed his wish.

But only, she reflected dryly, to a certain point.

THE TROPICO CLUB was an elegant, fifties-style night spot situated high on a rocky palisade overlooking the Pacific. An instrumental version of "La Bamba" drifted through the ornate double-door entrance, and according to the uniformed valet who slid behind the wheel of Alex's Jeep, the party inside was already in full swing.

They mounted the red-carpeted steps and entered the lavish building, past the coat check and into the main room. White linen cloths covered a multitude of square tables. The Latin feeling was strong, particularly on the bandstand where the orchestra members were all decked out in flaming-red toreador pants, gold-piped vests and ornately embroidered shirts. There was a large, polished dance floor at the front of the room and a bank of glass doors at the rear. Beyond that, Sara could see a whitewashed patio liberally sprinkled with potted palms and various other exotic plants. The lights were low, the dance floor was packed and most of the tables were occupied.

A passing waiter deftly offered glasses of Dom Perignon from his silver tray. Alex took two of them, handed one to Sara and inclined his head in the direction of the patio doors where Robin had managed to corner Jack. "She's still upset about those altered lines in her script," he said, amusement evident in his voice.

Sara sipped her champagne. "She's not the only one who's upset. Noel and Dieter look like they're arm wrestling with Alvin to keep him in his seat."

Alex's expression was wry. "The pitfalls of being in charge," he remarked with no trace of envy for Jack's position. He finished his drink in one swallow and smiled a seductively lazy smile. "Come on, let's go watch the fireworks."

They joined Noel, Dieter and Alvin at the small table. Like Alex, Dieter was totally transformed by his formal attire. He would have looked remarkably handsome, had his Scandinavian features not been drawn into a frown.

"Forrest at five o'clock, Alex," he stated flatly. "He's heading this way."

"Then I'm heading out," Noel said. "That dirty old man's not getting his pincers into me again. You feel like a trip to the ladies' room, Sara?"

Sara opened her mouth to refuse, then reconsidered the matter. Forrest wasn't likely to slip up with too many people around. Not that he was likely to slip up under any circumstances, but at least with Noel and her absent, Alex might be able to get something out of him.

"Sure, why not?" she agreed. "Where is it?"

"Just follow me, and watch your backside," Noel instructed her. "Forrest has the reach of an orangutan. And you—" she tapped Alex's shoulder "—make sure you save me a pack of slow dances. I didn't get myself all dolled up just to sit around like a bump on a log all night."

Sara saw the ironic look that Dieter bestowed on Alex, but had no chance to ponder it. Forrest Clements was closing in fast. She barely managed to evade him as he drew alongside the table.

"I don't know how Robin puts up with that old coot," Noel said when they'd reached the sanctuary of the floral-patterned washroom.

Sara sank onto one of the padded velvet chairs. "Somehow, I can't see him pinching her," she commented dryly. "Does she ever wear any other color than black?"

"Nope." Noel gave her low-cut chiffon dress a tug. "That's Morganna's color, honey. She figures if she wears the character's garb, old Gus'll eventually see the light and give her the part. So far, it hasn't worked— Aw, damn!" she interrupted herself. "Is that a snag?"

"Turn around," Sara told her. She inspected the swirls of purple and red chiffon. "No, you're okay. It's just a crease." She lifted her eyes to Noel's reflection in the gilt-edged mirror. "How badly does Robin want the part of Morganna anyway?"

"About as badly as Forrest wants the Sketch Shop. I don't suppose she's much different than the rest of us, though. We all want something, and it's usually something we can't have. I guess I can understand how she feels. You gotta keep on trying. Stick with it, and maybe your dreams'll come true."

"Maybe," Sara allowed, but she had her doubts in that area. Deep down inside, she had an inkling as to what, or rather, whom, she wanted. Yet, at the same time, she recognized the foolishness of her growing desire. Alex appeared perfectly happy with his life as it was. She couldn't see him complicating things by becoming emotionally involved in a relationship. Which was to her benefit, she reminded herself sharply. Just because she was attracted to him didn't mean she wanted to become involved, either. This was nothing more than a passing fascination. It was bound to fade—if she could just manage to keep a firm rein on her feelings long enough for that to happen.

"I'm going back, Noel," she announced, standing and smoothing her dress. "Are you coming?"

"Yeah, I guess so." Noel sighed. "Much as I'd like to, I can't hole up in here forever."

Sara started back for the main room, but Robin caught her before she could reach the doors. "You left your purse on the table, Sara," she said, tossing the small bag over. "I thought you big-city types were smarter than that. Noel, if you want a shot at Jack, you'd better get in there. He's on his fifth round of bubbly, and as far as I can tell, he's about ready to slide under the table. And if the Dom Perignon doesn't get to him, it's a good bet Alvin will. He's thoroughly ticked off about the size of Warwick's part in the film."

Sara peered through the crowd of slow-dancing bodies to the balcony doors. Alvin and Jack were indeed embroiled in a conversation. So, too, were Dieter and Forrest. Now that, she decided, was very interesting. Possibly worth watching. Dieter was, after all, on Forrest Clements's payroll.

Conscious of Noel close on her heels, she located Alex among a group of Sketch Shop coworkers. He was at her side within seconds.

"Let's dance," he said, taking her by the hand.

"Sure, strand me," Noel sulked, then she chuckled. "Oh well, maybe Robin's right. I should probably let Jack have it with both barrels before he turns up his toes and topples over onto the carpet."

She moved purposefully off, and Sara let Alex guide her onto the dance floor. "The Girl from Ipanema" floated in the air around them. It was a swaying samba beat, soft and sensuous, perfect for such a sultry summer night.

Unlike the wild crowd at the luau, this was a less-manic gathering. The exotic scents of Oscar and Opium mingled with the muskier scents of expensive male colognes. Whispers of silk and satin rose above the gentle shake of maracas, supplementing the mood, igniting it with a stirring Latin rhythm.

Of her own volition Sara found herself moving closer to Alex's firmly muscled body. She felt his arm encircling her waist, his warm breath caressing her temple, the soft cotton of his shirt brushing against her collarbone. And when he gazed down into her eyes, she saw a glimmer of something she hadn't expected from him. A flicker of desire not quite hidden from view.

"You remind me of a timber wolf," she said with a smile, in a half-hearted attempt at humor.

His lips twitched. "Fair enough. You remind me of Princess Aurelia." He slid his fingers along the delicate column of her spine, drawing an involuntary shiver of anticipation. "Princess Aurelia in blue velvet. Electric honey."

She laughed. "What?"

"You've never heard that before, huh? Must be the farm boy in me coming out."

Gently he urged her head onto his shoulder, and Sara gave up trying to talk. Alex's hands on her skin were incredibly distracting. It was hard enough thinking let alone speaking.

There would be time for talk later, she decided. For now, she wanted only to dance with him, to feel the hardened contours of his body pressed against hers. To know that Morganna's curse couldn't touch her tonight....

The music played on...and on, and on. Caught up in the Latin beat, Sara failed to see the figure that slipped through the door of the Tropico's dining room. She didn't feel the eyes that fastened themselves on her silver-blue evening bag, didn't notice the small, cryptic smile that played upon a pair of red-painted lips. She saw nothing, felt nothing, noticed nothing.

And that was precisely the way Robin Danvers wanted it.

Chapter Eleven

"Quite the party, don't you think?" Forrest Clements's gruff voice reverberated through the crowded room, jarring the evil, causing it to stiffen and tense.

Answer, it ordered its carrier.

"Yes, it is," the human replied carefully, albeit through clenched teeth.

Forrest's gray eyes studied his companion's face intently. "You, uh, want a refill for that drink of yours?" he asked just a trifle too perceptively.

Shake your head, the evil hissed, *and for heaven's sake, try to look bored.*

The human's head moved dutifully from side to side. A stifled yawn was added for effect.

Nice touch, the evil applauded. *Now, just say good night, and move away. That's it. Quickly. We both know that Forrest Clements isn't a man to be trusted. He's a ruthless old weasel, and he likes Alex. If we give him any reason to suspect us, he just might say something. And we wouldn't want that, now, would we?*

"Leaving, are you?" Like a hound on the scent of a raccoon, the big Texan dogged the carrier's movements.

"Yes, I am." This time it was the evil that spoke. It backed off, though, as Forrest's bushy brows lifted. "It's been a long day," the human carrier hastened to add in a less snappish tone.

"Well, yeah, I guess it has been at that." Forrest's gaze roamed the room, his attention shifting to some indistinct point near the patio doors. "I guess it has been at that," he repeated, moving off.

Okay, he's leaving. We can go now. And don't you dare say it, the evil warned as the carrier began to sidle for the exit. *Don't even think it. The man's an irritant. He deserved to be snapped at. He bothers me.*

"Everyone bothers you," the carrier muttered in a hushed voice.

No, not everyone, the evil corrected. *I'm quite fond of some people.*

"Like who?"

Like Alex. The evil smiled, wickedly. *Yes, indeed, I'm very fond of Alex. I'd have gone to him a long time ago if he would have let me. Unfortunately his mind is entirely his own.*

The carrier said nothing to the gibe, but Morganna's curse felt the shimmer of anger that rose up just as Alex and Sara came into view. *Good. Perhaps, now, this weakling would begin to channel that anger into something useful. Something that would rid them of their mutual problem.*

Effortlessly the evil urged the body that harbored it into the solitude of the night.

"WHERE DID HE GO, Alex?" Out on the carpeted stoop, Sara twisted her head, searching for Forrest Clements, who'd ducked through the Tropico's balcony doors less than sixty seconds earlier.

Alex took her firmly by the wrist, pulling her into the shadows of the overhanging canopy. With his hand he motioned toward the street. "He's making tracks for that cab over there."

Sara barely had a chance to locate the taxi he'd indicated before Alex was dragging her along beside him into the parking lot.

"Keep down," he told her as they reached the open area.

Oh, sure, fine for him, Sara thought sourly, inching up the hem of her dress with difficulty. He wasn't wearing a snug, strapless dress and high heels. He might at least have had the decency to warn her that they'd be skulking about in the shadows tonight. If she'd known beforehand, she could have brought a change of clothes with her.

"Where is he now?" she demanded, keeping her eyes more or less glued on the cracked pavement beneath her feet. The last thing she needed to do out here was trip and break her leg.

Alex halted and pulled her behind a red Ford van. "He's getting into the cab."

"Alone?"

"No, there's someone else inside. Damn," he muttered under his breath. "I should have stopped and picked up my keys."

Cautiously Sara ventured a look from behind the van. The taxi door was wide open, and Forrest was in the process of wedging himself into the rather confined back seat. Even so, she managed to catch a quick glimpse of the second occupant. Nothing much, but enough to know that whoever it was had blond hair.

She turned her eyes back to Alex. Evidently he'd seen the same thing she had. She wondered why he didn't look more pleased by the discovery. Even if they couldn't follow the twosome, there couldn't be much doubt as to the identity of that second person in the cab.

"Do you think it was Jack?" she asked, one eye on the sleek blue vehicle pulling away from the curb.

Alex's jaw set in an uncompromising line. "It could have been," he allowed through clenched teeth, and with a start, Sara realized what he meant.

Jack wasn't the only person at the Shop with blond hair. Dieter Haas was equally as fair—and perhaps equally as motivated to be meeting with the owner of the Cartoon Emporium.

And of course, Alvin's white hair could readily have been mistaken for blond in the filtered light on the street. Certainly Warwick's voice wouldn't lack for motive, either.

Still, it had been Jack Kensington Sara had seen skulking out of the club fifteen minutes ago, not Dieter or Alvin. Jack, who'd neatly avoided getting caught in any long-winded conversations with Forrest. Jack, who'd seemed to be keeping his eyes on Alex for most of the evening.

Sara scoured the still-full parking lot. There were more cars out here than people left inside the club, she realized. Obviously several of the guests had opted to play it safe and use an alternate means of transportation to get home.

"It has to have been Jack in that cab," she maintained stubbornly, when Alex didn't speak. "You told me before that Robin isn't a technician, that she probably couldn't tamper with the audio tapes. Well, the same is true of Dieter and Alvin, isn't it? Neither of them are engineers."

Alex's eyes slid down the busy boulevard in front of them. "No, I think it was Jack, all right," he said. "I'm just mad at myself for not realizing that he and Forrest might try something like this. They probably set their rendezvous up long before the dinner."

Sara glanced at Jack's black BMW several yards ahead of her. "Maybe so, but at least we saw them together. That is," she amended, moving her shoulders, "we sort of saw them together."

"Sort of," Alex agreed in a wry voice. "I don't know about you, Sara, but I didn't see anything except a quick flash of hair that could have been blond, white or light brown."

She couldn't resist a small, teasing grin. "Noel has light brown hair. Maybe she doesn't dislike Forrest as much as she pretends."

Alex arched a mocking brow. "If she doesn't, she should be up for an Academy Award. In any event, it's a moot point right now. About the only person who couldn't have been in that cab is Robin."

"Not unless her white wings are spreading," Sara said dryly.

Alex's smile widened a bit at that remark. Chuckling, he cupped her elbow in his hand, indicating a rocky parapet that stretched along the towering palisade behind the Tropico. "Well, now that we've run the gamut of possible suspects and gotten absolutely nowhere, how would you like to walk home? I can pick up my Jeep tomorrow."

Sara looked out over the darkened water, then back at the boulevard. The taxi had been swiftly swallowed up in the late-night traffic. There was no way they'd be able to pick up its trail at this point. And the beach did look awfully inviting.

Nodding, she made her choice. Morganna's curse would have to wait its turn. For now, she just wanted to spend some time with Alex.

Under the curving mantle of a black velvet sky, they descended a set of cracked stone steps to the beach. Alex had removed his tie and loosened his shirt; Sara had kicked off her shoes and draped her wrap over one bare shoulder.

It was a beautiful night. Above them, the constellations glittered, creating silver-studded outlines around the opaque circle of a nearly full moon. It was truly a midsummer-night's dream, and she relished the feel of the balmy breeze on her cheeks, the silken texture of the sand beneath her feet, the company of the man with whom she was walking.

This was mainland paradise, a beautiful evening with no overtones of malice or evil. Nothing but foamy waves rolling up onto the shore and, in the distance, a sailboat in silhouette, rocking lazily. Most of all, though, this was she and Alex, alone on the moon-drenched beach, temporarily removed from the problems at the Sketch Shop.

Glancing at his face in profile, Sara ventured a conversational, "When did you move to Los Angeles, Alex? Right after your parents sold their farm?"

"Not quite," he said. "They sold out when I was eighteen, and since there wasn't a helluva lot I could do about it, I took off for New York. I met Dieter in a dive on the Lower West Side. He was taking art courses at college and kicking around with a street-corner rock band that played gigs for pennies.''

"Sounds glamorous."

Alex grinned at her sarcasm. "It had its moments. I'd never lived in a big city before. I had visions of becoming a commercial artist and settling into a penthouse overlooking the East River. Big dreams for a small-town kid."

"So how in the world did you end up out here?"

"Twist of fate. I got a night job working with a cartoonist who did comic strips for an east-coast syndicate, and he introduced me to Gus. I'd never really thought about animating as a career, but it seemed like it might be worth a shot. And since Dieter had nothing better going, and Gus was interested in both of us, we decided to pack up and move west. I almost chucked the job after I met Forrest, but the Cartoon Emporium's a big place, and fortunately, it was Gus who did most of the dealing with the staff." He squinted out at the silvered water, at the sailboat anchored some four hundred yards offshore. "The old guy took close to two hundred people with him when he and Forrest split."

Lifting the heavy fall of hair off the back of her neck, Sara murmured a dubious, "That's a pretty high number, isn't it? I know Los Angeles isn't all that far down the coast, but it's not exactly within commuting distance, either. Those people must have had to uproot themselves and move to Santa Vera."

A reminiscent smile touched the corners of Alex's mouth. "The ones who could manage it made the move," he confirmed. "The rest stayed on at the Emporium. Only a handful continued to work at both places."

"A handful..." Sara echoed. "I thought Robin and Dieter were the only two."

"Now, not then. Two of the others stuck it out for a couple of years, then gave up and decided to go with Gus.

Alvin stayed on for a while, and you already know what happened to Elke.''

Well, maybe she knew what had happened to the woman, Sara reflected, a trifle uncertain about the circumstances surrounding the first Morganna's suicide. "I didn't realize that Elke Stevens was working at the Emporium, too," she said. Then she hesitated, shivering slightly as her fears began to mount all over again. Morganna's curse might be a sham, but it was beginning to take its toll on her nerves.

"You cold?" Alex asked, removing his jacket.

She shook her head. "No, I was just . . . thinking."

"That sounds dangerous." Grinning, he slid the jacket over her shoulders, and Sara enjoyed the warmth from his body that still lingered in the fabric. "What are you thinking about?"

"About Elke. About how she died." Sara drew a deep breath. "Alex, are you positive she committed suicide?"

Even with all the luminous moonbeams flooding the beach, the expression in Alex's eyes remained hidden from Sara's view.

"She killed herself," he said quietly, starting to walk once more.

"There's no chance that anyone else had a hand in her death?"

"Uh-huh."

They had rounded a bend in the beach. The Apple Shack cabanas appeared to their left, and Sara could see the starving artist hunting around beneath a cluster of palm trees, frantically searching for fallen fronds.

"Come on, Sara," Alex drawled, urging her past her own cabin and over to his. "Since your curiosity's obviously killing you, we'll have a nightcap together, and I'll tell you what you want to hear. Maybe."

The unreadable smile that hovered on his lips made Sara's skin heat up. He'd tell her what she wanted to hear, would he? Even allowing for the cryptic rider, she had her doubts.

Nonetheless, she accompanied him across the sand to his sheltered veranda and then inside.

Alex flicked on the light and dug out from his kitchen cupboards what appeared to be the contents for a martini. "You mix. I'll change," he told her, tugging at his shirt.

Smiling, Sara slid his jacket from her shoulders, trying to ignore the loss she felt in doing so. "Tell you what," she countered with a laugh. "You change, I'll change, and we'll have a beer nightcap out on the beach."

He arched a humorous brow. "You don't trust my unlabeled bottles, huh?"

"Do you?"

"Nope. I'll meet you on the beach in five minutes. And bring something edible, okay? I'm hungry and out of food."

Of course he was hungry. He was always hungry. The man had a cast-iron stomach, Sara decided as she left through the screen door. Considering his penchant for junk food and cigarettes, it was a miracle he was in such good shape.

Five minutes later, dressed in a pair of shorts and an oversize orange cotton shirt, and armed with a bag of trail mix, she hopped from her front porch to join Alex on the warm sand. He was perched atop a flat rock down by the water, wearing his customary faded jeans and a charcoal-gray T-shirt he hadn't bothered to tuck in.

"What are you smiling about?" he asked, moving over to make room for her on the rock.

She climbed up and dropped beside him, glancing at her shorts. "Nothing really. It's just that I practically used to live in blue velvet. Blue velvet from Bloomingdale's. It must be something in the air out here that changes a person's way of thinking."

"To a point," he agreed, giving her one of those lazy grins that made her breath catch in her throat. "But I don't see you ever turning into a Valley Girl." Twisting the top off a bottle of light beer, he handed it to her. "Here we go, honey. Now shoot."

"What?"

"Hit me with your questions." After raising his own bottle to his lips, Alex stretched out on the rock, propping himself up on one elbow to face her. "You want to know about Elke, right?"

Did she? Sara wasn't so sure she cared anymore. "Right," she said, drawing herself into a cross-legged position. "Noel said a bunch of you found her behind your trailer in the middle of a wild party."

"Noel said that, did she?" Alex said in faint amusement. "Well, at least she's accurate." He looked out over the ocean, his expression distant and rather wistful. "Actually it was Noel who first mentioned that Elke was missing—although I was surprised she noticed because she'd been so busy trying to catch Dieter's eye for most of the night."

Confused, Sara retorted, "But I thought it was you she...uh...never mind. Go on. Did Dieter have something to do with Noel's noticing that Elke was gone?"

Alex's lips twitched at the near slip, but he let it slide. "Nothing much. Dieter and Elke were good friends. The four of us used to spend a lot of time together. And at the time Noel just happened to be interested in him."

"So you think Noel was jealous of their friendship?"

Alex stared at her. "Did I say that?"

"Well, no, but—"

"You just assumed she was," Alex finished for her. A laugh escaped him. It was a deep pleasant sound that seemed to match the sultry evening air. "I'd be willing to bet that imagination of yours keeps you awake at night, Sara."

"It has been lately," she admitted, hunching her shoulders. "Okay, so Noel noticed that Elke was missing. What happened then?"

"We went looking for her. And we found her." He lowered his lashes. "We also found a note—a piece of paper clutched in her hand. When the police cleaned it up, they told us she'd written something about having problems with her voice."

"She killed herself because she thought she was losing her voice?" In the back of her mind, Sara recalled Alex mentioning that Robin might be tempted to make a doll of her and stick pins in its throat to damage her voice. She shook off the absurd notion, however, before it could take root. Alex had been joking when he'd said that. Even the witchy Robin Danvers wouldn't do anything so vile.

In response to her question, Alex's muscles tightened. "No, it was more than that," he revealed, his tone troubled. "The problem was real enough, and I gather from what she wrote that she knew exactly how serious it was." His eyes clouded. "She had a great voice, a lot like yours really. It had been her livelihood for eight years. She realized that her career would end if it deserted her, but at the same time, she was terrified of having an operation to try to correct the problem."

That made no sense to Sara. "Why was she afraid of an operation, Alex? And don't tell me she couldn't stand the sight of blood. No one with a fear like that would have slashed her wrists."

"It wasn't the sight of blood that scared her," Alex said, toying absently with his cold beer. "According to the doctor who'd been treating her, her voice would not, in all likelihood, be the same after surgery. She had to know her days as Morganna were over. I imagine she just couldn't accept the fact that her career was on the verge of ending. Everything she'd worked toward for eight years hinged on her voice. And suddenly that voice was shot."

Emitting a resigned breath, Sara endeavored to digest all that Alex had told her. It wasn't easy. For one thing, his story shot down her burgeoning theory that Morganna's curse might possibly extend back three years to Elke Stevens's death. And for another, he was stretched out disturbingly close to her on their stony perch, the breeze lifting the slightly curled ends of his hair and his hazy eyes surveying her through the veil of his sinfully long lashes.

Now, how could she be expected to think rationally when all she really wanted to do was reach out and touch him, to explore the sleek, sinewy contours of his body, to see if she could elicit in him the kind of response he called forth so strongly in her?

"Is your curiosity satisfied now, Sara?" he asked, having apparently shaken off his somewhat melancholy mood. His eyes, just a little too knowing, just a little too steady, stared into hers.

"It's never satisfied," she answered truthfully, and the response carried a double-edged meaning that he could take any way he chose.

His thoughts must have been running parallel to hers, for she saw his expression alter perceptibly, felt the light touch of his knuckles on her leg. "I just knew you were going to be trouble," he murmured, bending his head and brushing his lips across her knee.

Then, he was curling his fingers around her wrist, drawing her gently down beside him, tracing a lazy circle on her cheekbone with his thumb, while his gaze traveled down her throat to the cotton fabric of her shirt.

A shiver of anticipation swept through her, and she ran her own hand along his right arm, over the smooth line of muscle and skin to the soft covering of hair on his forearm and wrist.

He wore no cologne; nothing but a soapy clean scent mingled with the heat of his body. Beneath her fingertips, she felt the tension he was controlling, and she met his eyes without hesitation. Deep green and seductive... Beautiful eyes, staring into hers, as he shifted closer to her on the rock.

Lowering her lashes, Sara slid her fingers through the curling length of his hair. Smiling, she moved her hand close to trace a path across his jaw with her lips. She heard the sharp intake of his breath, felt him shudder as he pulled her firmly against him, half covering her with his hardened body. Then he sought out her mouth in a kiss that sent a rush of desire skidding through her limbs.

There was nothing tentative or teasing about it. His tongue, moist and warm, probed beyond her damp lips, finding hers, familiarizing himself with the contours of her mouth as his hands pushed the cotton material of her shirt aside.

She felt her nipples harden in response as his thumb grazed the sensitive tips. And when at last he replaced his thumb with his mouth, she gasped in pleasure, arching against him, turning her face into his neck while her own hungry hands tugged the T-shirt higher up on his back.

His skin was like hot satin beneath her fingers. Sleek satin over bone, and lean, strong muscle. She inhaled the warm, male scent of him, relished the riot of sensation he evoked in her. She wanted to feel more of him, to explore completely every inch of his body. She longed to make love to him, to have him make love to her. Here, on the beach with the surf washing onto the sand around them, and the stars glittering brightly overhead.

Placing her palms on his shoulders, she closed her eyes tightly, aware of the soft ocean breeze on her face, far more aware of Alex's tongue rasping across one of her nipples, of the hands that caressed and held her and the aroused state of his body digging into the soft flesh of her upper thigh.

She heard him groan deep in his throat when he lifted his head from her breast. She was damp and trembling inside, startled by the force of her reaction to him, pleased that he could look so shaken himself. The obscure smile that curved his lips had her wrapping her arms around his neck, pulling his mouth back over hers.

She tasted the damp tang of salt on his lips, felt the heat of his breath on her face, the solid surface of the rock beneath her. And she wanted more of him, all of him. Right here, right now, under the stars.

He groaned again and shifted his weight slightly. His mouth trailed over her cheek to her ear, and the feel of his warm breath sent a spasm of pure pleasure to every nerve of her body. She twined her fingers in his hair, arching up to meet him, uncaring that they were on a public beach, maybe not even realizing it...

...until one of the rising ocean swells suddenly broke over the rock, soaking them both and causing Sara to choke back a startled gasp as the salty, wet reality hit her.

Smiling a little ruefully, Alex lifted his head to stare down at her. "If I didn't know better, I'd say Robin summoned that wave just to spoil our fun," he murmured, touching her lower lip with his thumb.

Sara couldn't resist a small grin. "If you didn't know better, Alex?" she challenged. "You mean to tell me that you actually doubt her spiteful powers? I'm almost afraid to look at the color of the wave that hit us. If it's purple, I'm going to phone Gus right now and tell him to let her play Morganna."

"Still worried about her purple-cloud chant?" Eyes gleaming with amusement, Alex reached down and drew Sara gently to a sitting position mere seconds before another wave washed up over the rock.

There had to be a message in all of this, Sara thought as she and Alex clambered down onto the drenched sand, but she didn't want to acknowledge it. Damn the high rollers anyway. Why did they have to choose now to make their presence felt?

"Come on, Sara," Alex said, sliding an arm around her waist while she tried to wring the excess salt water from her hair. "The temperature's starting to drop. You'd better go change out of those wet clothes."

Resolutely Sara shook the damp tendrils of hair from her eyes, at the same time struggling to regain control of her tangled emotions.

In retrospect, it was probably just as well that things hadn't gotten out of hand between them. Morganna's curse was still out there somewhere, and doubtless the person behind it was just waiting for another chance to strike. If she lost sight of that unsettling fact for any length of time, heaven only knew what might happen to her.

Fighting off an apprehensive shudder, she rescued the beer bottles from the rock and tried not to dwell on the strangely divergent thoughts spinning through her brain.

A full step behind her on the sand, Alex was having a wrestling match with his own conscience. A disastrous affair four years earlier had left him gun-shy and mistrustful, but the last remnants of that hurt were finally starting to fade. Sara was helping him dispose of them one by one. Soon there would be none left—which would have been great had it not been for the whole new crop of problems confronting him.

Aware that she was likely feeling skittish after the day's events, Alex slid a comforting arm around her waist. But even as he tried to reassure her, he could feel his anger beginning to build. Anger at a curse his rational mind couldn't believe existed and anger at someone whose actions were, to say the least, gruesome.

Was Jack Kensington really capable of such viciousness, he wondered, reaching around Sara to shove open her cabin door. Or was he merely Forrest Clements's willing servant? His pawn? Had Jack been the person in the cab tonight? Or had it been Dieter, or Noel, or even the eccentric Alvin?

As Sara started for her bedroom to change, Alex flicked on the overhead light and, mindless of his wet clothes, tossed himself onto the sofa to wait for her. Swearing at Morganna's curse and whatever soulless travesty of humanity was using it, he glared through the front window at the pounding surf beyond.

But it wasn't the surf that captured his attention when he turned his head. It wasn't the play of moonlight on the water, nor was it the dark, looming shadows on the sand. It was something else, something dangling from the eaves that caught his eye. Something that had no place on Sara's porch.

Careful to keep his movements quiet, he shot from the couch, opened the screen door and slipped outside. The darkness of the beach seemed to press in on him as his eyes lifted to the piece of twine that bobbed with chilling mockery in the breeze.

At the end of that twine he made out the unmistakable shape of a single red rose, an effigy that bore an eerie resemblance to a human swinging from the gallows. The red petals hung forward, drooping as they withered and curled on their thorny stem.

And as Alex reached up to snatch the wilted flower from the eaves, the hard knot of fear in his stomach erupted into a blast of uncontrolled rage.

Morganna's curse would have hell to pay when he got ahold of the person using it, he vowed savagely. Man or woman, he didn't care. He'd tear the perpetrator limb from limb until there was nothing left of the damned curse but a blackened memory.

Curling his fingers around the rose, he crushed the delicate petals. Then, shoving the broken pieces into the pocket of his jeans, he went back inside Sara's cabana.

UP ON CORONADO BOULEVARD, the Apple Shack lights dimmed. So, too, did the lights in a dozen other establishments. But the evil was ablaze. For Morganna's curse there would be no rest.

Alex and Sara had left the Tropico...together. They were in her cabana now...together. The evil took great pleasure in reminding its carrier of that fact. Moonlight and roses. Pleasure and pain. Life. And death....

It wouldn't be long now.

Chapter Twelve

"Morning, Alex. Dieter." Jack mumbled the uncomfortable greeting as the three men met up in the Tropico's parking lot on Tuesday to pick up their cars left the night before.

Alex glanced at the dipping sun. "Try evening, Jack," he drawled, lounging against the fender of his Jeep.

"Whatever." Jack adjusted his designer sunglasses, wincing as he inadvertently followed the line of Alex's gaze. "How did things go at the Shop today?"

"No problems, for a change." Alex hoisted himself onto the fender. "Just a few residual setbacks from yesterday."

"Oh yeah?" Jack glanced across at Dieter who was eating a hot dog over by his convertible. "Well, I, uh, guess that's to be expected, isn't it?"

For an answer Alex withdrew a scorched camera switch from the pocket of his jeans and tossed it to the pale assistant production supervisor. "Is it, Jack?" he retorted calmly. "You expect brand-new equipment to short out like this, do you?"

Jack's fingers closed about the blackened switch. "What do you want from me, Alex?" he demanded, scowling. "Of course I don't expect things like this to happen. They just do. Can I help it if Gus's luck has gone sour?"

"You tell me," Alex suggested.

Jack's pinched features reddened. "I don't have to tell you a damned thing," he snapped, ignoring his hangover and firing the switch back. "I'm the one who's in charge of the Shop when Gus is away. I answer to him, not you."

Alex shrugged. "In that case, you might want to think about fixing up the wine cellar before Gus gets back to town. I doubt if he'll take kindly to having his California reserves demolished."

"His what?" Jack demanded, yanking off his sunglasses. Bloodshot eyes stared at Alex and Dieter in turn. "What the hell are you talking about?"

Consideringly, Alex returned the stare. "You're going to tell me you don't know about the demolished wine casks?" he asked, studying the man for any glimmer of uneasiness.

"Wine casks!" Jack's roar cut through the rumble of a passing truck. "Good God, why wasn't I told about this? I have several bottles of my own stored down in that cellar."

"You *had* several bottles," Alex corrected him dispassionately. "All that's left now is some California white."

Spinning on his heel, Jack marched over to his BMW. "I'm going to sue someone for this," he howled, clearly outraged. "Ten bottles of Country French! How could such a thing have happened?"

Good question, Alex thought, watching as Jack squealed out of the parking lot, unable to decide whether the man had been faking his anger or merely using it to avoid further interrogation.

Dieter strolled over to the Jeep, eyes following the departing BMW. "Did you buy that?" he asked, offering Alex a satirical, sideways look.

"Not much of it," Alex replied. He closed his eyes against the relentless glare of the dipping sun. "It's possible that Jack and Forrest took off together last night after the party."

Dieter stretched his arms over his head. "Together?" he repeated. "Are you sure?"

"Sure enough. Sara and I saw him getting into a cab around one. It looked to me like there was someone with him."

A surprised frown knit Dieter's brow. "You saw him at one?"

Alex lit a cigarette, grimacing at the taste of the stale tobacco. "Yeah. Why? Does that time mean something to you?"

"Not really, no. It's just that I saw Forrest around quarter after one, getting out of a cab at the Palisade Hotel. The driver picked up a fare right after that. It didn't look to me like Jack or anyone was with him."

"Did you have a clear view of all this?" Alex demanded, sliding from the Jeep's fender.

"Well, to be honest, no. I was on my second cup of coffee with Noel, in a window booth over at Maxie's." Dieter's grin was rueful. "Those windows aren't exactly the cleanest in town. However, if you've missed any of the running gossip at the Shop, I'll be glad to fill you in. Noel caught me up real good. At least she did until I fell asleep on her. When Maxie finally woke me up, Noel was gone, and lucky me, I got stuck with the check."

Alex leaned against his car, smoking his cigarette distractedly. So Noel and Dieter had been together, had they? Good. For what it was worth, that took care of them. Now all he had to do was figure out the rest of this damned puzzle, and everything would be just fine.

He thought back to the wilted red rose he'd found hanging on Sara's front porch. He hadn't told her about it, yet, but there was no doubt in his mind that it was another dose of Morganna's curse. What did it mean, though? And more importantly, what was it leading up to?

Controlling a deep shudder, Alex tossed the damaged camera switch to his friend. "I talked to a tech at the Cartoon Emporium," he said. "If we can get to L.A. before Forrest, he'll let us have one of theirs."

"We?" Dieter swiveled his head around. "We, who?"

"We, us. Forrest's assistant isn't about to let anyone from the Sketch Shop walk out with a piece of the Emporium's video equipment. You'll have to distract him while I get the switch.''

"Terrific." Dieter grimaced. "When are we planning to take this fun-filled jaunt?"

"In about half an hour. I just want to stop by the Shop and talk to a couple of people before we go."

"Okay, you're the boss." Dieter stuck his keys in the pocket of his rugby pants. "But let's make tracks, huh? I'd like to get in a set with the band at the Cellar Door tonight. I would have done it last night, but Noel insisted on talking my ear off."

Alex squinted at the dying sun and the ominous backdrop of bunched black clouds on the horizon. He didn't want to go to Los Angeles any more than Dieter did, but he had no choice. Still, he reminded himself, this was the best time to make the trip. Sara would be recording well into the night, locked in a soundstage with Alvin and Robin and a swarm of other people. With any luck at all he'd be back long before she finished taping.

Even if he wasn't, though, he planned to make sure she was safe. One of the layout artists at the Sketch Shop was an ex-bouncer. For a bottle of Napoleon brandy, he'd be happy enough keeping an eye on Sara for a few hours until Alex returned.

And that was all that really mattered, right now, Alex thought darkly. Making sure that Sara remained alive and out of the clutches of Morganna's curse.

"JUST GO DOWN TO MY CABANA when taping's finished, Todd." Alex's voice floated up the staircase to the morgue as he talked to the layout artist. "It shouldn't take me more than a couple of hours to pick up the camera switch."

Where are they standing? the evil demanded of its hidden carrier.

The human stole a look at the two men below. "Right by the door" came the whispered reply. "No, wait.... Alex is leaving. He must be going to find Sara."

Perfect. Let's get to work, shall we?

Nodding, the carrier crept quietly through the high shelves....

Near the foot of the morgue stairwell, Todd paused. Frowning slightly at the clatter of metal canisters that suddenly erupted from above, he stuck his head through the open doorway.

"Hey, is everything all right up there?"

The only response was another echoing, metallic crash, followed closely by a heavy thud on the dusty floor.

Sneakered feet immediately bounded up the steps. "Who's up here?" Todd called out, concerned. "Are you okay?"

In a far corner of the room, a row of tightly packed canisters seemed to dislodge themselves from their wooden shelf and, like a wall of dominoes, toppled one by one to the floor. Todd skidded to a halt just in time to see the last of them wobble drunkenly then plunge from their high ledge.

A disbelieving smile lit the man's freckled face. "Poltergeist," he murmured, bending to retrieve the fallen reels. "Watch out, Steven Spielberg."

The tinny containers made a loud clacking noise as the big layout artist began to shove them back into place on the shelf. A noise just loud enough to cover the stealthy footsteps that approached him from the rear.

As Todd began to search for the reel needed to complete the row, the human carrier smiled, a cold anticipatory smile. Then, above the young man's flaming red head, the elusive canister was raised. Raised and brought down sharply against his skull.

Seconds later, the ex-bouncer was lying facedown on the floor of the morgue. Then, with deliberate slowness, the last segment of the second Rainbow Forest feature was slipped back into its proper place.

All too easy, the evil reflected, surveying the unconscious man with satisfaction. *In the end, this would be written off as just another unfortunate accident. One more setback. One more mishap that couldn't be explained.*

For Sara Moreland, however, it would be oh so much more than that. Yes, indeed, for Sara, this night would be a living hell. A living, breathing hell....

"KEEP IT DOWN, Alvin," the director cautioned from the fourth-floor control booth. "You sound more like a screaming banshee than an ancient wizard. Now, let's take it again, from the top of page eleven."

The old man's shoulders quivered as he hunched over his script. "Powers of the Moonstone Orb arise," he incanted in Warwick's ogreish tones. "Strike my wayward apprentice down where she stands."

Sara took a deep breath, refusing to meet Alvin's myopic eyes, spearing her now from behind his thick glasses. "Save your breath, Warwick," she jeered as Morganna. "Your magic words can no longer serve you. I have destroyed your power. The Purple Mist rises at my call from this moment forth. No more shall the red glow of your Moonstone Orb hold me in its sway. I am the strength in the Rainbow Forest. Soon the mighty Scepter will be in my hands, and it will be my turn to banish you to the Mountain of Shadows."

From the stool beside her came Princess Aurelia's voice. "This is madness," she stated tearfully. "The Rainbow Forest is a peaceful realm, not a place for you to fight your battles. I appeal to thee, Sorceress Morganna, take your struggle with Warwick to the distant mountain, to the land of the Purple Mist."

"Without the Rainbow Scepter?" Morganna's laugh was cruel. "Foolish princess. Do you think your pleas can touch my heart after all this time? No, I shall not leave this forest world until that which I seek is in my possession."

"The Scepter is lost, Morganna," Warwick said dourly. "You wrested it from me, to be sure, but in doing so, you have sent it off into oblivion. Even Croatia cannot locate it."

"Ah, but Croatia is not a sorceress, is she, Master War-wick?" Morganna taunted. "She does not possess my clairvoyance. My vision. I shall find the Scepter," she vowed. "This I promise all of you. And when I do, the Rainbow Forest will be my domain. The battle will be over, and you will be the one who is banished. Trapped forever in the swirls of Lord Dracos's Purple Mist."

As the scene drew to a close, Alvin's droopy features contorted into a mask of outrage. He said nothing, how-ever, until the director called a halt to the action and an-nounced, "Okay, that's it for you, Robin. Sara and Alvin, fifteen minutes."

"Respect and obedience, Morganna," Alvin hissed, clearly still caught up in his evil role. "This matter shall not go unpunished. I am not so feeble as you think."

While Sara stared uneasily at the trembling man, Robin waved her hands back and forth in front of her. "Purple Mist," she predicted in a whispery undertone. "You'd bet-ter watch it, Sara. The mist over you is growing denser and more virulent by the minute. Midnight fire and brimstone burn. Purple vespers roil and churn. Clouds of fury, scorn and hate. Hover low in silent wait."

Having issued that unearthly warning, she jumped from her stool and exited the booth, leaving Sara to deal with Al-vin's resentful glares alone.

THERE WAS STILL a large number of people left in the maze of winding corridors as the woman began making her way toward the rear of the building.

If there was one thing she hated doing, it was sneaking around like a second-rate burglar. But she had to do this, she told herself forcefully. She had to finish what she'd started. And she had to do it now. Squaring her shoulders, she made the necessary detour into the lunchroom.

The key to the cupboard was hanging in its usual place by the fridge. A quick glance behind her revealed that no one was paying the slightest bit of attention to what she was doing. Fine. Now all that remained was to locate Sara's bag in among the jumble of other purses, and she could get out of here.

She clawed her way past macramé, canvas and cracked vinyl until she spied what she was searching for. Hastily she extracted the taupe handbag, unzipped it and began rifling through the contents.

Hairbrush, car keys, checkbook, pen, pieces of paper.... She shoved aside all those things and continued to hunt. Seconds later she latched on to the item she wanted.

There it was, right where she'd left it. Obviously Sara hadn't found it when she'd transferred her essentials from her evening bag. But it was where it belonged, and if all went well, it would do its job very nicely.

Her mouth set in an unrelenting line, the woman allowed her fingers to rest on a folded sheet of parchment. Then slowly, deliberately, she unfolded it. Her eyes fastened instantly on the black-and-white image.

"Morganna's curse," she murmured, tracing the bold charcoal lines etched there with the nail of her thumb. "Sara Moreland, you're in more trouble than you know."

An unreadable smile curved her lips as she refolded the paper and returned it to Sara's purse. Then with a toss of her hair, she slammed the cupboard closed, returned the key to its hook and left the lunchroom.

"LONGEST NIGHT OF MY LIFE," Noel grumbled, coming out of the fourth-floor control room at eleven-thirty, her hands crammed into the pockets of her baggy cotton pants. "Is Alex back yet?"

Sara shook her head, at the same time striving to ignore the furious lash of rain and wind against the studio building. "Not as far as I know. How long does a round trip to Los Angeles usually take, anyway?"

Noel headed for the lunchroom. "Depends on the traffic and the weather, and how hard it is to infiltrate the inner sanctum of the Cartoon Emporium." She unlocked the cupboard door and handed Sara her purse, pausing for only a moment to grab an apple from the bowl on the counter. "If the rain's as bad down there as it is up here, he and Dieter might not get back for hours."

That wasn't exactly reassuring news; nonetheless, Sara refused to submit to the attack of uneasiness that welled up inside her. She'd been alone in rainstorms before. This didn't have to be so terrible. Alex had told her that a friend of his would be using his cabana tonight. If anything happened, she could go to him. So, really, all she had to do was drive down to the beach, lock all her doors and windows, and hope that the storm passed quickly.

She parted company with Noel near the morgue, glad to note that Alvin was nowhere to be found. The old man's attitude had been almost as venomous as Robin's tonight. It hadn't been until the director had literally shouted him out of his role that he'd finally returned to being a mild-mannered eccentric.

The rain was a deluge when Sara reached the muraled foyer. It pelted against the old mansion and had turned the parking lot into a giant mud puddle. There was no moon out tonight, only an endless expanse of black sky that showed no signs of clearing.

She ran the thirty yards to her car, relieved to see that the top had been pulled up and secured in place. Alex's doing, no doubt, she thought on a wistful note of pleasure. Maybe she'd offer to cook dinner for him in return for saving her the trouble of having to bail out her MG.

The dark, slippery drive along the tree-lined road that snaked down Wizard's Hill took much longer than it would have under normal conditions. With each hairpin turn she navigated, Sara thought about Jasmine O'Rourke's fall from the train depot's platform less than two months ago. Morganna's second voice had died on a rainy night likely very similar to this one.

But had her death been accidental? The question still lingered in Sara's mind. And when she supplemented it with the string of weird occurrences that she herself had been subjected to, she couldn't help but feel skittish about what might yet lie in store for her.

She drove through the center of town, noting dispiritedly the lack of traffic on the streets. The parking lots near the three big movie theaters on Alvarez were packed with cars. So, too, were those outside the clubs. Even the soda shop across from Maxie's Grill appeared to be hopping. Obviously everyone in Santa Vera had decided to live it up indoors on this cool, wet evening, which in turn meant that there would be no action whatsoever down on the beach. With the exception of her rather eccentric neighbours, and Alex's friend, she would be virtually alone there. It was a creepy prospect at best.

On impulse Sara halted her car in front of a small convenience store on Coronado Boulevard. Maybe if she picked up a video or two she'd be able to keep her mind off her problems for a while.

Before climbing out of the car, she reached for her purse and shook it. There was nothing worse than standing by the cash register and discovering you had nothing but a few pennies with you. And who knew if a place like this took credit cards?

Switching on the interior light, she began hunting through her large, leather bag. Naturally her wallet had worked its way to the very bottom. She could hardly see it under the jumble of bulky paraphernalia she habitually carried with her.

But suddenly, she spied something else. Something folded and stuffed beside her cosmetic bag. It was ivory in color, grainy and thick just like...

"Oh, no," she groaned, her heart automatically beginning to pound. "Not again. Not another one."

Her desperate plea went unanswered, as she'd somehow known it would. Fingers trembling, she opened the innocuous-looking paper to stare transfixed at the charcoal drawing on it. She hadn't seen this one in the book she'd found in the morgue, but doubtless it had been there with the other rough sketches.

This time, Morganna was shown from the back, apparently gazing into the coffin she was standing over. A few of the red petals were scattered about the stone floor at her feet, having fallen from the top of the long stem she still clutched between her fingers.

Morganna and an open coffin... Despite her growing terror, Sara could understand the ramifications of those two symbols. The sketch represented death. Her death. And perhaps Jasmine O'Rourke's as well.

Swallowing hard, she jammed the parchment back into her bag. While the pictures were doing an all-too-effective job of scaring the hell out of her, she had enough reason left to know that a photocopied sketch couldn't harm her. The real danger stemmed from a very different source. A living source. A sick, demented source she felt certain would ultimately go far beyond shadowy warnings and hollow images of death.

That morbid thought had her driving the remaining distance to her cabana as though she were being chased by a horde of invisible fiends. It wasn't until she'd skidded her car to stop beneath the palms and dashed into the dubious sanctuary of her rented cabana that she permitted any real reaction to set in.

The moment the door was closed and bolted, she dropped her false bravado and allowed the icy shards of fear to explode inside her. Like a hundred tiny atom bombs, they impacted and mushroomed, fanning outward from the pit of her stomach to her limbs, until her knees very nearly buckled beneath her.

Hastily she snatched up the phone and dialed Alex's number. After ten unanswered rings, she slammed the receiver back in place.

There was nowhere she could run, her terrified brain informed her, no one she could trust or turn to. Alex's cabin was bathed in darkness. His friend wasn't there. She was alone on the beach. Alone and frightened half out of her mind. Drawing a shaky breath, she made her way to the TV set and turned it on—loud. Next came all the lights in the cabana. Then the stereo.

Twenty minutes later, with Tina Turner blasting, a car dealer bragging about his low discount prices and rain still drumming sonorously against the roof, she shed her jacket, along with a small portion of her panic, and started for the front window.

The sound of the telephone startled her, breaking through the cacophony just as she was debating whether or not to close the curtains. She hesitated for several long seconds, then backtracked to the desk by the door.

Let it be Alex, she prayed, reaching for the receiver. Just hearing his voice would help. It wouldn't change anything, but at least she could tell him what she'd found. Maybe his business in the city would be finished, and he'd be getting ready to come back to Santa Vera. Keeping that slim thread of hope in mind, she picked up the phone.

She realized instantly that this wasn't destined to be her lucky night. The word, hello, had scarcely passed her lips when she heard a faint click from the other end of the line. A click, and a soft scratchy sound she couldn't quite identify.

At first, the caller's voice was indistinct, but it grew clearer with each syllable. So clear, in fact, that the low-pitched words sliced right through the background noise, right through her own stunned silence, like fingernails across a blackboard.

"You've been warned many times," an all-too-familiar voice informed her. "Now the time for warnings is past. Soon you will face your destiny. You, and all others like you. Hear this and know. The time has come for you to die...."

The sentence trailed off to static while Sara stood there, too shocked and horrified to do anything more than stare at the receiver. This couldn't be happening, her brain screamed! It wasn't possible! It wasn't!

But it *was* possible, and it *had* happened. Her imagination couldn't be this vivid or gruesome. A death threat had just been issued to her over the telephone. A verbal death threat, from the throat of Warwick, the Master Wizard!

In a single panicky motion, she dropped the receiver and backed away from the table. An icy film of perspiration broke out over her heated skin. Fear and anger clawed at her insides, warring with each other as the dreadful realization of what she'd heard began to sink in.

Someone really did want her dead. Her…and all the other Morgannas. Someone, using Warwick's voice. Maybe a tape. Or maybe even Warwick himself.

Her throat as parched and dry as the Mojave Desert, Sara made an attempt to offset the worst of her alarm. She couldn't do it. Regardless of the fact that all her doors and windows were tightly bolted, she knew she was far from safe. Windows were made of glass, and glass was easily shattered.

A trickle of sweat slid down her spine. Battling a wave of light-headedness, she forced herself to walk into the kitchen, and gritting her teeth, she pulled a weighty meat cleaver from the utensil drawer. It gleamed dully in the overhead light. But only for a split second. She'd no sooner wound her fingers around the stainless-steel handle when a fierce gust of wind buffeted the tiny cabin. And with that gust her most harrowing fear was realized.

Without so much as a warning flicker, the cabin was plunged into total darkness.

"DID YOU GET HOLD OF HER?" Dieter demanded, huddling deeper into his sodden windbreaker and rubbing his hands together for warmth.

Alex shook the excess moisture from his hair as he climbed back into the Jeep. "No, the line's still busy."

Dieter reached down to switch off the radio newscast blasting from the rear speaker. "Maybe she and Noel are having a marathon gab session."

"At one in the morning?"

"Well, okay, so it's late. It could be the phone lines have been knocked down."

"Could be," Alex agreed. He pulled the door closed. "What've you got there?"

From a wet paper bag on the floor, Dieter produced two plastic-wrapped sandwiches and a take-out thermos of coffee. They were parked at a truck stop a few miles north of Los Angeles, a small, out-of-the-way place that was surprisingly busy considering its back-road location.

"The owner's wife runs the restaurant," Dieter told him, cocking a thumb over his shoulder at the brightly lit building behind the gas pumps. "I went in to warm up, and she insisted that I buy a couple of her spicy, ham-on-rye specials. She said there's nothing like a good case of heartburn to keep a person wide awake on the road."

Absently Alex reached for one of the thick slabs. Around a mouthful of spiced ham, he asked, "Where's the nearest access road to the freeway?"

"Good question," Dieter said. "If I could read the map, we'd be all set. You got a light in here anywhere?"

"It's burnt out."

"Great." Squinting, Dieter held the ratty road map up to the windshield. "Aw, I can't read this thing," he grumbled. "Where's your lighter?"

"Back at my cabin." Alex ground the Jeep's engine to life. "Try the glove compartment. There should be a dozen books of matches in there."

"Try about three dozen." Dieter held up one of the distinctive checkerboard covers for closer inspection. "Uncle Abe's Chicken Stop, Alex? Since when did you chow down in Yazoo City, Mississippi?"

"Read the map, Dieter," Alex told him.

"Uh-huh." With a sly grin, the blond man struck one of the flat wooden matches and bent his head over the crisscross of red lines. "You sure there isn't some sordid little tale you want to tell me? I mean, hey, it's none of my business what you and a certain ex-teacher might have done once upon a time, but I'd have thought you'd let me in on your little secret."

Alex finished his sandwich in one big bite. "Shut up and read the map. Noel quit smoking three years ago. You know that. This is just part of her match stash."

"Uh-huh," Dieter said again, still smiling. Then abruptly he changed the subject. "Okay, here we go. The closest access road's about two miles from here. We should be home free once we hit Highway 101."

And the sooner they did that the better, Alex thought, sipping the coffee Dieter handed him. Their mission in the city had been completely successful. The camera would be back in working order when the Sketch Shop opened tomorrow. Yet, strangely enough that didn't make him feel a whole lot better.

Suspicion was still gnawing away at his gut. More so now than ever. Even allowing for the precautions he'd taken, he didn't like the fact that he'd had to leave Sara alone in Santa Vera. He didn't feel comfortable about the things that had been happening to her. He still didn't trust Forrest Clements, and he sure as hell didn't trust Jack. But there was more to his gut feeling than that. He just couldn't put his finger on the reasons for the discordant sensation.

"Turn right here," Dieter told him, breaking into his meditative train of thought. "The freeway's about a mile farther on. Unless we run into a jackknifed rig, we should be home in ninety minutes or so."

Ninety minutes. Mindless of the streaming rain, Alex shoved the Jeep into a higher gear. If he could have gotten in touch with Sara, made certain she was all right, he might have been less wound up, more inclined to take it easy on the slick roads. But her line had been busy every time he'd called. Sixty minutes worth of busy... and still counting.

He glanced thoughtfully at a small service station near the freeway's on-ramp. Maybe he should try to reach her again.

DEEP INSIDE A TORTURED MIND, the evil laughed, wallowing in the dark, hollow pit of its carrier's conscience. How delightful this was. All the anguish and suffering, the uncertainty, the pain. My, but this really was good. Much, much better than the last time. The human had been right for a change.

Sara was scared, so scared she hadn't even said goodbye on the telephone tonight. Pity. It would have been delicious to have heard the unbridled terror in her voice.

Ah well, such was life. Now that its weakling human carrier had given it free rein, the evil knew it would be able to see this thing through any way it pleased. And it was pleased to watch Sara suffer.

Oh heavens, yes, it mocked humorously, that was the ticket all right. It was more of a ticket than anyone knew. It was a one-way ticket. From Morganna's curse to death....

Chapter Thirteen

The time has come for you to die.

The hideous words shot back and forth through Alex's head. Automatically, he tightened his grip on Sara's hand as they walked along the shore Wednesday evening. "Did you see anything after you got the phone call from Alvin?" he asked her, launching a stick into the water for Cabot.

"Warwick," she corrected him firmly. "The voice sounded strange, Alex. It could have been a tape."

"Whatever. Did anyone try to break into your cabana?"

"I don't think so." Sara kicked at a foamy roller that had washed up around her ankles. "I kept imagining I saw shadows out on the veranda, but then everything looks shadowy by candlelight. Anyway, I didn't really feel like going outside to investigate. I figured if one of those shadows did decide to come after me, it was going to have to get past my meat cleaver first."

Alex ground his back teeth, furious with himself for leaving town the night before, cursing the eighteen wheeler that had blocked the highway for more than three hours preventing his return, swearing at the accident in the Sketch Shop morgue that had sent Todd to the hospital for stitches. The very convenient accident, he tacked on grimly. Another mishap that might or might not have been planned.

The film's director had stumbled across a groggy Todd in the attic morgue sometime after Sara had left the Shop. But even now Todd wasn't able to shed much light on the situation. He said he must have tripped and fallen, hitting his head against one of the bookshelves in the process. What he chalked up to clumsiness, however, Alex couldn't help questioning. How handy for last night's warped phone caller that Sara had been alone on the rain-soaked beach. No, there seemed to be little doubt that Morganna's curse had scored yet another obscure victory.

"I talked to Gus," Alex said quietly as Cabot jumped and splashed around in the water. "He thinks we should go to the police."

"With what?" Sara demanded. "Alex, we still don't have anything to show them. Just three photocopied sketches, another 'accident'—and a rose you didn't tell me about," she added in a slightly accusing voice. "You know they'd need a lot more than that to open an investigation."

Well, yes, he did know that, Alex admitted. But he sure as hell didn't have to like it. Unfortunately, he couldn't see any point in arguing with Sara on that score. She was right. There wasn't a thing the police could do to stop what was happening. Any involvement by the authorities would only drive the person behind the curse into hiding. And only until the pressure subsided. Then the incidents would undoubtedly start up all over again.

Clamping down his anger, he glanced out at the ocean. It was a beautiful night. Last night's rain was gone and the sun was beginning to set, its waning rays streaking the sky with vibrant shades of red, orange and purple.

In an attempt to lighten both his mood and Sara's, Alex rested his arm across her shoulders and turned her toward a group of boisterous young surfers who had congregated several hundred yards offshore.

"Hot doggers," he revealed, mustering a dry smile. "If they catch a decent wave, they'll try all sorts of acrobatic routines on their boards."

"You mean just standing up isn't enough for them?" Sara replied, leaning back against him. Clearly she was more than happy to change the subject. "What kind of acrobatics do they do?"

"Handstands, back flips, that sort of thing." In one final burst of frustration, Alex tossed another stick for his barking dog, glad to see that Sara's expression had lightened.

"Have you ever tried anything like that?" she asked, grinning.

"Once." He pulled her down onto the sand, allowing himself to enjoy the sight of her long legs exposed by her off-white shorts. "At Ventura Beach. Noel and Elke and Dieter and I crashed a wild party there one night and wound up drinking too much beer for our own good. I don't remember doing it, but according to Noel, I tried a handstand."

"Did you make it?"

Alex chuckled. "Not quite. I broke my right wrist—and very nicely messed up production on the third film in the Rainbow Forest trilogy."

Sara's expression grew curious. "The third film, Alex? I don't understand. I thought Elke killed herself before the picture even got started."

"She did. Everything happened about the same time. She slashed her wrists less than ten days after I broke mine. We were doing preliminaries at the time," he explained, brushing the hair from her cheek. "When I hurt myself, Gus asked Dieter to do the rough drafts of Morganna. The switch immediately got Alvin up in arms, because if Dieter had to animate the sorceress's character, that meant someone else had to do Warwick." He shook his head. "The whole thing was a mess. The Shop was in an uproar, and everyone there was caught up in their own problems."

"Including Elke," Sara assumed.

"Uh-huh, including her. Unfortunately no one had any true idea of what she was going through with her voice. She'd been commuting to Los Angeles regularly. We thought she was working on a project at the Emporium, but apparently, she was talking to various throat specialists down there."

Sara lifted her eyes to his. "How could everyone have missed something like that?"

Alex shrugged. "I don't know. Somehow we just did. The only person who managed to make his feelings clear back then was Alvin. He was climbing all over Dieter about drawing Morganna instead of Warwick."

"But I thought Alvin didn't like the way Dieter drew Warwick."

"Well, he gripes a lot, but then, he griped about the way I drew Warwick in the last feature. Don't forget, Alvin's an ex-animator. The only way he'd really be happy is if he could bring the old wizard to life himself."

"And keep Morganna in exile forever," Sara added.

Alex heard the slight quaver in her voice, saw the way she tensed and knew immediately what she was thinking. "Don't," he cautioned gently, resting his arm on one upraised knee and reaching for her hand. "You'll drive yourself crazy if you start taking blind shots at this. There aren't going to be any phone calls tonight. There isn't going to be anything tonight."

A reluctant smile curved her lips. "The buck stops here, huh?"

"Nope. Just Morganna's curse." In one fluid motion, Alex rose to his feet and scooped her off the sand and into his arms. "The buck hasn't even started yet."

She kicked his hip accusingly with her heel. "One more arrogant crack like that, Alex, and the buck'll be singing falsetto for a week."

"Thanks for the warning, honey," he drawled, but his grin was unrepentant. "I'll try to watch my mouth."

"Oh, you don't have to do that," she murmured, touching his lower lips with her finger. "You just watch your step. I'll watch your mouth."

A ripple of surprise mixed with a healthy dose of desire tore through Alex's body as she lifted her head to kiss him.

It was fortunate they were so close to his cabana. If they'd been any great distance away, the temptation to make love to her right there on the beach would have been too strong to resist. Even the rough denim of his cutoffs couldn't allay the sudden, fiery surge of heat in his lower limbs.

He didn't bother with the lights when at last they entered his place. The moon was up, its pale silvery beams pouring through the windows like the misty spray of a waterfall. He deposited Sara gently on the carpet of the living room, his mouth never leaving hers, his tongue delving deeply into the sweet, warm darkness beyond her lips. He could feel the dampness on his skin, the tightening of his muscles as he pulled her to him, and his hands began a covetous exploration of her slender body.

A soft gasp of pleasure broke from her throat as he slid his lips along the side of her jaw and caught the delicate lobe of her ear between his teeth. There was little doubt in his mind that she wanted him, absolutely no doubt about how badly he wanted her. But he had to be sure. He'd passed the stage in his life when sex was all that mattered. He wanted something more from Sara, something he'd never thought he would want again.

In some far distant part of his mind, Alex recognized an unaccustomed pricking of his conscience. Not only were the pangs present, but they were growing stronger with each passing second, right along with the strength of his desire. If he hadn't been so caught up in her, he might have been amused by the strange sensation. It was one hell of a time to be having chivalrous thoughts.

"What's wrong?" He heard the fine thread of bemusement in Sara's voice when he raised his head to stare at her, and he almost forgot what he'd been about to say. Her eyes were large and round, a bewitching shade of blue in the tumbling moonlight. Her lips, soft and inviting and moist, were subtly marked by his kisses.

"Nothing's wrong," he said, his thumb grazing lightly across her chin. "I just want you to be sure about this."

She pressed closer to him, her fingers entwined in the ends of his hair, her breasts crushed against his bare chest. "I'm sure," she replied with just a hint of a smile. "I don't know what you've been through in the past and I'm not sure I really want to know. But believe me, Alex, I do know what I want... who I want."

He believed her. It had been all he needed to hear.

Groaning, he swept her into his arms once more, carrying her up to the raised dais where his bed stood. His mouth covered hers in a slow, delicious kiss that drew a shudder from deep inside him. With his hands, he eased the hem of her tank top upward, welcoming the completeness of the moment, totally entranced by all that Sara was, fascinated by the way she moved against him, touched him, held him.

The timeless wash of the ocean in the background was a soothing sound. The air was filled with the scents of summer, of sunbaked sand and salt water, of driftwood and palm fronds and coastal wildflowers. Muted music drifted from the boulevard, creating a soothing harmony that blended with the ocean and the whisper of skin against skin.

Sara felt hot and shuddery inside, immersed in the rush of sensations streaking through her. Alex's fingers, resolute and sure, pulled away the clingy fabric of her white tank top, then gently cupped her breasts, his thumb rubbing the hardened nipple of one while his mouth and tongue teased the other. She arched her head on the cotton-encased pillow, digging her nails into the smooth, satiny skin of his shoulders when his free hand slid beneath her hips to lift her so that he could dispose of her clothing completely. And when he'd done that, she let her own hands seek out the snap of his cutoffs.

If there was anything harder to undo than a metal zipper, Sara didn't know what it was. Yet, even as she confronted that minor obstacle, her desire for him grew—her desire and a host of other feelings she'd never experienced before. She sensed he'd had a bad relationship sometime in the not-too-distant past. But that was then, she reminded herself firmly. This was now. And now was going to be perfect.

Raising himself above her slightly, Alex finally shed his cutoffs, kicking them away and shifting his weight on the bed, making it possible for her to explore his body fully. He had such an exquisite body, tanned and sleek, responsible to the eager touch of her hands. He urged her to seek out and caress every part of him. She heard the sharp intake of his breath in her ear when her fingers slid over the hardened muscles of his thighs. And she heard her own breath catch in her throat as he ran his hand along her narrow rib cage over her stomach and lower still....

Her reaction was spontaneous, immediate, a burst of pleasure so intense she couldn't hold back the little cry of delight that burst from deep in her throat. She sifted her fingers through the damp layers of his hair, feeling the slick sheen of perspiration on his skin and on hers, relishing every sensation that skidded through her. Then he changed position again and moved between her legs.

His breathing grew ragged, his eyes unusually dark. Sara could feel his heart pounding as he poised himself just above her. And when he entered her for the first time, she instinctively wrapped her legs around him, wanting him deep inside her, wanting everything he could give her...and more.

A low moan escaped him as the rhythm of their lovemaking increased. Sara thought there was nothing on earth that would ever again be so perfect. She felt as though she'd been swept from one dimension into another, wonderfully immersed in a world of pure erotic pleasure, an intimate sphere of taste and touch and heated sensation.

Beneath her questing fingers, Alex's muscles bunched. His mouth traveled, hot and wet over hers, drawing her up almost out of herself. She heard her name on his lips, then felt a fierce shudder rip through him, through her, as the moment she'd been waiting for erupted between them.

It was exquisite. A unique, indescribable feeling of excitement and joy and discovery all rolled into one. It was the two of them alone, just she and Alex, giving and taking and sharing.

Even when the waves of exultation began to recede, Sara didn't experience any loss. How could she experience one when Alex was still a part of her, still holding her, caressing her, covering her with his beautiful, warm body?

For the longest time, they remained together on the bed, moving occasionally, but never out of reach. Alex draped his arm limply across Sara's breasts, angled his right leg over her thighs. He inhaled deeply the wonderfully exotic scent of her hair, relished the fine, silken texture of her skin. And as spent as he was, found himself wanting to do it all again...and again and again and again. Then he wanted to wrap himself around her and sleep with her, knowing that she would be there when he awoke.

Of course, there were no guarantees in life, but Alex knew he could live with that. Sara was worth any risk he might have to take; she meant more to him than anyone else ever had. Yet as vulnerable as that made him feel, he wasn't afraid to give to her. She wasn't someone who would tear him apart emotionally. He might have made a big mistake once before in his life but he wasn't about to make another by letting Sara go.

His face was pressed against her neck and when she stirred beside him, he kissed her ear. Then he forced himself to roll over onto his back, bringing her with him as he did so.

"I thought you'd fallen asleep," she said, her drowsy voice as soft as lush velvet.

Smiling, he pulled her more firmly against him, sliding his hand with deliberate slowness over the creamy skin of her collarbone. He'd fallen all right, but not asleep. He wondered if now might not be the perfect time to tell her that, along with a few other things.

Still...the night was long, and there was a great deal more pleasure to be taken from it. The words could wait, he decided. For now he'd let his actions say it all. "No, honey,

I'm wide awake," he told her. And with a grin, he swept her on top of his heated body.

To Sara, the night seemed as timeless as the one before it. But there was no terror in the darkness around her now, no fear or trepidation, no trace of evil. This was a warm, embracing darkness. Alex was here with her, making love to her, holding her, talking to her, calling forth a feverish intimacy that left no room for the faceless danger stalking her.

It was three in the morning, and her energy level had never been higher. Nor, it appeared, had his. His eyes were open; she could feel him watching her as she traced an imaginary line through the dark, curling hair on his chest.

"You look like you want to say something," she said, propping her chin on his shoulder, conscious of his hand stroking the hair at her temple.

He lowered his lashes to look at her and she saw a cryptic smile playing upon his lips. "I'm thinking about it," he murmured. "It's just a little hard to concentrate when only a quarter of my mind is functioning."

"That much, huh? Sounds like the novelty's wearing off."

He grinned, and catching her hand, guided it down his body. "Not likely, honey," he said, his voice a deceptively lazy drawl. "I was thinking clearer three hours ago. A couple more and I'll be reduced to an automaton."

"An automatic man? Well, that'd be different, but I think I like you better as flesh-and-blood mortal.... Oh, my God," she groaned, squeezing her eyes closed. "I'm starting to sound like Robin."

"I don't think I'd worry too much about that..." he began, then stopped and frowned as the telephone started to ring in the living room.

Although she tried not to, Sara recoiled at the sound. It was an instinctive reaction, and while Alex looked as if he would have preferred to ignore the strident summons, he seemed to change his mind when her muscles tensed.

Sliding lithely from the bed, he reached the phone in a few easy strides. If Sara hadn't been so riveted by the sight of his naked body in the pearly glow of the stars outside, she might have caught more of the conversation from his end of the line. As it was, she only knew that the caller was not issuing any dire threats. Alex wouldn't have been responding so calmly to anything as grisly as that. And besides, Morganna's curse was stalking her, not him.

Less than ninety seconds later, he dropped the receiver back into its cradle. His facial expression was thoughtful, his ensuing actions less than encouraging. Picking up a pair of jeans, he came back to the bed and began dragging them on.

"That was one of the cops over at the Santa Vera police station," he revealed as he zipped up his fly. "There's been a report of a prowler at the Sketch Shop."

Chapter Fourteen

"I don't get it, Alex," Sara said. "Why did the police call you?"

Alex sent her a wry, sideways glance from the driver's seat. "Because they couldn't get in touch with Jack." He flipped the headlights on bright as they began their ascent along the dense, tree-lined road that wound up Wizard's Hill. "They have to contact someone even if the report turns out to be a dud. I'm next in line."

Sara tried not to watch the twisting ribbon of road before them. She'd quickly learned that when Alex was driving it was best not to look much beyond the dashboard. "Since the police have obviously checked the report out and come to the conclusion that there's nothing to it, I assume you feel they missed something," she theorized, bending down to tie the laces of her hastily donned sneakers. At his silent nod, she frowned. "Do you really think there might be a prowler...?" she started, then trailed off as something in her brain clicked. "Jack," she stated flatly. "He's not home, so he just might be up at the Shop, right?"

"Seems reasonable enough, doesn't it?" Alex replied. He doused the Jeep's headlights as they neared the rocky bluff where the animation studio was perched.

Sara lifted her eyes to the huge old monolith. No lights burned in any of the shuttered windows, but of course, there wouldn't be any, would there? Jack might possess the scruples of a modern-day Rumplestiltskin, but he wasn't a total idiot. If he was here, it was a good bet he was doing his utmost to keep his presence a secret.

"Did the police say whether or not they checked inside?" she asked, more than a little unnerved by the blackened building that rose like a towering medieval obelisk in front of them.

Alex switched off the engine a good distance from the mansion and climbed out. "No. They said the alarm was still on, so they saw no reason to go inside. They're convinced the report was a sham. They only called because they were obliged to." He glanced consideringly at her. "Maybe you should wait for me out here."

Sara's stare was one of utter disbelief. "You can't be serious," she exclaimed. "Wait out here, near the edge of a rocky cliff, at three-thirty in the morning?"

"Yeah, well, it was just a thought. You might be safer out here than in there."

"Somehow I doubt that."

Alex sighed. "Maybe you're right," he agreed, turning his gaze to the faintly menacing-looking studio. "Just make sure you stay beside me, okay? If there's any chance Jack is in there, or worse, that he's responsible for Morganna's curse, I don't want him anywhere near you."

"Believe me, I don't want that, either. I guarantee I'll stay right beside you."

For some crazy reason, Sara felt they should be creeping across the deserted parking lot. Alex, however, didn't seem to share her sentiments. He cut straight through the clearing and bounded up the steps to the main door, making no effort to conceal his movements. But that was outside. Once he'd slipped his key into the lock, he assumed all the stealth of a seasoned cat burglar.

"Stay here," he instructed her in a low voice, placing a cautionary hand on her arm once they'd crossed the threshold. "I'll shut off the alarm."

He vanished into the inky blackness of the foyer, leaving Sara alone, hovering motionless in the open doorway. It was silly, she knew, but she couldn't stem the icy slivers of fear that skated along her spine. She felt as though the Sketch Shop had come alive around her, as though the figures on the muraled walls were no longer mere images of the Rainbow Forest, but living, breathing creatures, waiting for her to stray too close. It was the same way she'd felt in the basement on Monday.

In the dim, shadowy light filtering into the hall, the shapes gradually became more distinct. There was Warwick, standing next to a gnarled oak tree, his wizened hands holding aloft the powerful Rainbow Scepter, and Lord Dracos, his evil servant, astride his black charger, covered with a gleaming coat of mail. There was also Croatia, the Scepter's ancient guardian, huddled beneath the protective arm of a suddenly demonic-visaged Princess Aurelia. And, of course, there was Morganna, the beautiful, beguiling sorceress, clad in a full-length black cape, her amber eyes glowing wickedly, a satisfied smirk grazing her red lips.

Sara forced herself to look away from all of the phantom characters, chiding herself for her foolishness. These were figments of Gus's imagination, for heaven's sake. None of them could possibly harm her. They were two-dimensional drawings with no life beyond that given to them on the silver screen.

Good. Now that she'd resolved that in her mind, where was Alex? How hard could it be to turn off an alarm system anyway? She decided to give him two more minutes before she went searching for him....

Or maybe, she'd give him three. Or four. The last thing she wanted to do was grope her way blindly around this spooky old mansion at night. Doubtless a move like that would land her right in the clutches of whatever maniac was trying to frighten her. After all, neither she nor Alex could be certain that their hunch about Jack had been correct. If there was any truth whatsoever to the report the Santa Vera police had received, it might very well have been someone other than Jack Kensington who was skulking around the Shop.

In the pervading darkness of the hall, Sara's senses grew increasingly attuned to every creak and groan in the building. For a second, she even thought she heard a car engine outside. But when she glanced behind her at the top of the winding road, she saw nothing, and an instant later, the sound was gone, swallowed up by the night.

She leaned against the doorjamb, counting as the seconds ticked by in arduous succession. Before her eyes, the figures adorning the walls assumed hideous proportions, and the night seemed bound and determined to close in and smother her.

"Okay, it's off."

Alex's quiet voice might as well have been the wail of a crazed phantom, so badly did it startle her. It came out of nowhere, with absolutely no forewarning, and Sara didn't think her heart would ever beat properly again. If it ever even beat again, that was. Had she not been so relieved to see him she would have punched him for frightening her half to death.

Drawing a steadying breath, she whispered a snappish, "I'm not the prowler, Alex. You don't have to sneak up on me."

"Sorry," he murmured, taking her hand and nodding toward the central staircase. "There's no sign of Jack in his office. The next best bet would be the fourth floor." Keeping her close beside him, he angled the beam of the flashlight he'd picked up in Jack's office and led the way up the stairs.

The air in the old mansion was hot and stuffy, the shadows around them menacing and faintly oppressive. There was no sound or movement on either the second or third floor, nothing to indicate that they weren't completely alone in the building. Regardless, Sara continued to cast apprehensive looks over her shoulder.

Maybe it was just paranoia, she reasoned staunchly as Alex cracked open the door leading into the fourth-floor soundstage area. The place was like a tomb.

Controlling her uneasiness, she pressed herself closer to Alex, glad of his reassuring presence. Then a tiny sound issued from deep within the maze of glass booths, and the now-familiar talons of fear began clawing at her insides with renewed fervor.

Giving his head a quick nod to let her know he'd heard the noise, too, Alex pulled her with him down one of the narrow passageways. Their sneakers were silent on the hardwood floor, yet Sara felt certain that whoever was here would be alerted to their presence by the rustle of denim that just couldn't be avoided when they walked.

She took the flashlight, which Alex handed to her, but her eyes were glued to an arc of moving light less than twenty feet ahead of them in the corridor. There was someone here all right, she acknowledged. Fortunately that person seemed oblivious to their presence.

God, let it end tonight, Sara prayed as she and Alex crept ever closer to the shifting beam. Let whoever's behind Morganna's curse be caught. Let the nightmare be over.

She felt the pressure of Alex's fingers on her shoulder, halting her not five feet from the dusky ray of light. Unable to restrain her curiosity, Sara craned her neck for a better look. She could just barely make out a pair of gray-and-white sneakers sticking out from beneath one of the sound panels. Not the panel that had shorted on Monday, but one used primarily for large ensemble recordings of the type she hadn't yet been involved in.

Not a breath of air was circulating on the fourth floor. Only the muted clunk of a wrench and the grate of a stubborn bolt were audible from underneath the extensive panel. That and a muffled curse, which could only have come from the throat of a man.

Pressing her down into a crouched position, Alex moved over to the booth and reached for the overhead light switch. After pausing for a second, he flicked it on.

The corridor was immediately bathed in stark fluorescent light, and Sara saw the sneaker-shod feet give a convulsive jerk. They froze, then the legs above them began a slow, inexorable slide from their hiding place. Sneakers, dark blue jeans, alligator belt, black polo shirt...and finally, the pale, piquant features of the Sketch Shop's assistant production supervisor.

The prowler was indeed Jack Kensington.

"I'VE TOLD YOU the truth five times already," Jack mumbled, cheeks mottled, head bent over his clenched fingers. He was seated on one of the vinyl-covered chairs in the lunchroom, looking every inch the guilty party he was. Sara was across the table from him, and Alex was lounging casually against the windowpane. "Nothing would have happened if you'd just let me finish wiring the panel. I was trying to, uh, fix it."

"Like you fixed the one on Monday?" Alex inquired mildly.

Jack's thin-lipped mouth clamped shut, but Sara had a feeling he recognized the futility of his defiant stance. How could he possibly expect either she or Alex to believe his story when they'd caught him red-handed?

"There's no way out, Jack," Alex told him with an uncaring shrug. "You might as well tell us the truth. You know Gus isn't going to swallow this story any more than Sara or I do."

Jack's knuckles went white in his lap. He maintained his silence. But only for a few tense moments. Then he raised his head and muttered a caustic, "You have no proof of anything, Alex. Gus isn't going to listen to your wild tales." He glared at Sara. "Or yours, either, for that matter."

"Well, we'll see about that," Alex drawled. "And as for proof, I think there's more than enough to hang you with.

Every audio tape was fine until it got to you. And then, of course, there's the little matter of Morganna's curse to consider. Broken ladders, rolling wine casks—''

"What, you mean that wine cellar thing?" Jack interrupted, swallowing hard and clearing his throat. "There's no way in hell you can pin that on me, Alex. I was told it happened in the middle of the morning, right? Well, that's when you were in my office chewing me out for all the other problems that cropped up that day. No way could I have been in two places at once.''

Sara regaled him with an accusing stare. "Maybe you couldn't have done it, Jack, but an accomplice of yours could have.''

"What do you mean, an accomplice?" the man spluttered.

"She means Forrest," Alex supplied flatly. "Or more likely, some slimy little flunky you managed to con into doing your dirty work. The point's moot, Jack. No matter how you look at it, you're guilty of sabotage, possibly even murder, and God only knows how many other crimes.''

"Murder!" Jack's voice rose to a crackling squawk. "What are you talking about? Murder? No damned way, Alex! Uh-uh. Not that. Hell, not even vandalism, or whatever you call that wine-cellar thing. I swear to you, both of you, I didn't have anything to do with what happened in the basement on Monday.''

"What about what happened up in the morgue on Saturday?" Sara demanded.

"Saturday?" Jack blinked. "I was in Oxnard on Saturday. All day. My father'll swear to it. And what are you talking about, anyway? What happened Saturday?"

Alex pushed himself away from the windowpane. "The same sort of thing that's been happening for the past week. A mishap that's just a little too convenient to be believable. Now, are you going to tell us the truth, or would you rather I called the cops and let them question you?"

"I . . ." Jack faltered, his elfin features taut with strain. "Oh hell, yeah, all right, fine, so I did cross-wire a few panels. And maybe I messed up a tape or two. But you don't know what it's like to have your entire family expecting you to take Washington by storm, insisting that you do it all on your own and not knowing how to tell them that maybe you don't have what it takes to get there. I needed big bucks, and it was a cinch my old man wasn't going to cough them up."

"So you made a deal with Forrest Clements, huh?" Alex prompted softly. "You'd hand him the Sketch Shop, and in return, he'd finance your political career. What did you do, confirm the deal in the cab after the fund-raiser on Monday?"

Jack's eyes narrowed to slits. "A lot you know, farm boy," he snarled. "That old snake's nothing more than a big bag of Texas wind. Sure, I offered him a deal. Before the fund-raiser and after it. But he wouldn't give me any firm commitments. Said it was none of his business what went on here at the Shop. Still, I knew Gus would never sell out. He's too damned stubborn to give up. So what else could I do? I had to slow production down. I had no choice. I knew Forrest wouldn't question anything that happened, and I also knew he'd be more than willing to fork over a few greenbacks in return for the unasked favor."

"In other words, he was smart enough not to get involved," Sara clarified, "but you assumed he'd come through in the end."

"Yeah, something like that," Jack muttered.

Alex perched himself on the edge of the table. "What about Morganna's curse?" he pressed evenly.

"What about it?" Jack snapped, his tone testy and terse.

"The mirror messages, the photocopied drawings, the hanging rose, the phone call last night, the camera switch. . . ."

An uncomprehending frown invaded Jack's pinched features. "You're talking gibberish, Alex," he retorted. "I don't know anything about any of that. Well—" he hesitated and shifted uncomfortably in his chair "—except for maybe the camera. I mean, maybe I might have messed it up a little Monday morning, but that's all. It was no big deal in the end, was it? You managed to scrounge up a spare part from the Cartoon Emporium without too much effort."

"So it was you in the cab with Forrest on Monday, wasn't it?" Alex demanded.

"Yes."

"But you didn't phone Sara last night?"

"No."

"You didn't steal a book of preliminary sketches from the morgue?"

"Book of...? No."

"And you didn't push Jasmine from the depot platform back in April?"

"Push Jasmine from the depot platform!" Jack gulped air. His face was chalk white. "No! I swear to you, I didn't do any of those things. Alex, for God's sake, give me a break. You know I couldn't have done that. I'm not a murderer!"

"Just a crook," Alex said with a disgusted shake of his head. He slid from the table and motioned for Jack to stand. "Okay, let's go, hotshot. I'm sure Gus'll want to hear what you have to say. We'll call him from your office."

Although Sara half expected the man to bolt, he merely plodded along ahead of them, shoulders slumped in defeat, eyes downcast, staring blankly at the worn wood beneath his feet. He didn't say a word, just continued to walk, his fingers curling and uncurling at his sides.

She had to wonder how much of a confession Jack might have made had he not been confronted with such a barrage of vicious allegations. And it disturbed her greatly that she was inclined to believe him in terms of the charges he'd denied. After all, how difficult would it be to prove whether or not he'd really been in Oxnard on Saturday as he claimed? Not very, she decided glumly.

But if he hadn't caused her to topple from the ladder in the morgue, who had? No doubt about it, he'd been with Alex when those heavy casks had been untied in the wine cellar. Therefore, barring the presence of an as-yet-unknown accomplice, it was conceivable that he'd had nothing whatsoever to do with any of those curse-related incidents.

When they reached the first floor, Jack stood to one side while Alex opened the office door. His attitude was one of utter docility—which, in Sara's mind, only served to weaken the lingering possibility that he'd had any help in his mercenary plot. Jack was in no way a noble human being. If he could have pinned any part of his rotten scheme on someone else, he would have done so in a minute. Sara knew that as surely as she knew her own name.

With that disheartening thought came one that was far more devastating, one she'd touched on a few times in the past week, but had hoped and prayed would not turn out to be true: what if Jack and the person behind Morganna's curse were not connected in any way? What if there really was a sick soul floating free here at the Sketch Shop? Perhaps that individual, and not Jack, had copied Alex's sketches and slipped them to her. Perhaps that individual had done all sorts of unspeakable things.

But why? Who in this place could be so depraved, yet remain so well hidden? What was his or her motivation? What could he or she possibly hope to gain in the end?

Sara sank down onto the pub-style sofa in Jack's office, squeezing her eyes closed against the onslaught of discouraging conjectures flying through her head. Maybe she was wrong, she thought numbly. Maybe Jack was simply a terrific liar.

Somehow she didn't think that was the case.

Hunching her shoulders, she leaned back against the leather cushions, and listened as Jack stammered out his incoherent story to Gus...

...while, in the background, the evil continued to plan the death of its next victim....

Chapter Fifteen

"I tell ya, it's like the entire Sketch Shop's been dipped in a vat of sunshine," Noel declared to Sara on Friday afternoon. "Jack's gone, and the picture's humming along like a well-oiled machine. Imagine having Christmas in June."

"Imagine that." Sara grinned, then winced as one of the layout supervisors accidentally trod on her foot.

All one hundred and fifty members of the Shop's staff had somehow managed to squeeze into the fourth-floor meeting room, and every last one of them looked positively ecstatic. The only person who wasn't beaming was Alvin Medwin. His nose was buried in his notebook, his trusty pen flying across the lined pages at a fast and furious pace.

Sara decided Noel was right. For the past two days things at the studio had been running like clockwork. At Gus's request, Jack had been packed off to Dallas without benefit of police intervention. Gus had insisted on dealing with his wife's relative in his own way, and judging from the tone of his voice when Sara had spoken to him, she didn't have a single doubt that Gus would do just that. In fact, she could almost dredge up a feeling of pity for Jack. He'd left town Thursday morning under escort, looking like a resigned prisoner on his way to face a firing squad.

As for Morganna's curse, well, she wasn't altogether sure what to think about that anymore. Two days had passed, and not a single awful thing had happened to her. It was almost as if the curse had tucked itself in Jack's back pocket and flown off into the sunset with him. Maybe it was wishful thinking on her part, but she preferred to believe that was the case. It was infinitely easier than believing that there was a lunatic lurking in the ranks.

"Hey, what's going on here, anyway?" Dieter appeared at Sara's side, his expression puzzled. "I thought we were all going to get together over at the Cellar Door tonight for a celebration. Are we starting early or something?"

"You've been bopped on the head by that surfboard of yours once too many times." Noel chuckled. "This here's an official business meeting, Dieter. Best I can figure is Alex is gonna tell us he'll be taking over for Jack. It's about time, too," she tacked on, giving her head an emphatic nod. "I always figured he should be running the show."

Again, Noel was right, Sara thought silently. Alex wasn't very happy about it, but he'd agreed to take on Jack's job temporarily, until Gus could find someone else to fill the position. Evidently administrative work didn't agree with him.

She spotted Alex then, at the front of the meeting room and, excusing herself from Dieter and Noel, made her way to his side.

"What's the matter?" she asked in response to the frown invading his darkly handsome features. "You look more forlorn than Jack did when he left here."

"I am," Alex replied, sighing. "The ledgers in this place are unbelievable." A rueful smile worked its way across his mouth. "I don't suppose you happen to be an accountant as well as an actress?"

"Uh-uh." Sara grinned. "Actually, it's all I can do to balance my own checkbook. I'm afraid you'll have to look elsewhere for help."

"But not too far elsewhere," Noel inserted, wedging her ample body through the throng to join them. "It's your lucky day, Alex. You're forgetting, I used to teach accounting back in Yazoo City. Twist my arm enough, and I might just be willing to give you a hand in the office."

Sara couldn't fail to notice the anticipatory gleam in Noel's hazel eyes. Doubtless this was a dream come true for her. A heaven-sent opportunity to work in close quarters with Alex.

She wondered if she should be feeling in any way jealous over Noel's offer, then swiftly decided that such a notion was absurd, not to mention totally unworthy. She'd just spent two blissful nights wrapped in Alex's arms. She knew very well he was where he wanted to be. His feelings for her were real, just as real as hers were for him.

"Come on, Alex," Noel laughed when he hesitated. "I'm only trying to make things easier for you. If I do the books, you can keep right on animating, and we'll all be happy."

"Oh, absolutely," Robin supplied smugly. "We'll all be as happy as pigs in Mississippi mud." She'd sauntered over from the window in time to catch the gist of the conversation. Her red lips were drawn into a malicious smirk as she turned her attention to Sara. "That's the order of the day, isn't it, Sara? Or maybe—" her black brows arched guilelessly "—I should say, it's the order of the night. We're all fairly oozing happiness lately, aren't we? Especially at night. My, yes, those are the magic hours, don't you agree?"

Sara had long since resolved not to let Robin Danvers provoke her. "I think your X-ray vision's giving you negatives, Robin," she retorted, conscious of Noel's guardedly curious stare and Alex's suppressed amusement.

"X-ray vision..." Alvin echoed, shuffling into the growing circle. He planted the tip of his pen on an empty line. "Alex, how do you spell binoculars?"

Alex grinned at Robin's poisonous glower. "He has a knack for paraphrasing, doesn't he?"

Robin grunted disdainfully and clamped her fingers around Alvin's plump arm. "Come with me, Warwick," she muttered. "I'll spell out some words that'll make your medieval toes curl."

"Binoculars, huh?" After Robin and Alvin had moved off, Noel's eyes flicked to Alex and Sara in turn. "Sounds like things are hopping over at the cabanas."

"Only the bathrobed beachcomber and the sand flies," Sara said, not really sure how to interpret the slight tightening of Noel's smile, relatively certain she didn't want to try.

"Uh-huh." Noel sounded unconvinced. Then she relaxed and chuckled. "Oh well, whatever. I think maybe it's time you and I found a couple of seats, Sara. And, Alex, you'd better think about bringing this meeting to order, before Robin's language puts poor old Warwick in a permanent state of shock. Look at him, will ya? I swear his hair's starting to stand up on end. Our resident witch must be letting him have it with both barrels."

Sara spared the twosome by the window a brief glance. Not only did Alvin seemed shocked by whatever Robin was saying, he appeared to have relinquished his journal to her. She was scowling ferociously over something he'd scribbled down at an earlier date.

But was it just a scowl? Sara wondered, taking a second look, or was there a trace of concern in her expression? Could it be that Alvin had written some incriminating little tidbit in that book of his?

There was only one way to find out, she realized. She'd have to get hold of Alvin Medwin's journal and have a look at it herself.

THE CELLAR DOOR was buzzing by nine o'clock Friday night. Everyone who'd been at the meeting earlier had arrived. The small underground coffeehouse-turned-club was packed to the rafters. Somehow Dieter had talked the manager into letting him rent the place for the entire evening. There wasn't an empty seat in the place, or an unfamiliar face, either, Alex reflected, taking a sip of his light beer. This was a Sketch Shop crowd, a private party, and undoubtedly the biggest celebration in the animation studio's history.

He was lounging on a leather sofa in the manager's office, drinking his beer and watching the goings-on in the large, table-strewn area beyond the open door. The other five members of Dieter's combo were prowling around behind him, talking music and generally loosening up before they took to the stage. Alex felt loose enough already. As loose as he was going to get at any rate, he thought, his eyes combing the dance floor just outside and to the left of the office.

His gaze was pretty much fastened on Sara and one of the layout artists as they danced to an old sixties tune on the jukebox. The lady was definitely a stunner, he acknowledged dryly. She'd stunned him, hadn't she? These days, all he had to do was think about her, and his entire body was suffused with desire.

With that desire, however, there also came an edgy sense of foreboding. No matter how hard he tried, he couldn't quash it. Jack Kensington was gone; his days as a saboteur were over, as well as any political aspirations the man might have had. But had he taken Morganna's curse with him? Or was the person responsible for that out there still? Alex didn't know the answer to that, and the uncertainty bothered him. There were too many things that couldn't be explained.

Jack had confessed to a number of minor crimes, which would ultimately have ruined Gus had they continued to mount; yet he'd denied having anything to do with the incidents involving Sara alone. He'd had no accomplice Alex could discern; according to Jack's father he had indeed been in Oxnard last Saturday, and he couldn't possibly have been in the wine cellar Monday morning.

Even when he tried to rationalize all of that, Alex couldn't rid himself of the persistent fear that there was another person behind the incidents. Maybe accidents did happen, but what about the book that had disappeared from the morgue? Unless Jack had been lying, and he had photocopied those sketches, there was no answer for that one. Absently he lit a cigarette. It tasted like shredded bark, and he crushed it out after a few unpleasant drags.

"Alex, honey." Noel stepped through the open doorway just as he doused the last ember. "You got a cigarette I can mooch? Put a beer in my hand and I've just gotta have a puff."

"Looks like my bad habits are contagious." Alex smiled lazily and tossed his cigarette pack and matches at her. "Is everyone here?"

"I hope so. This old place won't hold many more steamy bodies. The graffiti's starting to melt on the wall posters. Pretty soon, James Dean's leather jacket'll be a grease spot on the floor." Noel held up the half-crushed cigarette pack. "Thanks for the apple, honey. I'd better get back to Eden before someone steals my seat. Remember, I wanna hear 'Light my Fire' sometime tonight."

Dieter passed her in the doorway, but waited until she'd moved back into the crowd before lifting a wry brow at Alex. "'Light My Fire,' huh? Has kind of a suggestive ring to it, don't you think?"

"Not particularly, no." Alex drank the last of his beer and crumpled the can. "What were you doing out there for so long?"

"Trying to unjam Alvin's camera. He's on a new kick. Now he wants pictures of everything and everyone in sight. He brought six rolls of film along with him tonight. So far he's got some great shots of knees and elbows, along with a dirty dozen he must've snapped in the men's room." Dieter chuckled. "Word of caution, Alex. You might want to back off on the beer for a while, until the old guy's exhausted his film supply."

Alex grinned. "It's too late for warnings." He stood and stretched his arms over his head. "You about ready to start, or have I got time for a dance?"

"I figure we'll be set in about ten minutes."

"Okay, just yell when you need me."

Sara was on the verge of returning to her seat when Alex reached her table. Noel was puffing away on a cigarette, Robin was studying Alvin's rather voyeuristic pictures, the lights were low, and the entire place was jumping. The cabdrivers in town were going to do a booming business tonight, judging from the number of glasses and bottles being raised in toasts to Jack Kensington's departure.

"It's like New Year's Eve," Sara remarked as Alex guided her onto the teeming dance floor. "I've never seen so many happy faces. Didn't anyone like Jack?"

"Not many, no," Alex replied, his tone bland. Then he lifted his head to frown at the jukebox. "Who punched in that song?"

Sara stopped to listen. "What song?"

Maybe it was a coincidence, but Alex didn't like the selection. And neither did Sara when she realized what it was.

"'Red Roses for a Blue Lady,'" she murmured. "Someone's got an awfully sick sense of humor."

"I hope so."

"I beg your pardon?"

"Nothing." He slid an arm abut her waist and pressed his mouth against her ear. "Do you see anyone who looks overly smug anywhere out there?"

"I can't see anything out there, Alex," she said, pushing herself away from him a bit. "The way you're holding me, I can hardly even breathe."

"Sorry, honey." A rueful smile curved his lips, and he slackened his grip. "My suspicious mind must be working overtime tonight."

"Yours and mine both. But I'll make a deal with you." She slid her arms around his neck and smiled up at him. "You give your suspicious mind a rest, and I'll be kind in my criticism of your drumming abilities."

He laughed. "Sounds like a fair-enough deal."

Fair or not, Alex couldn't stop his gaze from traveling around the crowded room. Things didn't feel quite right to him. But then Sara swayed closer, and his edginess began to dissipate. Maybe he was looking for trouble where there was none. The least he could do was keep up his end of the bargain.

Closing his eyes, he pulled her more firmly against him and allowed his reflexes to take over.

"DOWN IN FRONT," Noel shouted above the beat of the live music. "Alvin, if you don't park your butt in two seconds, I'm gonna take that camera—"

"Noel!" Sara couldn't help laughing. "Give him a break. He's just trying to take your picture."

"He's already done that." Noel waved her hand at the scattering of instant photos strewn across the lacquered tabletop. "Now sit down, Alvin. You're blocking my view.... Aw, hell." She raised her voice again. "Dieter, get outta the way. I can't see with you standing there."

"Why don't you toss a few banana peels in front of the drums," Robin suggested dryly from across the table. "Then you'd have a nice clear view."

Ignoring the gibe, Noel motioned again for Dieter to move aside. When he finally did, she settled back in her chair and reached for a cigarette from the pack Alex had left on the table. "Pass me those matches over there, will ya, Sara?" she asked, her eyes never leaving the stage.

Sara, whose own gaze was riveted on Alex, slid the gold-and-black checked packet over, then bent to search for her purse as a fresh round of drinks arrived at the table.

"Never mind," Robin piped up hastily, batting her hand away. "I'm feeling generous tonight. I'll buy."

"Well, as long as you put it so genially, be my guest," Sara returned with a mock-sweet smile.

"Quiet, you two," Noel ordered, pulling Sara back upright in her seat. "I can't hear the music."

If she couldn't, she was in the minority, Sara thought, squinting through the smoke in an effort to locate Alex behind the other men in Dieter's combo. It wasn't an easy feat. There always seemed to be someone walking in front of him.

Noel started singing an old Beach Boys song, tapping her fingers like drumsticks on the rim of the table. "God, but I love this song."

"Sure you do, Noel," Robin taunted, and her sarcasm wasn't lost on Sara. She opted to disregard the comment, however, and continued to watch Alex.

He looked incredibly sexy up there on the stage, a groupie's dream, all hot and sweaty, with his long, curling hair tumbling over the collar of his navy T-shirt. With every beat of the drums, the ache inside her grew. She could have stared at him all night, lost in the sight of him.

"Look up, Sara." As the song drew to its conclusion, Alvin sprang to his feet and snatched up his camera. "Yes, that's the ticket. Smile for me, now. You too, Noel. Smile." His stubby fingers pressed down on the shutter release. "Ah, there we are." Proudly he removed the blank square from the camera's mouth. "In a minute, you'll see yourselves in full color. Marvelous equipment," he declared. "Yes, indeed, marvelous."

"His marvelous camera's going to blow a fuse if he doesn't give it a rest," Robin noted sourly as Alvin moved to his next target group. "He's taken twenty shots of our table alone."

Sara wasn't overly concerned with the pictures that had been taken. Now that the band was beginning to file from the stage, she gave her full attention to the black notebook sitting in front of Alvin's empty chair. She'd been waiting for a chance to look through it all evening, and now here it was. If she could just reach the thing, she might be able to determine whether or not it held anything of value.

"Some actress you are, Sara," Robin sniped in an undertone. "If you're attempting to levitate that journal across the table, you're failing miserably."

Sara regarded her darkly. She was hardly in a position to deny the truth, so she didn't bother to try. "Okay, since you're so adept in the art of levitation, you do the honors."

"Be glad to." Robin's long fingers snaked out to trap the book. "Here you go." She dropped it squarely in Sara's lap. "Fastest way I know to transmit an object."

"Your sleight of hand's a little rusty, Robin," Sara said, unable to mask the sardonic inflection in her voice. "But thanks just the same."

"Oh, I don't know if you really want to thank me," Robin cooed, and Sara's hands froze on the journal's ratty cover.

Noel had gone over to chat with a group of people at the next table, and Alvin had disappeared into a smoky corner. Only Robin's eyes were on her; yet as cryptic as her stare was, Sara didn't sense any trace of lethal malice in it. Resolutely she bent her head and began flipping through the pages. She couldn't have cared less what Robin Danvers thought of her unethical behavior. If Alvin was hiding something, she wanted to know about it.

Halfway through the book, Jasmine O'Rourke's name, written in bold, black letters, jumped out at her. Slowly she turned the pages, skimming Alvin's long-winded and often misspelled account of the second Morganna's stay in Santa Vera. Then she turned one more page and saw it: a shakily drawn, but perfectly recognizable sketch of Morganna, the Medieval Sorceress. A miniature version of the picture she'd found in her purse on Tuesday night, the one where Morganna was staring into the open coffin. The only difference was that this sketch had been drawn entirely in ink. Even the rose petals were black.

Sara's breath caught tightly in her throat, and she snapped her head up to meet Robin's gleaming eyes. There was a self-satisfied smile on the woman's red lips.

It was a mirror image to the smile Morganna had worn when she'd overcome her banishment from the Rainbow Forest.

As ROBIN SMILED, the evil smiled, too. Slowly, the fingers of its human carrier traced the lightest of circles around a snapshot of Sara Moreland's head. Very soon, the final featureless sketch would have a face. A death mask she would recognize and understand...just as Jasmine had understood in the end.

You can't escape Morganna's curse, the evil decreed, laughing viciously. *I won't let you escape it. Not you. Nor anyone like you.*

Forever shall Morganna sleep, it chanted over and over in the mind of its human carrier. *For now and for all eternity. Forever shall the sorceress remain at rest. Forever...*

Chapter Sixteen

"The couch. Where's the couch?" Noel groped her way into Jack's former office late Monday morning, eyes closed, hands extended like feelers, searching for some place soft to alight. "My head feels like that volleyball we were banging around yesterday at Gus's beach house." She cracked open her bleary eyes and regarded Alex who was hunting through a clutter of papers on the desk for his keys. "How come you look so disgustingly wide awake today?"

"I don't," Alex told her, still hunting. "You're just seeing me through a fog." He lifted his head. "Listen, I'm going to take off for an early lunch. If you can bring yourself to face it, see what you can do with this mess of ledgers, okay?"

"Ledgers, right. I gotcha, honey," Noel eased to an upright position on the leather sofa. "Where're you going, anyway?"

"Over to Maxie's for some takeout. Is it still raining?"

"Spitting. Hey, bring me back a burger and a big piece of lemon meringue pie. My mouth tastes like the bottom of a bird cage."

"That's what you get for falling back into your old habits." Alex grinned, and at last located his keys.

"No lectures," Noel entreated dryly. "I've lit up for the last time. Have a nice lunch now, you hear?"

Oh, it was going to be a nice lunch, all right, Alex thought, tugging on his jacket. A nice, involved lunch during which he and Sara were going to try to make some sense of the sketches she'd received, plus the one she'd discovered in Alvin's journal Friday night.

"YOU KNOW, ALEX, the easiest thing to do would be to ask Alvin why he drew that picture," Sara pointed out when they arrived at his cabana.

Alex dipped into the bag of food they'd picked up at Maxie's. "Yeah, that'd be the easiest thing," he agreed. "But I can't see it getting us anywhere. If Alvin's the one who's been playing around with this curse, then he's a lot less absentminded than anyone realizes. And a lot more dangerous."

"I still think Robin's a better bet," Sara stated flatly. "You didn't see the way she was looking me over at the party. It was positively creepy. She knew exactly what I was going to find in Alvin's journal."

"I know, but unfortunately that doesn't prove anything."

"Nothing proves anything." She sighed. "There still isn't enough to take to the police. They'd think I was crazy if I told them I believed someone was after me. Either that, or they'd figure Jack was responsible for all of it."

"Maybe he was." Alex took a big bite of his steaming burger. "Some of it, anyway."

Smiling, Sara reached over and wiped a smudge of tomato sauce from the corner of his mouth. "You have a very optimistic mind, Alex. Does this mean you really believe that Morganna's curse is gone forever?"

He caught her wrist and brought it back to his lips. "Let's just say I want to believe it. With the exception of the drawing you saw in Alvin's notebook on Friday night and Robin's reaction to it, nothing's happened now for four days. We even got through that beach party out at Gus's place yesterday intact. Aside from the fact that my team got killed in the volleyball game, the day was perfect."

"That's because your team was trying to drink beer and play ball at the same time," Sara teased. "But you're right, the day was perfect. Not a sign of Morganna's curse anywhere."

Alex grinned and pulled her forward until she was straddling the hardened muscles of his thighs. "Not a sign of it here today, either," he drawled. And hungrily he covered her mouth with his.

AS THE BLACKENED CLOUDS OVERHEAD began to part, high up on Wizard's Hill, a pair of scissors snipped a rough circle around a glossy snapshot of Sara Moreland's face. *This is it,* the evil laughed. *Her death mask.* Morganna's curse was Sara's fate. And that fate was sealed. All that remained now was to kill her, to take back that which she had tried to steal.

Eyes glazed, the human carrier picked up a pastel crayon and began to color in the rose petals.

Roses are red, the evil prodded as the hand it controlled worked. *Yes, indeed, roses are red. And so is blood. Yes, so is blood....*

AFTER AN EXTENDED LUNCH HOUR, Sara and Alex returned to the Shop. The morning rain had eased up, and the sun had come out to bake the coast once again.

"A burger and a slice of lemon meringue pie. Sara, you're a doll." Noel bit first into the pie, then into the burger. "Where's Alex?"

"Up on the second floor going over some sketches with the other animators." Sara looked down at the ledger books Noel had laid out in semi-orderly fashion on the office floor. "Do you have any idea what you're doing?"

"Not a clue, but something's bound to come to me. It always does in a clinch."

Sara lifted a skeptical brow. "Well, good luck. At a guess, I'd say you're going to need it."

Leaving Noel to her mess of books and figures, Sara went up to the fourth floor, dropped her purse in the lunchroom cupboard and headed to the recording booth for another round of taping. She was relieved to see that neither Robin nor Alvin were listed on the sheet for that afternoon's session. Maybe she hoped, her luck was changing for the better.

In spite of the ground that the director wanted to cover, the afternoon seemed to zoom by. At eight o'clock the taping was wrapped, and Sara's day was finished. Although she made a quick search of the animation level and Jack's office, she couldn't locate Alex—which was to be expected, she supposed, since Jack had left a backlog in almost every aspect of his work.

"Thanks again for the lunch, and have a nice night," Noel called out on her way to the basement.

Nice? Well, yes, it would likely be that, once ten o'clock rolled around, and Alex was able to get out of here. Until then, though, Sara planned to take a long, relaxing swim, maybe even rent a horse from the stable a few blocks away from her cabana and go for a ride along the beach. A couple of hours alone would give her some time to think. About those few nagging questions still plaguing her in connection with Morganna's curse. About her future as the sorceress's voice. About Alex. . . .

The evening air was sticky as she drove down Wizard's hill, a portent of more rain, she thought, casting a quick look over the rooftops of the town to the hazy white overcast that was rolling in from the Pacific. If she wanted to go riding, she had a feeling she'd better do that first.

She glanced down at the apricot jersey, jeans and hiking boots she'd worn to work that day. Good enough, she decided, pointing her car in the direction of the oceanfront stable. A slight rumbling sound in her stomach, however, reminded her that she hadn't eaten since noon. And she'd long ago burned up that food energy. Being with Alex had to be the best form of exercise in the world, she reflected with a reminiscent smile.

Impulsively she braked her car outside a delicatessen on Alvarez, grabbed her wallet from her purse and ran inside. The submarine sandwiches looked fresh and delicious, so she ordered one; then, at the cashier's request for change, began hunting through her wallet for quarters. She found them easily enough...but at the same time she found something else. Something smooth and malleable that smelled very faintly of crushed herbs.

Grinding her teeth, Sara pulled a tiny, black satin pouch from deep inside her change purse. Since she was one of those people who invariably tossed loose coins into the bottom of her handbag, it occurred to her that the pouch—some sort of evil-charm bag, she supposed, could have been there for days without her realizing it. Still, no matter how long it had been in her possession, she knew instinctively who'd put it here. And she had a horrible feeling she knew the reason.

Hastily she shoved the pouch back in her wallet, paid for the submarine sandwich she no longer had any desire to eat, and returned to her car.

No way was Robin Danvers going to jerk her around anymore, she vowed, revving the MG's engine with more force than was necessary. The white-winged witch had gone too far this time. It was one thing to be warned off with photocopied sketches and threatening messages, another thing entirely to find that an evil charm bag had been planted in her purse.

Sara shot through town, mindless of the posted speed signs. Robin hadn't been at the Shop that afternoon, she recalled angrily. Chances were good the woman was reading tea leaves at the Apple Shack—or waxing her broomstick.

She skidded her car to a stop beside the restaurant, too angry to notice that the parking lot was virtually empty of vehicles. She took only distant note of the helmeted youths careening around the empty pavement on their skateboards. It wasn't until she encountered the closed sign on the front door that she realized something was wrong.

Luckily the door wasn't locked. Unconcerned with social amenities, she barged right in. "Robin!" she called as she entered. "Robin, I want to talk to you." No response. In fact, the only sign of life Sara could detect came in the form of a noxious odor drifting from the back of the restaurant.

With a quick glance back at the skateboarding youths who were still flying around the paved lot, she trailed the vile aroma to its source. Trailed it through the obscure reaches of the dining room and into the kitchen.

She paused for a moment on the threshold, keeping the swinging door open with her hand. Robin was in there all right, hovering over a bubbling black-bottomed pot on the stove. Around her head, she'd wound a bright red scarf, the pointed tails of which dangled forward like floppy rabbit's ears. She was dropping pinches of crushed herbs into the steaming pot and making a variety of incomprehensible hand motions over it. But at least she wasn't chanting. For that, Sara was grateful. Stiffening her spine, she ventured a calm, "Robin, I'd like to talk to you."

The woman's head swung around. If she'd been her own animated counterpart, her eyes would have shot forth a series of poison-tipped elf-bolts. But despite her witchy claims, she was only human, and as such she had to settle for spearing Sara with an icy glare.

"We're closed," she bit out, keeping her teeth locked together. "What's your problem, can't you read?"

Sara held her ground. "Yes, I can read," she retorted evenly.

"Then get out. You'll have to eat somewhere else tonight." She splayed her fingers over the blackened pot. "This isn't for public consumption."

Sara had no trouble believing that. "I didn't come here to eat," she stated flatly, letting the kitchen door swing closed behind her.

"Good thing," Robin said, her eyes filling with an odd blend of amusement and acerbity. "Ants can be such pesky creatures. Single-minded, too. We found a whole swarm of them in the basement today. The boss figured it would be bad for business if the troops decided to move upstairs, so he closed down. You got that, Sara? The restaurant's not open."

"I told you, I didn't come here to eat. I came to talk to you. You got that, Robin?" Sara mocked. "Talk. You do know how to hold a normal conversation, don't you?"

Lips curving, Robin dropped a lid on her simmering brew and sauntered away from the stove. Her expression had changed subtly from one of amused hostility to one of droll contempt. "You're in an awful snit tonight, aren't you, Sara? What's the gripe? Is Morganna's curse finally starting to get to you? Can you feel it now?"

Sara regarded her balefully. "Feel it? No. But I think I've figured out where it comes from."

"Really?" Robin's eyes narrowed, and she folded her arms across her chest. "Well, isn't that interesting. Tell me, when did you suddenly develop this extraordinary sixth sense? I've certainly never noticed it before."

"It doesn't take a sixth sense to recognize your touch."

"My touch, huh? Okay, I'll play along. Tell me all about my touch." She moved closer, her red-tipped fingers beginning to curl.

"Morganna's curse," Sara told her, determined not to back away. "You believe in it, and you want me to believe in it. You put a symbol of it in my wallet."

"Did I?" Robin's features tautened marginally, then relaxed into an enigmatic smile. In one fluid movement, she bent to scoop up her Siamese cat, who had wrapped itself around her ankles. "Now why do you suppose I'd do something like that?"

"If I were a witch, I'd probably know why. Since I'm not, I can only assume you had your twisted reasons. After all, curses are your specialty, aren't they? Curses, spells…black satin charm bags." Sara watched the woman who was rhythmically stroking the cat's fur. "Why did you put it there, Robin?" she demanded. "What did you hope to gain?"

"Purple clouds," Robin hissed darkly, her meaning clear enough to Sara. She glanced through the kitchen window at the passing skateboarders. "All right," she announced, her tone brusque. "You want to talk? Fine, we'll talk. But not here. This isn't for curious little ears to hear. Besides, the exterminators could show up any time now."

"You mean you're not trying to kill the ants off with that potion of yours?" Sara muttered under her breath.

Robin's eyes again narrowed, but she said nothing. Whirling around, she yanked the back door open and deposited Pyewackett on the stoop. "Go chase beach varmints," she instructed the purring feline. "I won't be needing you for a while." She sent Sara a withering glance. "In here," she said, flinging an arm at what appeared to be a pantry.

Drawing a deep, bolstering breath, Sara followed her inside. Even someone with bionic ears would have been hard pressed to eavesdrop on a conversation in such a stuffy little place, she thought. Still, she didn't care about eavesdroppers. She wanted answers, and Robin was damned well going to give them to her.

Wordlessly she extracted the black pouch from her wallet. "Go ahead, Robin," she said. "Tell me that this isn't yours. Tell me you didn't put it in my purse. Tell me it hasn't got anything to do with this supposed curse you're so fond of.''

With a toss of her wild black mane, Robin moved to stand beside a shelf laden with peach preserves. In the streaky light tumbling through a high window on the far side of the room, her features appeared cold, closed. She wasn't about to admit anything, Sara realized, her anger rallying all over again. But nor was she attempting to deny what she'd obviously done. How could she when her handiwork was dangling in front of her nose?

"Why did you do it, Robin?" Sara persisted, anger making her brazen enough to push the matter to the edge. "Does the part of Morganna really mean that much to you?"

Robin's expression transformed itself into a spiteful mask. "It should have been mine," she snarled through clenched teeth. "You had no business waltzing in and stealing it from me. Not you—and certainly not Jasmine O'Rourke. She didn't have a clue how to play Morganna."

Damn! In her vexation, Sara had forgotten her earlier theory about Morganna's second voice. Of course, Robin hadn't actually come out and confessed to killing Jasmine, but it seemed like a strong possibility. Too late, she realized that she might have walked right into the clutches of a cold-blooded murderer. She found herself edging unobtrusively toward the door.

"Why didn't you talk to Gus if you felt that way?" she managed, refusing to cave in to her trepidation.

"Talk to Gus..." Robin's laugh was a rough, bitter sound. "Yeah, sure, talk to good old Gus. What do you think I did? I never stopped talking to Gus. He just wasn't listening. As far as he's concerned, I'm Princess Aurelia. Even after Jasmine died, all I got from him was a conciliatory smile and a jovial, 'You got the voice of a princess, Robin. Ain't no way I'm gonna mess with something so right.'"

Sara inched past a row of canned pears. "Well, what's wrong with that?" she questioned, unsure whether to make a dash for the door or just keep slowly working her way toward it. "Princess Aurelia's one of the most prominent characters in the Rainbow Forest."

Robin shrugged and, to Sara's consternation, picked up a large jar of peach preserves. "Big deal," she snorted, testing the weight of the Mason jar. "Prominent isn't good enough. I want opportunities, the kind that doing Morganna's voice could give me. I want what Elke had. What Jasmine had. What you have. Princess Aurelia's a sappy little do-gooder. About the only thing she's got going for her is that she's not cursed."

"I'd say that's a pretty big plus," Sara said.

"Naturally you would," Robin retorted, "since you don't have the foggiest notion of how to deal with a curse. Admit it, Sara, you're scared. I saw your face when you stumbled across that sketch in Alvin's journal. You looked like you'd seen a ghost. Or was it just that you'd seen that particular drawing before?"

A crafty smile flitted across her lips. Red lips—perhaps covered with the same red shade of lipstick that had been used to write the message on her mirror, Sara thought irritably, wishing she'd just gone horseback riding.

"I think you know very well I've seen that drawing before," she said as calmly as possible, now only a few feet from the pantry door. "What I'm curious about is why you put it in my purse. And why the pouch, Robin? Was it supposed to have some kind of evil effect on me?"

Lord, she must be getting brave in her old age. What on earth was making her ask those questions? She should be concentrating on getting away from the woman, not attempting to ignite her temper. And yet . . . Robin's reaction was not quite what she'd been expecting. In fact, the woman now went as far as to laugh, a genuinely incredulous laugh.

"Evil effect! Lady, you're so far off base, it's almost funny. For your information, witches deal in herbal potions and the power of the self."

"And charm bags," Sara added dryly.

"Yes, and charm bags. Do you have a problem with that?" Robin halted abruptly, her sneer changing to a scowl. "And what do you mean, why did I put that drawing in your purse? I didn't put it there. I just saw it there."

Sara stopped in her tracks. "You saw it?"

"I just said that, didn't I? Read my lips, Sara. I *saw* it."

"When?"

"When I was checking to see if my charm bag, as you call it, was still in your wallet."

It was Sara's turn to frown. "You mean to tell me that you put the bag in my purse, but not the sketch?"

"I shouldn't be telling you anything," Robin grumbled, flicking at a cracked red nail and shoving the peaches back in place with her elbow. "But since you're hell-bent on pinning your problems on me, I might as well spit out the truth—revolting as it is." A perceptible shudder of distaste enveloped her. "The bag's an amulet. In layman's terms, it would be called a good-luck charm."

A feeling of disbelief rushed through Sara's body. "You gave me a good-luck charm?"

"Oh, don't say it like that," Robin snapped. "You make me sound like a goody-goody. But just so you know, I'm a white witch. I don't delve into the black arts. And yes, I believe in my amulets, in their power. I stuck that pouch in your wallet the night of the Heart Association fund-raiser, and for some ridiculous reason, I felt compelled to make sure you still had it. So I decided to check your purse Tuesday night before I left the Shop. That's when I saw the sketch." Her smile grew positively nefarious. "I knew you'd be shocked when you found the same drawing in Alvin's journal. But you'd have been a hell of a lot more shocked if I hadn't offset the worst of Morganna's curse for you. I know what I know, Sara Moreland. There are forces in this world that can't be denied. This curse is one of them. You're just lucky I was here to counteract the worst of it, luckier still that you weren't in Jasmine O'Rourke's shoes. Until she died, even I didn't realize just how potent Morganna's curse really was.''

For some absolutely ludicrous reason, Sara believed her. She probably shouldn't, knowing as she did how desperately Robin wanted to do Morganna's voice, but she couldn't help it. She bought the story—at least the part about the amulet. For all her esoteric chanting and purple-cloud prophecies, Robin Danvers just didn't strike her as a deranged person.

Smiling, Sara ventured a wry, "So you're a good witch after all, huh?"

Robin moved a shoulder offhandedly. "Let's just say I don't like death. And it challenges me to combat a truly evil force. Gives me a chance to hone my skills, so to speak."

Sara's muscles constricted. "I don't suppose you'd care to give this evil force a name, would you?"

Robin's gray eyes darkened. "There is no name for evil, Sara. It simply exists. And it won't go away just because you don't believe in it. It's part of life. The eternal struggle."

A little discomforted, Sara reached for the doorknob. "I'll keep that in mind, Robin," she murmured, half-afraid the woman was going to launch into an occult chant. "And thanks for the am—" She cut herself off as the knob twisted ineffectually in her grip. She gave it a mighty tug, but the door wouldn't give.

"What's wrong?" Robin demanded, coming up behind her. Then, she lifted her head and sniffed the air. "Hey, what's that smell?"

Sara's startled gaze shifted to the base of the door. Through the tiny crack, she spied several filmy wisps of smoke curling into the pantry. Smoke—and a folded sheet of parchment that was slowly being nudged along the floor.

Robin must have seen it, too, for she immediately bent to snatch it up. Her features paled, turning a sickly shade of white as she opened the paper. "It's for you, Sara," she said woodenly, extending the macabre sketch. "And for what it's worth, I don't think my amulet worked."

IN THE DESERTED KITCHEN of the Apple Shack, the evil reveled in the sight of the lapping orange flames as they crawled up the grease-stained pantry door. Through the human's eyes, it watched the fire spread. But only for a few seconds. Its attention shifted swiftly when the carrier's fingers jerked convulsively.

Get away from the flames, it reproached angrily. *Just hurry up and deliver the damned sketch—before it catches fire.*

The human carrier gave the parchment one final nudge. "I don't like this," came the annoyed whisper, "What if someone sees the smoke? What if those kids come back? I just don't think I like doing it this way."

Well, that's too bad, isn't it? the evil flared. *You're going to have to learn that what you do and don't like are entirely irrelevant in the overall scheme of things. You'll do as I say from now on. No more. No less. Do you understand?*

The carrier stepped away from the fiery door, realizing the futility of retaliation. The evil had grown incredibly strong over the past few weeks. Stronger than ever before. To cross it was pointless. Its talons had taken deep root, twining themselves intrinsically throughout the mind it inhabited.

Do you understand? Morganna's curse thundered again, and meekly the human nodded.

That's better. Now, listen close. I'm tired of repeating myself. I want you to go outside to your car, and I want you to wait.

The carrier blinked. "Wait? But why?"

You're beginning to irritate me, the evil warned. *I said listen, not ask stupid questions. You'll wait because I want you to wait. Because I want to know that it's over.*

"But it has to be over," the carrier insisted, aware of the dangerous line being walked. "They can't possibly escape."

Be that as it may, I intend to make certain they're dead. It must end, once and for all. Jack is gone. Our unknowing little ally can't help us any more. Alex is in charge now. He knows what he's doing. And remember, he likes Sara.

"I know, but..."

Stop! the evil commanded, and the carrier was quick to back down. *I've put up with you long enough. You will obey me, or I will silence you forever.*

As that formidable decree was issued, Morganna's curse surged upward in a huge blackened mass. *Burn, Sara Moreland,* it charged in a brutal thrust of rancor. *Burn, witch! Both of you, burn in hell!*

Reeling from the force of the vengeful cry, the carrier cringed, fearful of the omnipotent force for the first time.

So you learn the truth at long last, do you, human? the evil shouted gleefully. *It's about time you saw the light. Foolish human. How well I've kept my true intentions hidden from you. How marvelously well.*

Numbly the carrier whispered, "What are you going to do?"

None of your business, the evil retorted. *Soon enough, your goals will have been realized. Sara will be dead. And so will Robin. A problem and a potential problem taken care of in one fiery blow. Beyond that, you need know nothing more.*

"But I don't..."

Understand? The evil finished the perplexed thought. *How unfortunate for you. But then, your pathetic human brain is no match for me, is it? No, I assure you it isn't. I can blot out conscious thought in an instant. And from this moment forth, I shall. Yes, indeed, I shall.*

Flinging back the human's head, the evil laughed out loud, enjoying the unfettered sound, the sense of complete control.

Ah, but it was a lovely feeling to be free. To know that the two women in the pantry would not be the only victims of Morganna's curse tonight....

Chapter Seventeen

"Shoving rags and aprons under the door isn't going to keep the smoke out forever, Robin," Sara snapped as she jammed a wad of cheesecloth between the hinges.

From her hands and knees, Robin muttered an acerbic, "Just shut up and keep shoving. I can't think with a smoke-clogged brain." She grabbed a box of disposable cloths. "Damn, damn, damn! How do I get myself into these situations?" She sat back on her heels, dragging in a deep breath. "Fire and smoke by nature's hand. Reduce these flames of evil brand. Beyond these walls, by my decree. The fire dies. So mote it be...."

Sara stood, staving off the panic clutching at her midsection, and began prowling the tiny room. "Save your breath, Robin," she shot over her shoulder. "I don't think the fire is listening to you."

"Disbeliever," Robin snarled. "Your skeptical attitude is interfering with my commands." She ducked as a roll of paper towels flew past her head. "What are you doing?"

Sara had wandered away from the door and was starting to clear the sturdy wooden shelves of their contents. There was only one thing she could think of that stood a chance of working, and time was definitely not on her side. With her head, she indicated the narrow aperture high above them.

"If we can move this shelf over a little, we might be able to climb up on it and reach the window."

"And then what?" Robin demanded, still waving her hands in front of the door. "I don't know about you, but I'm not too keen on jumping into a gully full of thorny bushes."

"Would you rather burn to death?"

"I'm trying to rectify that."

"Fine. But in the meantime, get over here and help me dump the stuff off these shelves."

"I..." Robin hesitated. "Oh, all right," she grunted. "You're messing up my powers anyway. But you go first and clear a path. I don't like heights, I don't like thorns, and most of all, right now, I don't like you."

Sara tossed the last of the Mason jars from the shelf, ignoring the other woman's grouchy tones. "Then you certainly won't want to die with me, will you? Now stop complaining and help me move this thing."

Together, the two women managed to lever the heavy shelf along the floor. The wadded rags had slowed the in-pouring smoke only marginally. The air was rapidly becoming unbreathable. In another few minutes...

Sara waved at the thick whorls curling in front of her face and applied all her strength to the weighty shelf. In her mind's eye, she could still picture the snapshot of her head pasted onto the body of Morganna. Morganna and her, lying there in the coffin, clutching a dying, blood-red rose.

Coughing, Robin motioned her upward. "Go," she gasped, smacking Sara's arm to get her attention. "My lungs are starting to sizzle."

Drawing a deep, smoke-filled breath, Sara shook her dire thoughts aside and scrambled onto the first shelf, only barely able to make out the window above her. If she hadn't been so averse to the idea of death by asphyxiation, she might have stopped to wonder whether or not the opening would be large enough for her to squeeze through. As it was, however, she could feel her lungs searing every time she inhaled. It was either climb or die... And she wasn't prepared to do the latter without one hell of a fight.

When at last her trembling legs had carried her to the top shelf, she dropped to her knees and began struggling with the rusted window latch. It didn't want to give, and for a moment she felt like screaming in sheer frustration—and fear. The crackle of flames outside the pantry had taken on monstrous dimensions in her head. It was the only sound she could hear. That and the thundering beat of her heart.

She gave the latch one final, frantic tug and managed to prise it loose. Thank God the window hadn't been painted shut. It swung outward with a screech of worn metal. Sara immediately poked her head out, gulping in welcome lungfuls of the fresh evening air.

"Move it," Robin shouted from directly behind her. "The door's going to come crashing down any second now, and being showered with sparks isn't high on my list of favorite things."

Hastily Sara twisted herself around on the shelf. Then cautiously she eased herself over the sill. Within seconds, she was hanging from the weathered frame by little more than her fingernails. Scrunching her eyes closed, she offered up a quick prayer that she wouldn't be speared by a mutant thorn, and she dropped into the prickly bush below.

Her six-foot fall was broken by a tangled thatch of spiky creepers that gouged her arms and hands and somehow even got snarled in her hair. Belatedly she realized she'd probably sat on a few when she'd landed flat on her backside; but now was not the time to worry about a bunch of overgrown thorns. She extricated herself from the gully as swiftly as possible and cast a quick look over her shoulder as Robin made her jump out the window.

For a moment the woman disappeared completely from sight. Several interminable seconds ticked by before she emerged from the shrubs, and when she finally did, her black mane was liberally laced with broken twigs and mangled leaves. She looked like a refugee from an old slapstick comedy as she crawled on her hands and knees from the ditch. If they hadn't just escaped such danger, Sara might have been tempted to laugh.

Robin, busy plucking brambles from her clothes, glowered at her. "I hate you," she breathed, her eyes fastening darkly on Sara's face. She rose stiffly to her feet, wrestling irritably with the strap of the handbag she'd slung around her neck. "I brought your purse," she said. "I'd hate for your keys and credit cards to get scorched. You'd be stuck in this town for God knows how long if that happened."

Biting back a cutting retort to Robin's barb, Sara ignored the woman's bid to disentangle herself from the twisted strap and just reached over and pulled her keys and wallet from the bag. Smoke was streaming through the open window now. Sara rushed to a pay phone near the rim of the Apple Shack's parking lot.

"Someone's probably already called the fire department," she called over her shoulder. "But I'll make sure the trucks are on their way. You take a look around the front of the building and see if there's anyone enjoying the spectacle."

"Yeah, sure, give me the easy job," Robin muttered, scooping up her cat. "I'll probably wind up with a knife in my throat, won't I, Pyewackett? And why? All because I wanted to try and get rid of an evil curse."

By the time Robin trudged around the side of the building, Sara had already contacted the Santa Vera fire department and been told that the trucks were indeed on the way. The instant the connection was broken, she inserted another coin and dialed the number of the Sketch Shop. It was a futile undertaking. The Shop's switchboard closed down at five. Only outgoing calls could be made after that.

"Damn." Sara slammed the receiver back into place and caught up with Robin on the sandy walkway that encircled the restaurant. "Do you see anyone?" she asked without a great deal of hope.

"See?" Robin glared at her. "You expect me to see with all these thorns stuck in my eyelashes? What are you doing now?" she demanded as Sara suddenly started rooting through a hedgerow next to the porch. "Do you have a bush fetish or something?"

Sara offered no response to the snide question. She was too absorbed by what she'd spotted lying beside the hard-sand path.

It was a crumpled matchbook cover. Her stunned mind acknowledged the discovery in a startled burst of recognition. A gold-and-black checked cover. Like the ones that had been on the table at the Cellar Door. Like the ones Noel had been using to light the cigarettes Alex had given her.

Swiftly Sara extricated herself from the flower bed and smoothed the wrinkled cardboard with her fingers until the printing on the book was legible. Uncle Abe's Chicken Stop. Yazoo City, Mississippi.

Gritting her teeth, Sara stood, fists clenching around the discarded cover. She turned automatically for her car.

"Where are you going?" Robin demanded, still pulling brambles from her hair and clothing.

"Up to the Shop to look for Alex," Sara told her, conscious of Robin's verbal bids to stop her but not paying the slightest bit of attention to them.

Yazoo City. Noel had taught school there, hadn't she? And she'd openly proclaimed her dislike for Jasmine O'Rourke. She'd also openly proclaimed her love for Alex—or if she hadn't, she'd come very close. But whether those things added up to Morganna's curse or not, Sara couldn't say. She only knew that jealousy had been the root of countless crimes over the centuries. And one thing was certain, she reflected grimly, those matches definitely hadn't sprouted legs and walked into the shrubs under their own steam.

But Noel? Sara wondered, hesitating. Was it possible she could be the person behind Morganna's curse? Noel, who'd befriended her almost from the moment she'd set foot in Santa Vera? Who'd warned her to watch out for Jack Kensington? Noel with her outspoken personality and cheerful good nature? Noel—who absolutely adored Alex?

With a vengeance, Sara twisted the key in the car's ignition. Don't let it be her, she prayed as she sped from the Apple Shack's parking lot. She had a feeling, though, that this was one prayer that wasn't going to be answered.

The road leading to the Sketch Shop ended at the fringe of the clearing that doubled as the staff parking lot. It surprised Sara a little to see Alvin Medwin's aging jalopy chugging well ahead of her into the cleared-out space. Now why on earth would he have come back here tonight?

She halted her car a good distance from the clearing and slid carefully from the driver's seat, her eyes locked distrustfully on Alvin, who was busy wiping a spot of dust from his car's front fender with the sleeve of his rumpled suit. As usual, his thoroughness was annoying. For all she knew, he might very well stand there half the night polishing every inch of the ancient vehicle. Sara waited for several long minutes, then gave up and decided to try to skirt the clearing without his spotting her.

It shouldn't be hard to do, she reasoned, striking off through the woods to her left, toward the rocky cliff that would wind her around to the rear entrance of the Shop. Maybe she'd be wiser to sneak in the back door in any event. It was within the realm of possibility that the person responsible for her so-called accidents had returned to the studio after locking her and Robin in the Apple Shack. Only a fool would have hung back to watch the fire. And despite the fact that the mind behind Morganna's curse was unspeakably mad, Sara sensed it also possessed a strong instinct of survival. How else could it have remained so well hidden for such a long time?

As she emerged from the woods and began creeping along the edge of the cliff, Sara's gaze traveled over the craggy ground to the open window of Jack's former office. Was Noel in there at this moment, she wondered apprehensively. Was she watching? Could she see? Was she plotting her next move? Was she, in fact, the person behind Morganna's curse?

So intent was her surveillance of the unshaded window that she forgot for a second about the precariousness of the ground beneath her feet. It took only that split second of diverted attention for one of the rocks to give way. And it did give way—jerking right out from under her, sending a spray of loose stones, gravel and dirt down the side of the steep slope, bringing a scream to her lips she couldn't quite choke back.

Reflex had her scrambling away from the shaky ledge before her balance could desert her completely, but she knew that anyone in the office couldn't possibly have failed to hear her. And she had a feeling it would have been asking too much for that someone to be Alex.

Sara gave up her attempt at stealth. As noiselessly as possible, she made her way inward from the cliff. She'd taken only a few steps, when, to her horror, the Sketch Shop's rear door was flung open and Noel strode out.

"Sara?" The woman's hazel eyes were unreadable in the evening shadows. "Is that you? What are you doing up here?"

Well, maybe the expression in her eyes couldn't be deciphered, but the incredulity in her voice seemed to say it all.

Sara dug her heels into the hard-packed dirt, watching with a creeping sense of terror as Noel advanced on her. *Say something,* her brain commanded. *Say anything. Just don't let her see what you think.*

"I—uh—wanted to talk to Alex," she managed, then winced inwardly. Of all the things she could have said, that had to be the dumbest. Still, what difference did it make?

One way or another, Morganna's curse appeared bent on killing her.

Noel continued to walk forward. The evening shadows cast a series of eerie patterns across her face, marbling her round features. Around them, the whisper of leaves intensified, as if issuing a warning. Like the haunting wail of the legendary Santa Ana winds, Sara felt that nature itself had taken up a portentous cry.

It startled her when Noel started to speak. Her dulcet southern tones rose above the prescient rustles of leaves. "Sorry, Sara," she said, a cryptic smile touching her lips. "With all that's happened lately, I must've forgotten to tell you. Alex isn't here. He left around eight-thirty. I was supposed to give you the message, but I guess I forgot. He wanted you to meet him at his place."

Alex wasn't here.... The words echoed hollowly in Sara's head. Automatically she felt herself moving backward. Slowly. Inexorably. Back toward the edge of the cliff, as though she'd been caught in the pull of a giant magnet. The ground beneath her grew rough and pitted. One false step, and she knew she'd plunge right over the side of the steep embankment.

Even in her retreat, she took note of the peculiar light in Noel's hazel eyes. A murderous gleam perhaps. Or maybe a glimmer of certain knowledge. Of déjà vu. After all, hadn't Jasmine O'Rourke died in a fall?

Biting her lip, Sara took another tentative step back from the woman. She was poised on the rim of the ledge now. Noel had taken a menacing stance, positioning herself squarely between the cliff and the Sketch Shop. And Sara had reached the outer limit of that cliff. She couldn't back up any farther.

From the rocks below a mournful gust of wind tunneled upward, swirling about her legs, ruffling her hair, sweeping over her skin, causing her to freeze where she stood.

In the dappled light of a high overcast, she saw Noel's mouth move. But then it seemed the earth moved, too. A threatening rumble filled the dusky air as the rock ledge groaned and slowly began to give way. She felt the sheering vibrations beneath her feet, saw Noel looming in front of her, heard the scream that burst from her own throat, underscored by the crack and clatter of tumbling rocks.

The ledge had broken off completely, Sara realized, clawing desperately at the loose wall of dirt and granite. She was falling, skidding down the side of the cliff, plunging straight to her death on the jagged rocks below.

Her mind became a riot of sound and sensation, a swirling jumble of fear and darkness, of pain and dread. Brutally sharp rock edges dug into her skin as she slid. A cloud of dust rose up and around her; a shower of pebbles cascaded over her head. Frantically she fought to gain a foothold, but it was futile.

Then suddenly, unexpectedly, she felt it—a wrenching jerk on her right wrist that very nearly tore her arm from its socket. The avalanche continued, yet somehow, miraculously, she'd ceased to be a part of it. With her foot, she sought out a tiny gouge in the side of the craggy precipice, a crack just big enough to take the agonizing strain off her arm.

Breathing a shaky sigh of relief, she snapped her head back. Shock ripped through her, followed swiftly by suspicion and a raw sense of doom.

Noel had twined the fingers of both hands around Sara's forearm. And that grip was the only thing between her and certain death.

What was the woman trying to do? Sara wondered in a surge of panic. Savor the moment of death? Or maybe she just wanted to be sure that the dust had settled sufficiently for her to have an unobstructed view of her death.

Whatever the case, Sara didn't waste any more precious time pondering it. Using every ounce of energy she possessed, she managed to wedge her foot deep into the crack and, with the other, hunted for a similar hold.

Mere inches from her outstretched arm, she spied a small jutting ledge, a rock shelf that looked to be sturdy enough to support her weight. If she could wrest her arm free, she might be able to reach it.

Noel's voice, tense and coarse, floated down to her as she began struggling to extricate herself. "What the hell's the matter with you, Sara? Are you crazy?"

Sara ground her teeth. "Not as crazy as you, Noel," she retorted. "Let me go. You won't get what you want this way."

She twisted again on her arm, but to no avail. Noel had the advantage of being firmly anchored on her stomach. All Sara had was a weak toehold and muscles too sore to even feel.

"For God's sake, stop struggling, will ya?" Noel growled. "At least let me get you over to that ledge."

Get her over to that ledge?

For the first time since she'd fallen, Sara took a moment to let her brain function rationally. Noel was holding her arm. Holding it tightly. The dust had pretty much settled now, and still the woman's grip showed no signs of slackening. Could it be she'd been mistaken? Sara wondered numbly. Was it possible that Noel was trying to help her rather than kill her?

She lifted faintly accusing eyes to the woman above her, noting the strained facial features, the grimace of determination, the definite upward tug on her wrist.

"Oh, my God," she murmured in open disbelief. "You're *not* trying to kill me, are you?"

"Kill you!" Noel hung her head over the side of the cliff and glared down. "What kind of crack is that to make? You're the one with the death wish here. Now knock it off, and give that pretty little butt of yours a boost. See if you can reach the shelf."

Sara immediately pushed herself up with her braced foot. It seemed to take forever for her groping fingers to latch onto the protruding rock, but she finally got it within her grasp. Employing her last vestige of strength, she hoisted her trembling body onto the narrow ledge. Then she sank to her knees and huddled there, too overwhelmed with relief to respond to the string of grumbling invectives being flung at her from above.

"What do you think I am? Some kind of a monster?" Noel charged, releasing her wrist. "Kill you! What are you, drunk or something?" Hazel eyes, both concerned and annoyed, peered downward. "Can you climb out now? Are you okay?"

Mutely Sara nodded. There were several tiny crevices between the ledge and the top of the cliff. If she could force her groaning muscles to respond, she should be able to make it without any more help.

"Get away from the edge, Noel," she called up to the frowning woman. "I think I can do this by myself."

An endless stretch of seconds passed before she actually began her ascent. Although the rocky wall seemed to go on forever, she was really only three or four feet from safety. Three or four of the longest feet she'd ever encountered.

Wisely Noel had removed herself from the dangerous rim of the precipice. Eyes focused straight ahead, Sara clawed her way to the top, not daring to look down at the clumps of gravel she dislodged in her wake. Moments later she crawled out onto the solid embankment and as far away from the treacherous edge as her tightly strung muscles would permit.

"Thank God," she gasped, pushing herself to her knees and shaking the hair from her face.

Suddenly she froze, her eyes clearing and focusing on a pair of feet planted firmly in front of her, blocking her path.

Almost instantly, terror assailed her, brushing through her soul like the blade of a spectral dagger. She sensed pure, unbridled hatred behind the eyes that stared her. Violence and fury and resentment. A twisted roil of emotions so malevolent and strong Sara recoiled.

Slowly Sara lifted her head. There, towering above her, stood the personification of all her fears. Evil in human form, glaring down at her through cold, glittering eyes.

It was the evil of Morganna's curse!

ALEX HEARD THE WAIL of sirens on Coronado Boulevard long before he caught sight of the fire trucks rolling into the paved lot outside Granny's Apple Shack. He debated for a second, then overshot the access road leading down to the cabanas and swung in behind them. Some obscure inner instinct warned him that the smoke pouring from the side windows of the building was not the result of a stove-top fire.

His eyes strayed automatically to the distant palm trees where Sara usually parked her car. It wasn't there. He left his Jeep running and strode over to where Robin stood, tapping her foot in annoyance while the fire fighters doused the last of the flames.

"What's going on?" he demanded.

Robin glowered at him. "Looks pretty obvious to me," she replied sourly, returning her gaze to the scorched restaurant. Then she did a sharp double take. "What are you doing here? Sara just went up to the Shop to find you."

Something coiled tightly in Alex's stomach. "To find me? What was she doing here in the first place? Didn't Noel give her my message?"

"Well, I don't know anything about any message, but as for your other question, trust me, it's a very long, very involved story. Suffice to say, Sara and I had ourselves quite a chat this evening. Or at least we were having one before the fire started, which must have been right after someone locked us in the pantry. Then of course we saw the sketch, but who could possibly care about a stupid sketch when a ton of smoke's billowing under the door? I hate to admit this, but it's a damned lucky thing there was a window in that room. It was worth a buttful of thorns just to get out unsinged. I'm just glad I put Pyewackett out earlier."

As difficult as it was to follow Robin's jerky, gesture-laden discourse, Alex managed to grasp the gist of it. He took her by the arms and turned her around to face him. "What sketch, Robin?" he grated, shaking her.

Her glare was one of exasperation. "A sketch of Morganna," she fired back. "She was lying in a coffin, holding onto a dead rose. Here," she said, snatching Sara's purse from around her neck and digging out the drawing. "Look for yourself."

Alex took the wrinkled sheet of parchment she thrust at him. It was Morganna all right, stretched out in a coffin. But this time, there was a snapshot of Sara's face pasted to the sorceress's head. His eyes lowered to the shakily drawn lines, to the smudges that revealed no trace of black ink beneath them. Alex paled visibly, and his heart began to slam against his ribs.

This wasn't one of his sketches. It was a copy of one he'd done, but it wasn't his.

"Hey, are you okay?" Robin's strident voice broke through the shock that gripped him. "What's wrong, Alex? Are you sick or something?"

He shoved the drawing at her. "Don't you recognize this, Robin?" he growled.

She slapped at it. "Well, of course I do. It's from the dead files at the Shop. Old Gus decided not to use this particular scene at the end of the second film because it seemed too final—more like death than banishment."

"It is death," Alex snarled. "The person who drew it wants Sara dead. Sara and Morganna."

Robin inspected the tremulous lines closely. "Hey, this isn't right," she said at last. "It's too... Alex where are you going?"

"To the Sketch Shop." He reached his Jeep in five long bounds. "Call the police," he shouted back at her. "Tell them to meet me up there. Do it, Robin," he ordered when she didn't move. "Now."

Her red lips thinned. "The police can't fight the evil power of Morganna's curse, Alex," she warned, but he cut her off.

"Morganna's curse isn't any evil power," he said in a dangerously low voice. "It isn't something you can chant away. It's a sickness. A deadly sickness."

Chapter Eighteen

"So. We finally meet face to face, Sara Moreland."

The voice that greeted her contained a note of hideous mockery, an undercurrent of laughter so cruelly tarnished that it no longer sounded human.

"I have to give you marks," the horrible voice continued. "You're extremely resourceful—you and Robin. We felt sure you'd both perish in that fire. Certainly we hoped you would."

From her hands and knees, Sara could only gape at the figure of the man who loomed above her. A man whose face was twisted into a ravaged mask, whose blue eyes glowed with a chilling intensity, and whose lips were drawn back into a cold, feral grin. A man Alex had known for years, yet had obviously never known at all. This man was Morganna's curse. This man she knew as Dieter Haas.

"What, nothing to say, Sara?" Dieter crowed, his tone one of triumph. "Did we fool you so very well? Ah, but of course we did. It stands to reason that you wouldn't have noticed the differences. After all, you're not an animator."

Somehow Sara managed to shake herself out of her shocked paralysis. At the same time she also caught a glimpse of Noel, lying on the grass behind Dieter. Thankfully she appeared to be breathing, but it was hard to say how long that state of affairs would last.

"What differences?" Sara forced herself to ask, not sure whether her question had been audible or merely an unspoken scream in her head. But she must have gotten it out, for the savage grin widened.

"The sketch, Sara. The one we gave you tonight."

Dieter squatted down, and hastily Sara pushed herself back onto her heels. Up close, his eyes radiated a maniacal sheen, like ice on fire, if such a thing were possible. Those eyes peered intently into hers despite her best efforts to avoid them, and the grin assumed crafty proportions.

"Robin saw that sketch, didn't she, Sara?" he inquired in a tone that a cartoon cobra might have used. "Yes, I can tell by your startled expression that she did. Well, no matter, we'll take care of her. We had a feeling we'd have to do it at some point anyway. That's why it was so perfect when you went down to the Apple Shack to talk to her. Wasn't it perfect, Dieter?"

To Sara's astonishment, Dieter's head bobbed up and down.

"Yes, it was," he murmured, his pitch lower now, less menacing. "We realized we'd have to kill her, too. Just in case. All threats, present and future, must be eliminated."

"Good boy," came the congratulatory response. One blond brow lifted. "He's so obedient, Sara. So wonderfully pliant. Don't you agree?"

Sara found herself nodding. Something told her she'd better if she hoped to have any kind of chance for escape. "Ah, Dieter—" she began, but he cut her off sharply.

"You're not talking to Dieter," he roared, his lips twisting into a ferocious snarl. "You're talking to me. I'll thank you to remember that."

Oh, God, now what? Desperately Sara swung her gaze to the empty windows of the Sketch Shop. Despite her most fervent prayers, there was no sign of movement in the aging building. She was alone out here. Alone with a raving lunatic—with the essence of Morganna's curse. Things couldn't get any worse.

Through the torturous swirl of thoughts in her head, she heard the low, reverberating chuckle that emanated from deep inside Dieter's throat. It was an odious sound that hung like an eerie vapor in the night air. And with that ghastly sound came the chilling words that had the last of her hopes evanescing around her.

"There's no one here, Sara," he revealed, his smirk brutal. "Silly woman. Do you think we'd be stupid enough not to cover ourselves?" One hand flapped at the air. "Perhaps this weakling human I'm forced to coexist with would overlook certain details, but there's little enough chance of that with me. You see, I know many things. For instance, I know that Noel's in love with Alex, that she didn't pass along his message asking you to meet him at his place. I know that Alvin is prowling around in the wine cellar even as we speak—and just for your edification, I wouldn't hold my breath waiting for him to find his way out. I had my human corollary here take a few precious minutes to rearrange some of the more significant posters down in the basement. Warwick's voice will be wandering around that maze for hours, searching for a way out."

Somehow Sara made herself confront Dieter's glassy gaze. "Why are you doing this?" she rasped, trying to clamp down the worst of her panic.

"Why?" Dieter's head shot up like a wolf about to bay at the moon. He shouted it again, and the unearthly sound rebounded through the neighboring hills.

Sara had a dreadful feeling she'd just asked the worst possible question—and had absolutely no idea to whom she'd posed it. What in God's name had so brutally ravaged Dieter's brain? What could possibly have caused him to split into two such divergent personalities?

"Dieter, I—" she tried again, but he leveled her with such a hateful glare that she didn't dare finish.

"Not Dieter," he bellowed. "You will not talk to this human creature unless I decide to let you. You will address me—Morganna's curse." Dieter's hand shot out, fingers snapping impatiently. "Now, give it to me."

Give it to him? Inhaling with difficulty, Sara stared at him. "Give you what?"

"The sketch, of course. I drew it; I want it back. In the wrong hands, it could be extremely damning...and don't tell me you haven't got it," he mocked her, his words filled with venomous sarcasm. "I know you, Sara. I've watched you. You always show the drawings to Alex. That's why you came back here tonight. To show him the final sketch."

"But, I don't, uh, have it. I really don't."

"Sara..." Dieter cautioned, his expression blackening. "I'm warning you. Don't play games with me. You do have it, because that's the way you are. You're a creature of habit. Just like every other simpering human creature on this planet. Now hand it over. I still have work to do. Once you're dead Robin will become a potential problem. She must be disposed of. And don't give me that shell-shocked look. You heard the human. All threats must be eliminated."

The human? "Threats to what, Die—I mean, Morganna?"

Dieter's eyes hardened. "Me, Morganna's curse," he snapped fiercely. "Get it straight, Sara. It bothers me to be wrongly identified. And the threat you so foolishly ask me about should be more than obvious by now." A grotesque parody of a smile flattened Dieter's lips. "It's the memory I protect. The memory of the sorceress's life. That memory must not be tainted. Not by you or any other imposter. Including the ever-hopeful Robin Danvers."

In the background the leaves rustled again, reminding Sara of the sinister presentiments she'd had earlier, heightened greatly now by Dieter's evil presence. By the presence of Morganna's curse.

The ominous whispers filled her ears, sweeping over her with each swirling gust of wind, pinning her there on the ground a mere three feet from the edge of the cliff. Above her the clouds had bunched, gathering themselves into an angry, black mass, as if in anticipation of the murder scene about to unfold below.

Too dazed to even blink, Sara forced herself to ask, "Is that why you killed Jasmine O'Rourke? Because she was doing your, ah, Morganna's voice? Because she was an imposter?"

A raw cackle rose up in the night air. "You finally understand, do you, Sara?"

Although she seriously doubted that she would ever understand any of this, Sara nodded. "You're what's left of Elke Stevens, aren't you?"

Dieter's lashes lowered, but his eyes never left hers. She saw his smile grow faintly reminiscent.

"In a manner of speaking, yes," the voice of Morganna's curse confirmed. "Long ago we were one. Elke, Morganna and me. Inseparable in life. Inseparable in death. Morganna was banished and Elke died. The powers that destroyed one crossed over to kill the other. Now only I remain. Morganna's curse. Her soul if you will. The essence of what she was, what she will always be. I am the protector, the sorceress's life beyond life. I am the force that cannot die. I am here, in the mind of this man, the answer to his anguished pleas, stronger than he could ever have hoped to be, with one, and only one, destiny to fulfill."

"To protect Morganna's memory," Sara said, still too shocked to really comprehend what was being said to her.

"Yes. To insure that it remains intact." A cunning light entered Dieter's eyes. "Go ahead," Morganna's curse instructed, turning its sights inward. "Tell her how you invited me to join you. Tell her what a willing host you have been. Tell her now, while I still permit you to speak."

The eerie light faded slowly, and Dieter's face resumed its normal cast. "I loved her," he croaked rather helplessly. "She was my Elke. And I failed her. I—"

Suddenly he stopped talking, and Sara thought for a startled second that the evil controlling him had taken over again. But then his attention shifted to Wizard's Hill, and a measure of confusion invaded his features.

Whatever had caused the lapse, Sara spent no time pondering it. Her chances for escape would be minimal at best. She knew she couldn't afford to waste any of them.

She shot to her feet and began to run. Away from the cliff. Away from Dieter. Away from the mad mind that harbored Morganna's curse.

But as fast as she was, Dieter was just that much faster. There was no eluding the arms that snaked out and grabbed her, no loosening the iron grip of Dieter Haas's well-developed muscles once they'd closed around her. With a jerk, his right forearm tightened chokingly about her throat, snatching her flat back against the solid wall of his chest.

"Dieter, don't! Let her go. She hasn't done anything to you."

To Sara's astonishment, Alex's voice, calm, yet authoritative, pierced the cloak of blackness that threatened to envelop her as she scratched and kicked to no avail in Dieter's hammerlock.

She dragged in a difficult breath, peering disbelievingly into the growing shadows, refusing to still her struggles. Thank God, it was Alex, she realized weakly, not just some ghostly apparition conjured up by her frantic brain. Alex, walking across the uneven ground, features taut, hazy green eyes intent on the distraught face of his old friend.

"Come on, Dieter," he urged, his tone tense, yet in a strange way almost conversational. "You don't really want to kill her."

"Ah, Alex." Morganna's curse was speaking now. Morganna's curse controlling Dieter's incredibly strong muscles, holding Sara fast in his arms. "Well, this is a pleasure indeed. An honor of sorts. I've wanted to talk to you for so very long. But of course I couldn't take the chance. You knew the human better than anyone. I had to hide away whenever you two were together. Please, allow me to introduce myself." The voice grew amused. "I'm that which you scorn. I am Morganna's curse."

If Alex was shocked in any way, he gave no outward indication. Sara was amazed that beyond the unrelenting set of his jaw, no expression registered on his face.

"Dieter—" he started.

"Not Dieter!" the voice cried out in a burst of fury. "I am Morganna's curse. You of all people should recognize me for what I am. You gave the sorceress life, Alex. You made her strong. You endowed her with great powers, powers that I now possess."

"I drew a picture," Alex corrected quietly.

"No, no, no," Morganna's curse admonished as its human carrier, Dieter, snatched Sara's fingernails from his arm. "No, Alex, you did much more than that. Gus drew a picture. But you... You gave the sorceress a soul. You, and Elke. I'm only sorry that it had to end. Sorry that what was can no longer be. Oh, I wouldn't come any closer if I were you. Unless, of course, you enjoy the sight of blood."

Reluctantly Alex slowed his steps. "Killing Sara won't solve anything," he grated in a low voice. "If Gus doesn't resurrect Morganna, the Sketch Shop will fold, and—"

"Well naturally it will fold," Morganna's curse interrupted. "Do you think I care about anything as inconsequential as Gus Sherman's animation studio?"

"You should." Alex took another forward step. "If the shop goes under, Forrest Clements will snap it up in a minute, along with all of Gus's Rainbow Forest characters."

"Oh, Alex, Alex, Alex. I'm disappointed in you. I know Forrest Clements will move in. But do you take me for an utter fool? I am Morganna's curse. I have come to protect the memory, and so I shall. At the Sketch Shop, at the Cartoon Emporium, the location is unimportant. I will eliminate any and all imposters, whenever and wherever the need arises. And, as always, the human will assist me.''

"You mean Dieter," Alex stated coldly.

Sara felt Dieter's biceps constrict around her neck. He dragged her back a pace, back to the rim of the cliff. "Stop where you are, Alex, or I'll throw her into the canyon right in front of you."

Alex watched the face of his old friend slowly transform itself from a caricature of evil into a tormented human mask.

"It has to be, Alex," Dieter told him in an agonized whisper. "Elke's death was my fault. By your hand, Morganna was banished from the Rainbow Forest. I had no right to try to bring her back. I had no control over her destiny. Only you had the power to revoke her banishment. I interfered. And when I did, Elke died. I caused her death. Don't you see that? First, she lost her voice, then she killed herself. And all because I interfered. I drew Morganna wrong. I dealt her the final death blow. And because of that, Elke died, too. My Elke. My love..."

"Elke's gone," Alex said softly, drawing closer still. "You can't change that, Dieter. Let her go. It's time for that. Just let her rest."

Dieter's only response was a howl of outrage and a sharp tug on Sara's throat. "Stay away from me, Alex," he warned, stepping back and dragging Sara with him. "We have to do this. Sara tried to desecrate Morganna's memory. She tried to steal what wasn't hers, and now she has to die. There's no other way. She has to die. Just like Jasmine."

"She..." Reluctantly Alex slowed his footsteps. Dieter had dragged Sara right to the edge of the cliff. Another couple of inches and they'd both be dead. "Dieter, none of this is Sara's fault," he said sharply, praying that a twisted form of logic would get through to his old friend. "Killing her isn't the answer. I'm the one who animates Morganna. I'm the one responsible for trying to bring her back. If I don't draw the sorceress, she can't return to the Rainbow Forest. Don't you see? It has nothing to do with Sara."

Dieter's eyes narrowed to blue slits. "You..." he breathed, and Alex knew Morganna's curse had seized control once more. "The animator. The controller. Not the voice, but the heart. Yes, I see it now. The fault is yours."

For the briefest of moments, Dieter's eyes closed, and the only thing Alex could do was make a lunge for Sara.

It didn't work. Dieter was simply too agile, too unpredictable in his crazed state. He jerked sideways, his arm still wrapped around Sara's throat, oblivious to the nails raking his arm. He crouched like a wild animal on the edge of the embankment, yanking Sara down with him, staring at Alex through vicious eyes. But when he spoke, his anger seemed to be directed inward.

"It was you who interfered," Morganna's curse shouted. "You who made the banishment complete. You killed Morganna!"

"No, I... I didn't mean to say that," Dieter denied, cringing from the unseen force inside his head.

With a start, Alex realized that the struggle taking place was between Dieter and what he'd come to regard as Morganna's curse.

"I didn't have a choice," Dieter was wailing. "Gus made me do it. He forced me to draw her."

"Ah, so you maintain that the fault is Alex's," Morganna's curse shot back, evidently delighted by Dieter's confusion. "Do we kill him, too?"

"No, I—"

"And what of Gus?" the evil prompted. "He is the creator, is he not? Oh, you are a limited creature. You function with such a small part of your brain. All this time, you have inhibited my growth, prevented me from seeing that which must be. It doesn't end with Jasmine or Sara. It scarcely even begins with them. We must eliminate everyone who poses a threat to the memory. Everyone and everything.''

Counting on Dieter's warring mind to keep the man distracted, Alex judged the distance between himself and Sara. She'd stopped clawing at Dieter's arm and was now holding herself perfectly still in his iron grasp. If he could just get close enough, Alex knew he might be able to stop Dieter from pitching her into the rocky canyon.

''Unrequited love,'' Morganna's curse chortled disdainfully, forcing Dieter's eyes upward to the blackened sky. ''You pitiful creature. See what you have done? You drew the sorceress, and she died. You killed that which you loved most. You allowed this to happen, and now it falls to me to make things right. No more shall you limit me, human. I will do what must be done.''

With each bitter word Morganna's curse uttered, Sara's terror intensified. Alex was edging nearer, but Dieter didn't seem to notice. Nor did he appear to notice the squeal of tires and brakes out on the road to Wizard's Hill. His breath rushed past her cheek in jerky spasms. Then from his throat issued an unearthly wail that ricocheted dolorously off the floor of the canyon beneath them.

The nightmarish sound slowly dissipated, swallowed up by the vast emptiness beyond the cliff. Sara saw Alex's hardened jaw and the coiled muscles of his body delineated in the shadowy light. He was still too far away to do anything should Dieter suddenly decide to throw her from the cliff. He knew it, she knew it, and so did the man holding her.

''Death,'' Morganna's curse howled, heedless of the stones beginning to shower beneath Dieter's feet. His eyes snapped open. ''Only death will keep Morganna's memory pure. Death to all. Death and blood. Morganna's blood...just like the petals of that rose. Ah, yes, a dying red rose. Your sketches, Alex. All of them, until the last one.

Until the death sketch, drawn by the human who caused the sorceress to perish."

Morganna's curse stopped speaking, and Dieter started to shake. Or was it the ground that was shaking? Sara couldn't tell anymore. She could hardly even breathe, so forcefully was Dieter's arm pressing into her throat.

She held her breath as the ground under him began to yaw. In her peripheral vision, she caught a fleeting glimpse of Robin Danvers skidding to an astonished halt on the rocky ground. Robin, followed by a group of police officers. Then she heard a gurgle of wild laughter in her ear.

But even though she was sure she should be falling, she wasn't. Not yet. An eternity passed in her dazed mind, a bleak endless stretch of time during which she seemed to be hovering on the brink of death. Hovering on the edge of the cliff, while the rocks beneath her slowly crumbled.

"Sara!" Her name burst from Alex's lips, and giving one last desperate kick, she managed to squirm from Dieter's strangling grasp.

Then Alex's arms were around her, pulling her forward, away from the quivering embankment, away from the hideous laughter and the shackle of Dieter's flailing limbs.

She watched in numbed horror as the wild-eyed man pitched backward over the edge of the precipice, his face contorted into a mask of madness, his hysterical laughter ringing shrilly through the suddenly still night air.

"You can't kill me," Morganna's curse shrieked. "I am a force that can never die. Never..."

Sara saw Robin's jaw drop in disbelief, felt Alex shudder as his arms tightened around her. And she pressed her face into his shoulder.

The laughter had stopped. The screams had stopped. Only the echoing crash of rocks could be heard from deep in the canyon.

Through the prevailing darkness, a shocked Robin stumbled over while the police swarmed to the edge of the precipice. "What happened?" she demanded, for once sounding completely stunned. "I called the cops as soon as you left, but I didn't know what to tell them. What the hell was Dieter doing anyway?"

"Doing?" Alex lifted his head, but his arms remained firmly locked around Sara. "Dieter wasn't doing anything, Robin," he said grimly. "As far as I can tell, he wasn't even here."

Chapter Nineteen

"He thought he was a cartoon sorceress?" The crusty police officer who'd been taking Sara's statement in the fourth-floor lunchroom rolled his eyes at his partner. "And here I figured he was just another kook addict who wanted to take a stab at flying."

"Sounded more like a looney tune to me," the second officer commented. "Okay, Miss Moreland, that'll be it for now. If we need anything else, we'll let you know."

Nodding, Sara looked up at the clock. Midnight. She couldn't believe that three whole hours had passed since Dieter had fallen to his death on the canyon floor. Three hours during which she'd repeated her detailed story to the police no less than four times.

She waited until the two men were gone, then pushed herself away from the table. Alex, she'd been told, was in the screening room, likely being subjected to far more questions than her. She could only imagine how hard this whole thing must be for him.

As she stood, Sara noticed Robin creeping around the corridor outside the lunchroom. The woman ducked through the door and began to prowl the wooden floor by the counter.

"It's gone," she said waving her hands in front of her waist like a geiger counter. "I can feel it. The evil's been exorcised."

All Sara felt was exhaustion, but she was more than willing to accept Robin's verdict. "How's Noel?" she asked as the woman began to sniff the air.

"What? Oh, she's fine. Concussion. She's been taken to the hospital clinic." She lifted her head to the ceiling. "I wonder where it went?" she mused aloud. Holding up two fingers, she traced an oblique pattern around the room. "It must've gone somewhere. Evil doesn't just disappear."

"Maybe it went south to the Cartoon Emporium," Sara suggested wryly.

Robin planted her hands on her hips. "You still don't believe, do you?"

"In Morganna's curse?" Sara shrugged. "Probably not the same way you do, but I believe that Dieter believed in it."

"Damn right he did. He not only believed in it, he lived with it. He wanted it to help him do something he couldn't stomach, and it wound up consuming him. You just can't trust an evil force," Robin maintained. "Evil thrives on trickery. Once it moves in, it takes over. It can break down the best defenses in the world, and Dieter's defenses were anything but the best. Mine, on the other hand, are unshakable. And my amulets aren't half-bad either—are they, Sara?"

"They're great," Sara agreed. She regarded Robin thoughtfully. "I still don't understand why you made one for me."

"I told you, I wanted to hone my skills." Robin moved her black-clad shoulders. "Besides, in case you hadn't noticed, Morganna's curse took a nasty little shot at me tonight. Either it didn't like the fact that I helped you deflect its power, or it figured Gus might give me the part of the sorceress if you died. Whatever, I was hardly its ally. Be warned, though, Sara." She lowered her dark lashes. "If you ever breathe so much as a word about that amulet to anyone, you'll wish I'd let Morganna's curse have its way with you. You got that?"

"Trust me, your secret's perfectly safe," Sara promised. Then she frowned. "Is Alex still in the screening room?"

"I guess so." Robin began to prowl the floor again, in search of the elusive evil force. "Last I heard, the cops were filling him in on the cache they found at Dieter's place." She pressed her fingers against the refrigerator door. "If you want to talk to him, you'd better get the lead out. Alvin's been rescued from the wine cellar. He's fired up and ready to lambaste Alex for letting Dieter defile Warwick's character." She paused and rubbed her fingers together. "Maybe that's where it went," she theorized, turning for the door. "Warwick's curse... It would have a real willing host there. I never thought about a human carrier until I saw Dieter. I'd better go check the old wizard out. That evil's just got to be around here somewhere."

Sara let Robin get well ahead of her before she began making her way to the screening room. She'd had enough of Morganna's curse to last a hundred lifetimes. She didn't particularly want to see the woman performing some occult ritual over Alvin Medwin.

Unfortunately, slow pace notwithstanding, that's exactly what she did see. At the end of the hall Robin's fingers were probing Alvin's head from behind while a uniformed officer scanned the old man's journal.

"Did you draw this?" he inquired, showing Alvin the sketch of Morganna that Sara had found at the Cellar Door.

Alvin nodded rather proudly. "Oh, yes, officer. Yes, indeed. I most certainly did draw it. I made a copy, you see, of a drawing that Jasmine O'Rourke found one night in her cabana. She showed it to me the very next day. I believe she thought that someone was playing a prank on her." Alvin pushed his glasses higher on his nose, evidently unconcerned that Robin had her palms pressed flat against his skull. "I wrote it down, of course. Everything she said to me that day. Here, let me find it for you."

As Alvin fumbled through his notebook, Sara slipped past the threesome and went into the dimly lit screening room. The police were just finishing up their business with Alex. Shaking their heads in apparent disbelief, they filed out the door, muttering to themselves as they left, casting surreptitious glances behind them at the animated movie that was rolling forward on videotape.

Alex was sprawled in one of the large padded chairs in front of the wide viewing screen, holding up a photocopy of the sketch Sara had been given in the Apple Shack earlier that night. Even with the Rainbow Forest chatter spilling from the wall speakers, he must have heard her come in, for he glanced over his shoulder and motioned for her to join him.

"Subtle differences," he said darkly, handing her the sheet of parchment and toying idly with the remote-control device in his lap.

Sara studied the picture curiously. Without Morganna's features to give the character clear definition, she couldn't really understand what he meant. Not until she encountered the rose the sorceress was clutching. Clutching between fingers that were less than human in appearance.

"Claws," she murmured, wondering how she could have missed such an obvious flaw in Morganna's image. "So that's why you didn't seem shocked to find Dieter here tonight. You knew it was him before you came up here."

"Robin showed me the drawing outside the restaurant," Alex confirmed. He sounded tired and drained. "Dieter had a tendency to make all his characters' hands look like claws."

Sara sighed, pulling the crumpled matchbook cover from the pocket of her jeans. "And I thought this checked matchbook I found in the bushes proved that Noel was behind Morganna's curse. Still," she mused absently, "maybe Dieter was the one who dropped it."

"He might have," Alex allowed, "but I doubt it. Noel distributed those matches to all sorts of different people at the Shop. Anyone could have tossed that cover in the bushes outside the Apple Shack. No, it was the claws that gave Dieter away."

"Is that why he used copies of your sketches at first? Because he knew you'd recognize his?"

"That was probably a big part of the reason." Reaching over, Alex stroked the hair away from her cheek with the back of his fingers, turning in his seat to look at her. "But I also know he had a strong aversion to drawing Morganna after Elke died. Deep down, he blamed himself for her death. I always suspected that. I just never thought he'd feel guilty enough about it to drive himself crazy. God, all those things he did to you—and to Jasmine—and I had no idea what was going on."

"He didn't want you to know," Sara reminded him. "He told you that out on the cliff. Or rather Morganna's curse told you. I've heard that truly insane people can do that. They learn how to hide their insanity from everyone, sometimes even from themselves." She bit down on her lower lip. "What I don't understand is why he bothered to warn Jasmine and me off. Jasmine was leaving town, and yet he still killed her. And I'm positive he intended to kill me. As a matter of fact, for a minute I thought he was going to try to kill you, too."

"So did I." Alex ran his thumb lightly across her collarbone. "Actually it sounded as though he was planning to kill a lot of people. What started out as a bid to preserve Morganna's memory was about to become a bloodbath."

"That was the evil talking, not Dieter," Sara said firmly. "I don't think he really knew what that other part of his mind was thinking. It seemed to me that Morganna's curse turned on him in the end. Almost as if it suddenly blamed him for killing Morganna and Elke.''

"Yeah, I guess that's about the size of it. Dieter's mind was totally messed up. What it likely boils down to, though, is torment.''

"You mean Dieter's torment?''

"Dieter's, yours, Jasmine's.'' Alex shrugged, his expression one of sadness. "I doubt if that other side of him much cared who was suffering as long as it could inflict pain on someone. At a guess, I'd say Dieter deliberately directed me onto the highway behind that jackknifed rig the night we went down to the Emporium, knowing that you'd be alone on the beach thinking about the phone call he'd made.'' He swore softly. "I should have seen it. He as much as admitted that he believed in Morganna's curse.''

"So did a lot of other people in town,'' Sara pointed out, crooking her leg underneath her and picking up the remote from Alex's lap. "Did the police find very much at his beach house?''

"Uh-huh.'' Alex continued to graze her throat with his knuckles. "They found a veritable treasure trove in his bedroom closet. A life-size poster of Morganna, a spliced tape of Warwick's voice that Dieter played over the phone to you, the book that was missing from the morgue, a trunk full of Elke's clothes, videotapes of the first two films in the Rainbow Forest trilogy, a cut-up snapshot of you and a similar one of Jasmine. They even found Jasmine's final death sketch tacked up in the palm of Morganna's hand.''

Sara glanced at the viewing screen. "Why are you playing this, Alex?'' she asked him gently. "In spite of the way you feel, none of what's happened is your fault. You couldn't have done anything to prevent it.''

A vague smile curved Alex's lips. "Thank you, Dr. Freud. In spite of the way I feel, I realize that. The police wanted to see the character in action.'' He looked over at Morganna who was conjuring up a horde of smoky demons in her dungeon laboratory. "I just feel bad about it all. Dieter was a good friend. He was completely devoted to Elke, and she killed herself. It's not the same as having someone you love simply leave you. There wasn't a damned thing he could do to change Elke's death. But he obviously couldn't accept it, either. To him, Morganna and Elke were a single entity. All he could do was try to protect that memory. The memory of his unrequited love."

On-screen, Morganna's amber eyes blazed. It was a scene from the first film in the trilogy. The sorceress was leaving her castle, laughing over her success in staving off one of Warwick's early spells.

"There is no one in this forest realm more powerful than me," she stated with absolute confidence. "Not the Purple Mist, not a wicked curse, not even the mighty Rainbow Scepter. Do you hear me, Warwick?" Her commanding voice echoed through the magic treetops. "I cannot be defeated. I am the Sorceress Morganna. My will to live is stronger than any spell you might cast upon me...."

Sara's gaze shifted to the film for a second. "I don't think Morganna wants to be a memory quite yet," she said in response to the sorceress's fierce statements. Then she shuddered. "I can't believe it. I'm actually starting to think of her as a real person."

Grinning slightly, Alex clasped his hand around the back of her neck. "We're all guilty of that to a certain extent," he told her. "Dieter just took his fantasies too far. He let love become an obsession, and you can't do that. I love you, Sara, but there's no way I'd ever confuse you with a cartoon character."

"In other words, if Robin were to subject you to her witchy probes, she'd find no trace of evil, huh?"

"Nope. Only good, healthy vibrations. I've been feeling a lot of those lately."

"Really?" Sara ran her hands over his shoulders. "Tell me, where do these good vibrations come from?"

"For an actress, honey, you miss a lot of cues."

"You mean like the one where you said you loved me?"

"Yeah, that might be a good place to start," he said, inclining his head.

Sara smiled. "Best place in the world," she agreed. "I love you, Alex."

"Enough to stay?" he murmured against her lips.

"More than enough to stay."

And as she sealed the promise with a kiss, Sara could feel Morganna's curse crumbling to dust around her.

There was no doubt left in her mind. The evil had been banished. Forever.

Step into a world of pulsing adventure, gripping emotion and lush sensuality with these evocative love stories penned by today's best-selling authors in the highest romantic tradition. Pursuing their passionate dreams against a backdrop of the past's most colorful and dramatic moments, our vibrant heroines and dashing heroes will make history come alive for you.

Watch for two new Harlequin Historicals each month, available wherever Harlequin books are sold. History was never so much fun—you won't want to miss a single moment!